Holiday
SPECTACULAR

FERN MICHAELS

SANTA'S *Holiday* SPECTACULAR

KENSINGTON
PUBLISHING CORP.

kensingtonbooks.com

Library of Congress Control Number: 2025936274

First Kensington Hardcover Printing: October 2025
ISBN: 978-1-4967-4683-2

First Trade Paperback Printing: October 2025
ISBN: 978-1-4967-5958-0

ISBN: 978-1-4201-5675-1 (e-book)

10 9 8 7 6 5 4 3 2 1

Printed in the United States of America

The authorized representative in the EU for product safety and compliance is eucomply OU, Parnu mnt 139b-14, Apt 123
Tallinn, Berlin 11317, hello@eucompliancepartner.com

Prologue

Four Friends—Santa's Crew

Frankie Cappella, Nina Hunter, Amy Blanchard, and Rachael Newmark were best buds at Ridgewood High School, in an upscale area of North Jersey, approximately thirty minutes outside of New York City. As with many friends, each went their separate ways after graduating, in search of fulfilling their dreams.

Ten years later, during their high school reunion, they easily became reacquainted, recalling their antics during class plays, where Nina acted, Frankie sang, Rachael danced, and Amy was the stage manager.

After college, Frankie moved to New York City to begin a career in publishing; Nina left for Los Angeles to pursue acting; Amy, the brainiac, eventually got her PhD and became an associate professor at Stanford; and Rachael got married, had a son, got divorced and started a dance studio, and was in constant search of a boy toy. While their personalities were distinctly different from one another, the friends shared many other traits. They were bright, talented, ambitious, and passionate. All four had a deep affection for animals—a trait Frankie felt very strongly about.

Within the first half hour of the reunion, the four women recounted the milestones and the mishaps of the last decade. Frankie had lamented about the corporate climate; Nina confirmed the difficulties of Hollywood; Amy bemoaned her feelings of confinement; and Rachael—well, Rachael always had something going on with a man or two. They discovered another thing they had in common was that none of them had a serious significant other, including Rachael. That's when they made a pact that if they didn't have dates for the forthcoming New Year's Eve, they would do the unthinkable: go on a singles cruise to the Caribbean.

The cruise proved fruitful, and each of them found romance—some at sea, and some upon returning home.

Frankie began a relationship with Giovanni, who owned a restaurant with his brother in her neighborhood. He had looked after Bandit, Frankie's kitty, while she was away on the cruise, and his genuine care for her fur-baby softened her heart. Nina met a successful lawyer named Richard Cooper, who lived and worked in Philadelphia, which wasn't terribly inconvenient, since she was moving back to New York. Amy had literally bumped into Peter Sullivan on the cruise, and he became her good buddy on the trip. The problem she faced was their geographical distance. She was in California, and he was in Boston. But as luck would have it, she was offered a position at MIT and moved her fur-family of two kitties east. Rachael, the dancing diehard, began a relationship with Henry Dugan, a world-renowned choreographer. Each year, he cruised the Caribbean teaching dance lessons to the ship's guests. The ten-year difference in their ages didn't seem to matter. At first.

The following year, Frankie had a falling-out with Rachael but didn't want to slight her, so she depended on the other gals to let Rachael know they were planning another adventure the week between Christmas and New Year's. Amy had an interview back at Stanford, and Nina had some business in Los Angeles, so they decided to meet in one of the most beautiful settings in the country: Lake Tahoe. Rachael had gone radio-silent, and it was unknown if she was going to join them, so the threesome made their travel plans accordingly. Frankie, being Frankie, made sure there was room for Rachael should she decide to meet them there.

The week after Christmas, Frankie, Nina, and Amy met in South Lake Tahoe, but Rachael's presence was yet to be determined. It wasn't until Frankie went missing that everyone in her orbit, including Rachael, gathered at the shores of the magnificent lake to find their friend. It was a reunion that bested their first, and Rachael found a new friend in Randy, a flamboyant and hilarious gay man.

For their third adventure, the girls and their significant others (well, in Rachael's case, her plus-one was Randy) embarked on a trip to Italy with their final destination in Salerno, where Giovanni's mother Rosevita and his Aunt Lucia lived in the family home. Giovanni was intent on getting his hands on his mother's well-kept secret recipe for panettone, Amy made a side trip to Geneva to see the Hadron Collider, Nina met a colleague in Milan, while Randy and Rachael stirred up the streets of Rome.

After three holidays of exhausting fun, the women decided to stay closer to home this year. Amy and Peter were going to spend Christmas with her father and his new wife, Nina's parents were coming up from Florida, Rachael still lived in Ridgewood, and Frankie was settled in New York. With plenty of activities in the city that never sleeps, Frankie—Ms. Bossy Pants to her friends—was determined to make plans for everyone to enjoy.

The Sisters of the Sisterhood

In the basement of an old farmhouse in Virginia is a War Room that would rival the Pentagon. It serves as the head-quarters for a group of women who provide justice when the system fails. Myra Rutledge, heir to a candy company fortune, and her childhood friend, Countess Anna De Silva, are the masterminds of the league of vigilantes.

Myra's husband, Charles Martin, is a former MI6 operative, who—along with Annie's other half, Fergus Duffy, the former head of Scotland Yard—work behind the scenes providing technical support and more, including Charles's culinary skills.

The Sisterhood began when Myra's daughter Barbara, and Barbara's unborn child, were killed by a driver who was never prosecuted because of diplomatic immunity. Myra vowed that she would do whatever she could to help other women who were denied their day of reckoning. Over the years, Myra and Annie have taken on corporate frauds, kidnappers, money-launderers, human traffickers, drug runners, rapists, and child molesters.

Several of the women who had been wronged and re-deemed became part of the alliance. Kathryn Lucas was the first. Her husband, Alan, had multiple sclerosis and Parkinson's disease. As his condition became worse, they left their engineering jobs and took to the highways. Kathryn worked as a long-haul trucker so Alan could enjoy the adventure of being on the road and seeing the country. One night at a truck stop, Kathryn was raped by three bikers while her husband was forced to watch. After he passed away, Kathryn became Myra and Annie's project, dishing out the revenge the bikers deserved. Kathryn maintains the big rig and continues to work as a long-distance driver.

Yoko Akia's mother had been duped into a relationship

with a movie star when she was fifteen. His brutality ended the woman's life, but his stardom kept his vile secrets from the public. It was the sisters who changed all that, including his face. Yoko now owns a nursery and is a highly regarded florist. She is also an expert in martial arts and well-trained in killing without a trace. She is the ninja of the group.

Alexis Thorn was an extraordinarily successful broker until she was imprisoned for fraud, set up to take the fall for Wall Street scammers. Once again, the Sisters took care of the problem. Alexis, a beautiful, tall, woman of color, is also an expert in disguises, a talent that comes in very handy during their operations.

Isabelle (Izzie) Flanders, an architect, also had her run-in with the law, but not because of any wrongdoing. She was framed by a coworker who manipulated a car accident to make it appear that Izzie was drunk; the accident resulted in the deaths of three people. With the help of the Sisterhood, Izzie was exonerated and regained her architectural license. She also has a hobby: computer hacking, trained by her husband Abner.

The group regularly enlists the investigative eye of Maggie Spritzer, a crackerjack reporter who works for Annie's newspaper.

Why do you need to know all of this? Because although the two groups had never met, circumstances beyond their control—something none of them relished—would propel both teams of women to embark on a new adventure of righting a few wrongs.

PART I

Chapter 1

Frankie

Mid-November
New York City

Frankie glanced out the window of her fourteenth-floor office that overlooked Rockefeller Center. The area was cordoned off for the arrival of the famous tree, which was scheduled to be delivered the following morning, then hoisted into place before noon. There was excitement in the air for the eighty-foot-high, forty-three-foot-wide spruce, which would be adorned with over five miles of 50,000 lights over the next coming weeks.

It was a tradition that began in the 1930s from a simple gathering with people singing holiday carols. Over the years, it became a phenomenon, with major recording artists performing at the event. The list of stars that have embraced the tradition includes Cher, Barry Manilow, Darlene Love, and Kelly Clarkson, to name just a few. In 2007, it was one of Taylor Swift's first live performances, and unless you are living in a cave or under a rock, you know how far she's come.

Frankie wasn't sure who was performing that particular

year, but she knew it would be grand. She also knew not to leave the building until the festivities were over, and began her own tradition of having Patsy's Italian Restaurant cater food for the late-working staff.

Frankie chuckled at the thought that her office party had grown over the years. *Must be the food*, she mused. Frankie was compulsively detail-oriented, which is why her friends counted on her to make the plans.

Her staff and colleagues often depended on her organizational skills for work-related situations, and sometimes for their personal lives, like the time Betsy from the art department begged Frankie to plan her baby shower. Frankie knew precious little about babies, especially baby showers, but she didn't want to disappoint the woman, who looked like she would give birth any minute. Frankie didn't ask why none of Betsy's friends or family could coordinate the event, but she overheard a conversation Betsy was having with her mother. Apparently, this was the first grandchild in the family, and there appeared to be a lot of competition as to who could throw the most fitting celebration. It was better to have someone outside the family circle just in case something went awry, eliminating any blame among the lot.

Frankie's generous soul graciously accepted the task. In spite of her being a childless cat lady, she was able to figure it out in short order, especially when she roped Giovanni into setting up the restaurant. It was an enormous success, and Betsy gave birth to a beautiful daughter three days later. Talk about a close call. As much as Frankie enjoyed party planning, she wasn't inclined to start a business and prayed she would be off the hook for future kids' parties.

Now it was time to plan her grown-up party for the tree-lighting evening. She called Matt into her office to go over the details. Even though the event was three weeks away, it was imperative they get their food order in ahead of time.

Matt strolled in with a few pages of invoices from the two

previous years. "You do realize the extravaganza starts at seven, and they light the tree at ten," Matt said, crossing his legs and tapping his pen on the clipboard.

"Yeah, I know. That really stinks, but proceed," she said, nodding. "I'll remind you to spread the word that people can leave whenever they want to, but don't say anything until the night of the party. I don't want to minimize it by making it sound unimportant."

"It is important, and I totally get it." Matt adjusted his chair and continued, "We've gone from a tray of eggplant rollatini to three, three dozen clams oreganata to five, and two trays of penne a la vodka to four." He paused. "How does Giovanni feel about you using Patsy's instead of his restaurant?"

"He couldn't be happier. Bringing the food to Midtown in all that chaos would make him *pazzo*!" Frankie used the Italian term for crazy. "Besides, he loves Sal and the Scognamillo family."

"Is it true that it was one of Frank Sinatra's favorite restaurants?" Matt asked.

"Yes, indeed. There must be dozens of photos of Frank through the ages on the walls, including tons of others: Pacino, De Niro, Michael Bublé, Ben Stiller, George Clooney, Calvin Klein, Carroll O'Connor, Jon Bon Jovi, and Oprah!"

Matt's mouth dropped. "Wow. Talk about a who's who in showbiz. And to think they cater our little office party."

"I copied the idea from an old friend, Nick Maria. He used to work at Atlantic Records and started that tradition in his office. It was on the second floor and faced directly at the tree. We could look straight out the window and watch the lights go on at seven. Now we have to wait until ten o'clock and crane our necks." She chuckled.

"Yeah, but the food is still good!" Matt added.

"Exactly!" Frankie said. "I hope people don't think they have to wait until ten. Every year the event gets longer and longer."

"People really appreciate that you do this, Frankie," Matt offered. "It's much better than the required company holiday party." He flopped down in the chair across from her desk. "I don't know why they bother."

"Neither do I, but I suppose they think it helps us bond."

"I'd rather bond with the fifty bucks it costs per head."

Frankie let out a howl. "It's probably more than that. I actually suggested it to upper management."

"I guess that didn't go over well." Matt smirked.

"Not one bit," Frankie said, grinning. "At least I tried. Besides, I think they use it as a company write-off."

Frankie returned to her desk and sat across from him. "Remember, on the night of the party, please let people know they are not being held against their will if they want to dine and dash."

"Will do." Matt made a note for himself.

"What are your plans for this year?" she asked.

"The usual. Dinner with people I don't speak to all year."

"Because?" she prompted him to explain further.

"Because they live completely different lives. You know, sister is a soccer mom and is on my back to get married. My mother got wise and no longer approached the subject."

Frankie smiled. "What about your brother?"

"Ah. My brother the bum."

"Bum?" Frankie said, and cocked her head.

"He's twenty-nine and hasn't ever had a real job."

Frankie crinkled her brow. "You're kidding, right?"

"Nope. He lives in my parents' basement." Matt thought for a moment; then he chuckled. "Maybe that's why my mom is off my back." He paused again. "At least he does the laundry."

"See. There is a bright side to everything." Frankie grinned. "Okay"—she began to rattle off the list—"conference room reserved?"

"Check."

"Tablecloths, dishes, flatware, napkins?"

"Check."

"Extra trash cans and liners?"

"Check." Matt stopped. "Only you would think about extra trash cans."

Frankie snorted. "Where else are all the dirty dishes going to go?"

"Good point."

"Menorah, Kwanzaa candles, and a small tabletop tree for the centerpiece?"

"Check."

"How many people have RSVP'd?"

Matt checked. "Twenty-four."

Frankie chuckled. "Word's out."

"Yep. And I cannot believe you pay for this out of your own pocket." Matt shook his head.

"Are Ira and Steven on the list?"

"Yep. Ira is a yes."

"Excellent. Nothing like having the COO come to your party. Maybe we can figure out a way to get the company to pay for it next year and make it the company holiday party instead."

"The conference room can't hold a hundred people," Matt said.

"I have some ideas." Frankie raised her eyebrows.

"Okaaay . . . shoot."

"The halls are wide enough on the executive floor to set up high-tops along the walls. We can have a service bar at each end, and the food can be set up in the large conference room. I am willing to bet it will save the company money, and no one will feel compelled to dance." She blinked several times. "Why do they do that? Hire a DJ and expect people to cut a rug? Nobody wants to hang around and pretend they're having fun. Besides, with my plan, people will be able to eat, drink, and mingle, which is what's supposed to happen." She sat back and folded her arms.

"Sounds like you've been to too many company holiday parties," Matt said, smirking.

"Oh, don't get me started. We used to go off-site for sales conferences, which in itself wasn't a bad thing. You had the opportunity to chat with people you never see. But"—she paused—"you were required to attend the evening banquets, dance, then spend the rest of the evening at the hospitality suite. Man, did I dread it. By the end of a long day, you just wanted to go to your room and order room service." She let out a huff. "There has to be a happy medium."

"If anyone can figure it out, it's you," Matt said.

Frankie smiled. "I have a few things to review, and then I am outta here. Why don't you stop for the day?"

Matt was a conscientious, loyal assistant. He never left work before Frankie unless she threw him out the door, a common state of affairs between the two of them. "Now, shoo." She waved him away.

"Right, boss."

"That's Ms. Bossy Pants, buster." Frankie feigned a frown.

He gave her a nod and disappeared.

Frankie began checking the project report to be sure everything was running on schedule. The cookbooks for spring were already copyedited and on their way for final proofing. Next was the batch of cookbooks for the following year. So far, no glitches. She checked the publicity plans for the books that were already on sale. All of her authors were behaving themselves, running on time to their TV appearances and book signings.

Over the years, Frankie knew how to keep her head down and her nose to the grindstone and was eventually promoted to an executive position running her own imprint at Grand Marshall Publishing. It was a star-studded roster of celebrity chefs, each book dedicated to raising money for a charity; hence, her imprint was called Cooking for a Cause.

Cookbooks were having a boom—books from celebrities, to kids, to real chefs. Short-form videos were turning into long-form books. But it wasn't all glamour all the time. Authors could be royal pains in the butt, especially celebrity chefs, whom she dealt with on a regular basis. Through trial and error, she found her own way to navigate the publishing world and the idiosyncrasies of her authors.

By the time she had finished checking her list, she noticed it was past seven and called Giovanni.

"*Amore mio!*" he greeted her with an affectionate pet name, and followed with, "*Che se dice?*"—an Italian term for "what is happening?"

"Just finishing up here. What's for dinner?"

"What would you like?" Giovanni asked.

"Something warm and delicious."

"Ah, but you are warm and delicious," he teased.

Frankie couldn't help but blush. "Stop," she said in a soft voice. "What's the pasta special?"

"It's-a Friday. Linguine with clam sauce."

"Make mine white, easy on the garlic."

"Do you want to come to the restaurant or bring to the apartment?"

"I'll come down to the restaurant. I want to go over the menu for the family and friends dinner for the night when everyone is here."

"*Positivo.* How soon?"

"I'll grab a ride. Should be there in a half hour."

"*Perfetto.* Be careful, bella." Frankie could feel the warmth in his sultry voice. "I will go feed Bandit and Sweet P so you can relax."

"You are the best! See you shortly." Frankie pulled up the app for one of the rideshare companies and made a request. She was happy it was only a five-minute wait, especially this time of year. Things were starting to get terribly busy. Everywhere. She unhooked her coat from the back of her door, pulled her tote from the bottom drawer of her desk, turned off the lights, and briskly walked to the elevator bank.

Chapter 2

Myra and Annie—The Sisterhood

Pinewood, Virginia

Myra padded into the kitchen, where Charles was fixing a traditional English breakfast of back bacon, fried eggs, grilled tomatoes, mushrooms, toast, baked beans, and sausages.

"You are going to make me so fat!" Myra pouted.

Charles swept her into his arms. "The more to love you, love." He kissed her on the forehead. "I skipped the blood pudding, as per your request."

"Thank you, dear." She reached for one of the mismatched mugs in the cupboard and placed it next to the barista coffee maker Charles had installed in the butler pantry.

"Fergus and Annie are on their way."

As if on cue, Lady, their beautiful golden retriever, lifted her head, then stood in anticipation of their guests, especially Fergus, who always had treats in his pocket. He said he learned to do that when he was a young constable during his first year at Scotland Yard. It was a good device when they encountered unfriendly dogs. He explained, "Ye toss one in the opposite direction, and if yer quick enough, you can make your way past 'em. Although I've had many a pants caught in the jaws of a few canines, but nobody was ever really hurt. Only my ego."

Lady was already at the door a couple of minutes before they heard the roar of Annie's souped-up golf cart followed by the sound of gravel flying about. Lady let out a soft *woof*.

"Good watchdog," Charles joked.

Annie, wearing her rhinestone cowgirl boots, was the first through the door.

"Good morning one and all!" she burst out. "How are my BFFs today?" She shimmied in Myra's direction and blew a kiss to Charles.

Fergus was being held hostage at the entry by Lady and her pups. They weren't going to let him into the room unless he greeted them accordingly. Of course, the dogs were polite and waited patiently, while Fergus dug into his pockets and presented them with a handful of crunchy morsels.

Myra grinned. "Between Charles making me fat, and you plumping up the dogs, we might have to move to a bigger place where we can fit our supersized behinds!"

Annie hooted at her lithe friend. "Ha! You couldn't get fat if you strapped a side of beef onto your skinny thighs!"

It was true. All the joking about weight gain was simply banter. Myra and Annie were impeccably fit for "women of a certain age," meaning that although they weren't running through the streets of New York wearing stiletto pumps, they were still agile and buff enough to scale a fence if necessary.

Charles handed a spatula and an apron to Fergus. "You oversee the bacon in the pan, and I'll manage the bacon on Myra's fanny." He gave her an affectionate pat on her behind.

"It's a good thing I have a sense of humor." Myra laughed, rolling her eyes.

Annie helped herself to another mismatched mug and fixed a coffee for herself and one for Fergus. "Charles, care for a cuppa?"

"*Cuppa* is for tea. *Coffee* is for coffee. You yanks." He shook his head and smirked.

"Pardon me," Annie said, bowing. "Care for a coffee?"

"Thanks, don't mind if I do." Charles winked.

Annie brought the coffee to the two men shuffling back and forth in front of the stove and went back to fix her own.

"So, Myra, what did you think of my idea about the Toys for Tots event?"

Annie and Myra served on the boards of several charities; for some, they asked for anonymity, and were only known to the executive directors. Over the years, both women of extreme wealth were constantly in the crosshairs of grifters and questionable organizations. They would make their donations privately and work behind the scenes. It was fitting, since their "other lives" functioned in the shadows.

"I think it's lovely they are honoring Camille this year," Myra said. Camille was an old chum of Annie's and owned a townhouse a few doors down from Annie's place in Manhattan. "That was a terrible ordeal they went through with their son." Myra was referring to an incident that involved a twenty-year-old kidnapping. When Camille's son J.R. was in college, he cleverly planned and carried out his own abduction. He owed a huge chunk of money to some extremely dangerous people, and he believed it was his only way out. The scheme worked. For almost two decades. It was a twist of fate that uncovered his long-hidden ploy and put the family into a tailspin.

"Things have greatly improved. J.R. dumped his crafty, greedy wife and cleaned up his act. He works with his father and has a new girlfriend. Camille said everyone is in a particularly good place now, except for his golf game," she said, chuckling.

"That's wonderful. Not the golf thing." Myra smiled. "Let's go over the plans after we feast on Charles's handiwork."

"Oi! What about me?" Fergus protested. "Do I not deserve some credit?"

"Don't be such a crybaby," Annie teased. "You're a good sort, Fergus."

"I suppose that's something, innit?" he said to the utensil in his hand.

Lady's head moved in sync with the platters as they were carried to the table. Fergus leaned over and whispered in her ear, "Don't worry, love. I'll be sure to save some for you."

"Oh, how you spoil them!" Myra faked a scolding.

"Sometimes I feel as if they're the only friends I have in the room," Fergus kidded.

"They're the *only* friends you have," Charles delivered a witty barb.

"Now that hurts, mate," he said, and frowned. "Can I still call you *mate*?"

" 'Til the cows come home." Charles slapped his pal on the back.

The four friends gathered around the table, said grace, and passed the lavish breakfast items. "Charles, you are going to make all of us fat!" Annie said, then dug into a wad of bacon.

"I told him the same thing just before you got here." Myra duplicated Annie's grab for the crispy slices.

"Not me." Fergus rubbed his belly. "I still run every day."

"Yeah, he runs from the kitchen to the lounge chair," Annie ribbed.

"Come on, love. Can't a man get a little break?"

She patted his stomach. "You're still in enough tip-top shape for me."

Charles steered the conversation to the reason for their gathering today. "Tell us, what do you women have planned?" He raised an eyebrow. The answer could be almost anything.

"We shall be working on the logistics to deliver a trailer of toys for Camille's event."

"Sounds like a lovely idea." Fergus slid two more eggs onto his plate.

"There is a grand holiday party at the Park Hyatt," Annie began. "They're honoring Camille this year, and we want to help her cause. They will be inviting a hundred children from some of the local orphanages. They'll get to meet Santa and get a gift. Plus, a good meal."

"Brilliant!" Charles said. "How can we help?" He pointed his fork at Fergus, then himself.

"Right now, we are in the planning stages, but you can be sure we'll find something for you to do." Annie smirked.

"We thought about posting a call to action on social media, but expecting people to send gifts is too complicated."

"Instead, we suggested when people have a holiday party, they ask people to bring an unwrapped gift. We'll provide them with the nearest drop-off point," Myra added.

"Lovely." Fergus dunked his toast in the gooey yolk.

"Myra and I are going to order toys from the manufacturers, have them delivered here, and then get Kathryn to drive the truck to a place outside of the city. We'll get help transferring the toys into smaller vehicles so they can navigate the gridlock."

"Right. The city can be a massive parking lot this time of year," Charles said.

Annie turned to Myra. "Kathryn is on board, correct?"

"Yes. She is doing a run to New Mexico and plans to be back the day before Thanksgiving. We should have most of the toys by then. They need to be at the hotel by December nineteenth, so we have some time. It will take her about six hours to get to the transfer station in New Jersey. After that, she said she was going to take the rest of the year off."

"As if!" Annie howled.

"I know. Every holiday is difficult, but we're here for each other. I suggested she spend the holidays with us in New York," Myra said.

"It will be a nice change of pace."

Charles looked over the rim of his coffee mug. "How long are we planning on staying?"

"Well"—Annie eyed Myra for support—"I was thinking we go up for a weekend for Camille's event. It's on a Saturday. Come home Monday. We can take the Gulfstream to Teterboro Airport. It will take thirty minutes to get to the townhouse from there."

"Without traffic," Fergus reminded her.

"We could take a helicopter," Annie suggested. "That would take ten minutes."

Myra gripped the edge of the table. "You *know* how I feel about those whirligigs."

"It's probably safer than the traffic that time of year," Charles added.

"Oh, I don't know, Annie. Do we have to decide right now?"

"Of course not. Just suggesting a way to eliminate most of the traffic buildup going into the city and minimize the gridlock."

Charles patted Myra's white knuckles. "Steady on, love. We'll get it sorted. It could be grand seeing the city lit up from above." His words were soothing, but not necessarily convincing.

"What about the train? It will bring us to Penn Station."

Annie pursed her lips. "We shall consider it."

"Thank you." Myra exhaled the long breath she had been holding.

Annie continued, "We will spend Christmas here, and then go back to celebrate New Year's Eve. We can go to the ballet."

"You can't help yourself when it comes to *The Nutcracker*, can you?" Fergus teased.

"And the fireworks in Central Park!" Annie squealed.

"If the word *fun* is involved, there is no question where we will be singing 'Auld Lang Syne.'"

Fergus raised his mug in a toast.

"Excellent! Then it's settled! It's been a long time since we had a party in New York!" Annie's face lit up like a Christmas tree. "We'll invite the Sisters. I'm sure most of them have plans, but in case someone doesn't, they shall have plans with us!"

"Terrific!" Myra smiled. "It will be nice to have us together for holiday festivities." She looked at Charles's dubious expression.

"Does this mean I have to brush up on a few more recipes?"

The three others looked at one another and burst out laughing. "What do *you* think, Charles?" Annie grinned.

"It will be bloody good to shop at Eataly and the Tin Building," Charles mused.

"Don't forget about the Union Square Greenmarket," Myra reminded him.

"Now that is what I call an amusement park for cooks!" Charles leaned into his chair, placed his hands behind his bald head, and shut his eyes. "Some people dream of a white Christmas; I dream about fresh rutabaga."

The laughs and cackling continued for another half hour until Myra and Annie decided to get to work and put their plans on paper. Fergus helped with the cleanup duty, while Myra and Annie retreated to the atrium and put pens to pads and began making lists for the toys and the parties, as there would be much entertaining going on.

Chapter 3

Rachael—Santa's Crew

Ridgewood, New Jersey

Rachael was loading her small music speakers into the back of her car. She had just finished a session at the local adult community center. Once a week, she picked a theme and encouraged those who were interested to "get up and dance." If they didn't know the steps, she patiently taught them. Normally she would be in a good mood after an evening like this, but tonight, her pal Randy had put a buzz-kill on her merriment.

Two years before, she'd met Randy in Lake Tahoe, where he had been the concierge at the hotel where everyone was staying. When she discovered Randy was a dancer, she immediately drew him into her flash-mob dance routine. When she returned to New York, she strong-armed her former partner Henry into helping Randy find a job on Broadway. Randy had natural talent and embarked on a new career moving from one musical to another. Rachael was happy her friend had found success, but that also meant he had less time for her. Now that he was involved with Jordan Pleasance, he had even less.

The year before, when everyone traveled to Italy, Nina caught up with one of her former colleagues, Jordan Pleasance. He was a highly regarded film producer who left the glitz of Hollywood behind and settled in Milan. He was dabbling with the idea of adapting a story into a screenplay and invited Nina to collaborate with him. Nina, a celebrated television actress turned screenwriter, had all but given up on the entertainment business when Jordan convinced her to join him on the project. Nina invited Jordan to come to Salerno to celebrate New Year's with her gang, which is where he met Randy. The two hit it off and, you know the phrase, "the rest is history." And as far as Rachael was concerned, so was her friendship with Randy.

It wasn't as if they had a falling-out, but if you weren't on Rachael's schedule, then you weren't necessarily her friend. It was something the other friends had become accustomed to. But long-term friendships get a lot of free passes, and Rachael was no exception. She wasn't mean-spirited, just a bit spoiled. She had been counting on Randy to spend more of the holidays with her, especially New Year's Eve.

The prior year, she'd met Salvatore Barone in Italy while he was on sabbatical from the University of Salerno. Several months later, he moved to New York to teach at NYU. Their relationship was steady until he announced he was going to Italy for the holidays to visit friends. What irked her was that he didn't invite her to join him. They had a huge row when he explained that he needed some free time to spend with his pals, with the underlying and unspoken words that Rachael monopolized people.

Rachael was the only one of the friends who had been married, had a son, and was divorced. Her aspirations of a life of luxury and flitting through life like a social butterfly were crushed when she discovered her husband went through her trust fund in less than three years. Yes, she had to bear some of the blame for allowing him access, but at the time, she was busy and fluttering about.

With her bank account drained, she needed a job. The idea was revolting. Her plan was to find another man of equal or better resources than she originally owned. But she discovered it was not that easy, especially as a single mother. Greg, her ex-husband, contributed to their son's child support, but the monthly nut was hers to crack. She began to teach classes at a local dance studio. When the owner announced her retirement, Rachael got financial assistance from her family and purchased the building and the client list. Dancing was something Rachael knew how to do, and she did it well. The business was a success, yet she was still in search of validation from another man, an error many women make.

Rachael couldn't shake her constant need for attention. For the most part, it was harmless, until people realized she was always talking over them, or she would compare an experience they were having with something she went through. If you were looking for empathy or just for someone to listen, Rachael wasn't necessarily the gal. It often felt like a competition, and it was exhausting. But she was loyal, which made it easier to forgive, knowing she will always have your back. No matter what.

And this is why she was angry with both Randy and Salvatore. Randy chose to welcome the new year with Jordan, and Salvatore chose to be with his former professor and fellow students. When Frankie suggested Rachael should be delighted for Salvatore instead of being upset, it started another battle between the two friends. "Listen, Rachael," Frankie had said, "I'm no expert on relationships, but one thing my mother tried to tell me was, if you push too hard, you push them away. If you act nonchalant, they wonder what's going on in your head." Frankie knew all too well how she had failed miserably in the past. It wasn't until she inadvertently ignored Giovanni and sent him into a tizzy that she realized her mother was right. "You've gotta trust me on this."

Rachael did not want to be the fifth, seventh, or ninth wheel over the holidays. As she flung her things into the car, she muttered the words "act nonchalant" to herself. She finished packing her belongings into the back of her SUV, raised her voice, and blurted, "I just might do that!"

A young man, a few years her junior, stopped and turned. "Sorry. Were you talking to me?" He had a nice smile.

Rachael was caught off guard and slightly embarrassed. "Uh, me? No. Just complaining to myself." She turned back to her car and realized what a mess she had made by just throwing everything into the vehicle. She leaned into the SUV to organize it a bit, but when she pulled out one of the speakers, the wires got tangled, almost causing both speakers to tumble out.

"Arrgh," Rachael muttered in frustration.

The young man walked over to her.

"Here. Let me give you a hand," he offered.

Rachael was about to protest, but she decided to allow the gentleman do the gentlemanly thing. "Thanks," she said, and smiled.

He grinned down at her. "I saw you working with those folks inside. You've got some rather good moves."

Rachael actually blushed. For real. "Thank you. That's truly kind of you to say." She waited a beat. "I'm Rachael."

"Nick. Nicholas Morrison." He extended his hand.

"Rachael Newmark. Nice to meet you, Nicholas Morrison."

"I've seen you around," he said, then paused. "Wait, that came off a little creepy. I actually work here."

"Oh?" Rachael hadn't noticed the clean-cut, clean-shaven, nice-looking man before. He was wearing what appeared to be a uniform from the medical staff.

"Yes. I'm a nurse practitioner. They call me 'Nurse Nick.'

I normally work the day shift, but someone called in sick, so I'm covering for him. I noticed you at the Halloween party. I believe you were dressed like a French maid?" He cleared his voice. "Now *that* sounded creepy, but you were hard to miss doing the salsa."

Rachael was almost embarrassed. "Thanks for noticing . . . I think." She shifted into her demure posture. "What was your costume?"

He chuckled. "You're looking at it." He spread his arms and glanced down at his scrubs.

"Duh," Rachael answered coquettishly.

"I was on duty. Just in case someone choked or fainted."

"There seems to be a lot of that going around, especially when there's a party." Rachael grimaced. "Oh, was that mean?"

He tilted his head. "It's accurate."

"So, tell me, how many Heimlich maneuvers have you maneuvered?"

"Too many to count." He snorted.

Then came an awkward moment of silence.

"Would I be too forward if I invited you for a coffee?" he asked.

"Be as forward as you like." Now *there* was the real Rachael. "I mean, yes. I mean sure. Coffee." Once again, she began to blush. She felt the heat on her face, which was something she hadn't experienced in a while.

"Just let me know when." He pulled his cell phone from his backpack. "May I text you my number?"

"Yes, you may." Rachael rattled off her number as he punched it into his phone. Her phone buzzed, indicating she had a text message.

"That would be me," he said, smiling.

Rachael shifted into a casual, nonchalant mode. "I'll let you know my schedule. And thank you for your assistance."

She walked toward the driver's door. "Have a good night." She quickly got inside the car and started the engine.

Nicholas stepped aside and held up his hand in a half-wave as she backed her vehicle from the spot. She did the same and drove off. Under normal circumstances, she would have planned a date with him before she got into her car. This time, she was going to ease up. If there was someone new in the picture, she was going to try a different approach. *Frankie would be proud of me,* she thought.

And why shouldn't there be someone new? Rachael and Salvatore were not in a committed relationship; at least, it was never solidified. Yes, they had a date almost every Saturday if she wasn't working. Yes, they'd celebrated their birthdays together over the past year, and yes, a few of the summer outings. But he was going back to Italy for the holidays and didn't invite her. She didn't like the idea of being ditched.

Maybe a little competition would shake Salvatore into a commitment or at least force a conversation about it. She had to admit she had to take some of the blame for not bringing it up. She secretly feared that if she did mention it, she may not like his answer.

She was about to call Frankie as she drove out of the parking lot but recalled another conversation the two friends had recently.

"You are always doing something when you call me," Frankie had complained.

"What do you mean?" Rachael said defensively.

"You're on your treadmill, taking a hike, paying for something in the grocery store. Can't you just sit still and have a conversation with me? I feel as if I'm competing for your attention."

"You? Are you kidding?" Rachael continued with her justifying tone.

"Seriously, Rach. A nice exchange without all the distractions in the background would be a nice change."

"Sorry you feel that way." Rachael was becoming indignant.

"Let's not blow this out of proportion. I am simply asking that we—you and I—have a conversation without the checkout cashier at ShopRite asking for your customer number, or you blowing the horn at the guy stopped at the traffic light."

"Fine. I'll call you some other time."

At least a month had passed before the two spoke again. Rachael couldn't remember who reached out first, but they managed to patch things up between them.

Tonight, she was going to honor Frankie's wishes and give her a buzz after she got home, fed the dog, and poured a glass of wine.

Twenty minutes later, she checked those items off her list and dialed Frankie's number. After Frankie answered, Rachael began, "I am sitting in my living room with a glass of sauvignon blanc. No distractions."

"Who is this?" Frankie teased.

"Ha ha. Listen, girlfriend, I have something to share that I think you'll be happy to hear."

"Splendid. Shoot."

"I met a guy in the parking lot tonight."

"Did you try to mug him?" Frankie continued to joke.

"Stop picking on me. I did two things based on your advice."

Frankie bit her lip and let her friend continue. This was a first: Rachael taking advice. "Sorry. Continue, please."

"So, I was packing my car after the dance class, and I was in a Rachael mood."

Frankie cringed when Rachael referred to herself in the third person, something she often did. "Which one is that?" Frankie couldn't help herself.

"When I get cranky. Anyway, I was tossing my equipment into the car while I was thinking about Salvatore going to Italy, and what you said about being nonchalant."

"Okay. And?"

"The speakers got tangled, and I was trying to rearrange everything when a nice, slightly younger man approached and offered to help."

"Chivalry is not dead," Frankie mused.

"He recognized me from the center and the Halloween party."

"Oh, I think I see where this is going. You were dressed like a French maid."

"Yep, but it was my dancing that caught his eye."

"He's tactful but sounds like he was flirting with you."

"Sorta. I mean he wasn't over the top or anything, but he asked me if I would like to have coffee."

"And?" Frankie dragged out the word.

"And I followed your advice. I was nonchalant."

Frankie perked up. "How so?"

"I took his number and said I would check my schedule. Then I got in my car, gave a brief wave, and drove off."

"You left? You didn't go for coffee? You let him leave the parking lot without making a date?" Frankie was incredibly surprised.

"I said I would get back to him."

"Brava!"

"I thought you might say that."

"What about Salvatore?" Frankie knew the relationship was "undefined."

"There is no ring on my finger," Rachael said smugly.

"Good. Are you going to tell him?"

"Nope. In fact, I have a plan."

"Uh-oh." Frankie feared what Rachael might have up her sleeve.

"No! Listen. I am shifting into Frankie mode. I am going to call him and apologize for being unreasonable and tell him that I hope he enjoys himself."

"And he won't think you're being sarcastic?"

"I think I can be convincing that I'm being sincere."

"And are you?" Frankie was dubious.

"No, but he doesn't need to know that." Rachael paused. "I shall be charming in my new nonchalant persona."

"Okay. What did you do with my friend Rachael?" Frankie laughed.

"Come on, Frankie, I'm serious. Obviously, my moves have only worked on the dance floor, so I'm going to change my routine."

"Good girl!" Frankie was pleased that Rachael was having a *man-piphony*, a word she'd created when she was first dating Giovanni. Something had clicked, and she took two steps back, and Giovanni took two steps forward. Her mother had been right all these years.

"Look, I realize most of my dating debacles have been self-inflicted, so I'm turning the page on my approach."

"Rach, I am happy to hear this. And I think you will enjoy playing cat and mouse."

"I agree. I knew I had it in me, but I guess I never had the confidence to try it."

"Not that I'm an expert, but I'll be glad to be your coach should you feel you're having a relationship relapse."

"Thanks, pal."

"Tell me a little more about your new friend."

"He's a nurse practitioner. My guess is he's about three or four years younger. Nice looking. Clean-cut. Not necessarily a heartthrob, but he seemed to be kind and witty."

"For me, that's a much bigger turn-on than a hunk."

"You got that right. Hunks can be oblivious. Self-involved."

"That's because they've gotten lots of attention their entire lives by simply looking good."

"So true," Rachael sighed. "Anyhoo, I figure I'll wait a few days, send him a text, and let him know when I'm available. I don't want to wait too long, though."

"My recommendation is to wait four days. That way you

will remain mysterious, and he'll keep wondering when you will get in touch."

"Perfect."

"What's his name?"

"Nicholas Morrison. Nurse Nick."

"Well, my friend, I am enormously proud of you. Not just for being nonchalant, but for looking out for yourself. Going out for coffee with someone is totally innocent." Then Frankie realized with whom she was speaking. "Well, if you can behave yourself." She chuckled.

"Very funny. If you ever get out of publishing, you should consider stand-up."

"Now who's being funny?" Frankie cracked back.

"I'm going to give the new Rachael a spin when we get off the phone. I'm going to call Salvatore and be sweet as pie."

Frankie laughed out loud.

"What's so funny?"

"I had a vision of a pie with a knife baked in it. You know, like the ones they give prisoners to help them break out of jail."

"Your imagination is running wild tonight, Francesca."

"Yep. I'm in overdrive." Frankie paused, then said, "Listen, no matter what happens, you will spend New Year's Eve with me, Nina, and Amy. Regardless."

"I don't want to be the odd girl out."

"But you're not 'out.' We are a team. Don't ever forget that."

"Thanks, Frankie." Rachael got a little choked up. "I know I can be demanding at times, but I love you guys and appreciate all of you. Even the guys."

"You bet. Love you, too. Keep me posted. And if you want to call me later and let me know how your conversation with Salvatore went, I'll be up until at least eleven. *Ciao!*"

"*Ciao!*" Rachael replied.

She waited for a few minutes to gather her strength and

muster up a sense of confidence and charm. She dialed Salvatore's number.

"Hey, Rach. What's going on?" He sounded in a pleasant mood. Lately he had to steady himself from Rachael's petulance over the trip.

"Hi. Listen, I want to apologize for all my whining about your plans to go to Italy." She could envision Salvatore giving his phone a double take. "The holidays are difficult, trying to parse out time with Ryan. Greg never sticks to the schedule and is always making other plans, and I took it out on you. I'm really sorry." Rachael was impressed at how sincere she sounded. Perhaps that was because she actually was sincere.

"Yeah, I can imagine it's tough, and I'm sorry that you took my trip as a personal affront. I was inconsiderate not to discuss it with you before I made the plans."

"You have every right to make plans, but I appreciate your apology." Again, sweet Rachael emerged.

"Are we still on for tomorrow?" Salvatore asked.

Rachael paused. She didn't want to start toying with his insecurities just yet, but she thought he was going to the game with his buddies. "Um, sure. Where are we going?"

"I have tickets for a Jets game."

"Don't you usually go with Bret and Danny?" Rachael was surprised at the invitation.

"Yes, but they have something with their kids." He quickly realized she may think she was an afterthought. "But I had already told them I wanted to take you to the game." He hoped it was a good save. "So you can see why I like to go, and why you'd probably hate it." He laughed nervously.

"That's sweet. Sounds like fun." Actually, it didn't. Salvatore was right in his thinking. Rachael wasn't big on huge crowds of drunken fans, but she was going to buck up and go.

"Great. We can grab a bite. The dogs are suspect at the stadium."

Rachael chuckled. "Reva's Steak House?"

"Sounds good. I'll pick you up at five."

"Perfect. See you then."

"Rach?"

"Yeah?"

"Thanks."

"You're welcome." She got off the phone as fast as she could. She was proud of her demeanor but wasn't sure how long it was going to last.

She immediately phoned Frankie. "Mission accomplished. I apologized, and he apologized for not talking to me about it before he made his plans."

"See? Sweetness and light. A little dab will do ya."

"And he's taking me to the game tomorrow."

"But you hate that stuff." Frankie winced.

"Yes, but I think he's trying to make it up to me, although a romantic dinner would be much better."

"Take it as a good sign. You've softened him up. Then you can peel his ego like an onion."

Rachael howled, "Frankie, you never cease to amaze me. You can be rather diabolical."

Frankie lowered her voice an octave. "I am your mentor."

"You sound more like Svengali." Rachael snickered.

Frankie maintained her baritone level. "Even better." Then she let out an evil laugh, one that you'd hear from a haunted house.

"Now you're starting to sound creepy," Rachael said, chuckling.

Frankie continued with her impersonation of Bela Lugosi, the first actor to play Count Dracula in the 1931 movie. She rolled her *R*s appropriately. "Yourr rrevenge has just begun."

"Okay, weirdo. I think it's time for you to go to bed," Rachael said jokingly.

"Ah, but the night is still young." Frankie let out the sinful laugh again. "Ha ha, ha ha ha."

"Okay. I am getting off the phone now. Let me know when my friend Frankie gets back. Nighty-night."

"See ya, toots!" Frankie signed off in her usual cheerful tone.

Rachael cranked up the music and did the cha-cha in front of her dog, Digger, slang for *jail cell*. The previous year, she and Randy had spent a few hours at the Grey-Bar Hotel after a big misunderstanding on the winding roads of the Amalfi Coast. Digger's head followed her every move; then he got up on his hind legs and slapped his paws on her shoulders.

Rachael laughed. "If I could post this on TikTok, you'd be a star!"

Digger *woof*ed in response.

Chapter 4

Amy—Santa's Crew

Boston

Amy Blanchard knew the holidays were going to be a head-ache this year. She was going to be pulled in so many different directions.

Her overbearing mother would insist Amy spend the holidays with her and her new husband, Lloyd Luttrell. Amy actually liked Lloyd. He had been her mother's and Rachael's divorce lawyer, but when Amy's mother planned to marry a grifter named Rusty Jacobs, Amy sought Lloyd's assistance. She urged Lloyd to speak to her mother about getting Rusty to sign a prenup. Amy was certain he wouldn't sign it and would bolt at the suggestion. It took a few weeks of Rusty trying to sweet-talk the new, lonely divorcée, but Lloyd was relentless, and kept nudging Dorothy to "get those papers signed. It's for your and Amy's protection." It came as no surprise when Rusty took a powder. Lloyd was sympathetic. He was a confidant. Someone to talk to. Spend time with. He nursed her bruised ego. That's not to say he didn't have an ulterior motive, but it was a good motive. He genuinely cared for Dorothy. The more time they spent together, the more Dorothy appreciated this fine man. Lloyd was decent, successful, kind, and age-appropriate.

Then there was her dad and his wife, Marilyn. Like her mom and Lloyd, they lived in New Jersey. But Marilyn had adult children and grandchildren who lived in Virginia. Amy thought Marilyn would surely want to spend time with them.

And she couldn't forget Peter's family, who lived in Connecticut.

She and Peter lived in Boston. Amy mulled the scenarios in her head. There were a lot of logistics involved, including arrangements for Gimpy and Blinky, her fittingly named cats. Then there was the fact that the rest of the world would be traveling at the same time. It was beginning to make her head hurt.

Amy was a scientist, and solving problems was part of her job, but when it came to social functions or simply getting from point A to point B, it could be a problem. She could recite quantum formulas, but if you asked her what bus she took to work, she would reply, "The one that stops in front of me." Her navigational skills were nowhere to be found, and often so was Amy. The year before, she got an invitation to see the Hadron Collider in Geneva. It was a scientific wonder, splitting atoms and delving into the origin of the universe. But while she was waiting for her escort, she got in the wrong line and was transported to another attraction several miles away, with a group of non-English-speaking tourists. Once again, it was Peter to the rescue of the absent-minded professor.

She decided to approach the holiday madness as if she were solving a mathematical problem. She went into their den and rolled the whiteboard out from behind the door and wiped it down. Using the blue marker, she began dividing it into sections:

PETER'S FAMILY
DAD & MARILYN
MOM & LLOYD

Under each heading, she listed the states she thought everyone would have to cover.

The bottom half of the board had a rudimentary sketch of the Northeast Corridor from Virginia to Massachusetts. She used the red marker to indicate the towns with an X. She stood back and pondered how she and Peter could accommodate everyone, including themselves.

Her first idea was to drive from Boston to Connecticut, spend Christmas Eve Day and Christmas Eve with Peter's family. The next morning, they would drive to New Jersey to spend Christmas Day with . . . ? She supposed it would depend on where Marilyn would be. If she was in Virginia, Amy's father would most likely be there, too. She scribbled a note in the corner: *talk to Dad*. Her mother and Lloyd shouldn't be an issue, since his kids were an hour from where they lived. She put a dot on Ramsey, New Jersey.

Blinky and Gimpy jumped off the desk, where they had been spying on Amy's graphics. They looked up when they heard the front door open.

"Daddy's home!" Amy squealed. "I'm in here," she called out to Peter.

Peter gave her a peck on the top of her head. "What is all this? A new equation?" He peered closer. "Christmas Eve?"

"I'm trying to figure out how we can spend as much time with as many people as possible." She stepped back and tapped the marker against her lips, turning them blue.

Peter burst out laughing.

"What's so funny?" She harrumphed.

He lifted her chin. "Your face." Then he kissed her on the nose.

"What's so funny about my face?" Amy asked again with indignance.

"Are you okay?" Peter asked. It was not like Amy to be touchy. Snarky. He took out a handkerchief, dipped it in a glass of water, and wiped her mouth. She was blinking the same way her cat blinked when he was confused. Peter showed her the now-blue piece of linen.

Amy immediately sighed. "Sorry, Peter. I'm trying to figure this out, and it's making my hair hurt."

Peter scanned the board. "Looks like a lot of dots, and is that a map?"

Amy snatched the soiled hankie from his hand and gave him an affectionate slap on the arm. "I'm a scientist. Not an artist."

"Science *is* an art." He took her hand and coaxed her into one of the overstuffed club chairs. "Let's talk about this. I'm a math guy; you're a science maven. I am sure we can figure it out together."

Amy appreciated Peter's level-headed yet lighter approach to things. She pointed to her amateur cartography. "It's going to be a highway nightmare getting from one place to another."

"Not if we plan carefully." Peter took the marker from her hand and approached the board. "Do you know what your mother and father have planned?"

"No." Amy lowered her gaze.

"So, you're getting yourself in a tizzy before you know anyone else's itinerary." He was patient and correct. "Let's call your dad now and ask him."

"I don't want him to think I'm being nosey." Amy was on the brink of whining.

"You're not being nosey. You are being proactive."

Amy sat up. "Yes. Proactive. Good word."

Peter couldn't help but smile at her cherub face. "I tell you what. How about if I call him? Then he won't think you're the one being nosey."

Her eyes brightened. "Really? That would be swell!"

Before she had a chance to change her mind, Peter pulled out his cell and dialed Willie B.'s number. With Frankie and Amy's fathers having the same name, they decided on a nickname for Amy's dad from when they were in high school.

"Willie B.! Peter here." He made sure his tone was upbeat. Parents don't normally like to hear from their children's significant others. Their parental instincts go immediately to thinking something is wrong. Before Willie B. had a moment to respond, Peter continued. "Amy and I are sitting here trying to' put holiday plans together." Peter realized Willie B. might wonder why Peter was shoehorning himself into a family situation, and quicky continued. "She's standing in front of a whiteboard that looks like a schematic of the interstate highway commission." Peter chuckled. "Yes, she likes to plan ahead. Not that she won't get lost along the way." He grinned at Amy, who gave him a sideways glance in return. "I'll put us on speaker."

"Hey, Daddy!" Amy called out.

"Hey, sugar pie. Getting yourself all flummoxed?"

Amy couldn't argue. As brilliant as she was, some of the simplest things could throw her off. "I am trying not to."

Peter smiled at the cute face before him that still had a few blotches of blue. "Do you and Marilyn know what you're doing for the holidays?"

"Marilyn wants to send her grandkids to Disney World. I told her to leave me out of the plans. I cannot imagine what the Magic Kingdom is like at that time of year."

"Good point," Peter remarked.

"And much to my surprise, Marilyn had the same sentiment and said she would send the parents and the kids. By themselves."

"Sounds like you escaped the fairy-tale nightmare." Peter laughed.

"Talk about an oxymoron," Willie B. added. "I didn't mind doing it once when Amy was little, but now? No way."

"I'm with you on that." Peter waited for Willie B. to discuss the rest of the holiday plans.

"Marilyn and I were thinking about going on another cruise. Would you kids mind?"

Amy's eyes got as big as saucers as she recalled how all of them met.

"The last one was certainly momentous," Peter added. "For all of us."

Willie B. continued, "Amy, honey, would you mind if Marilyn and I spent the holidays on the high seas?"

"Not at all!" she squealed. "That would be great for the two of you, and romantic."

"I thought so, but I didn't know how you would feel if we weren't here."

"Oh, Daddy, whatever makes you happy. Have you discussed this with Marilyn?"

"Yes, and she is all for it."

"Excellent! Where are you going?"

"We're going to cruise the Greek Islands."

"Fantastic! Even more romantic than a singles' cruise." Amy giggled, both with delight and relief. "We can make a plan either before or after you get back."

Peter scribbled *Thanksgiving?* on a piece of paper. He and Amy had talked about having their own quiet dinner together. No traveling. There would be enough of that in December. Amy nodded.

"Dad? Would you be mad if Peter and I decided to stay home for Thanksgiving? The end of the semester is coming up right behind the holidays, and I know I'll have a ton of work. I could use the days to get a lot done and give myself a day or two to chill."

"Honey, that's perfectly fine with me. I'll check with Marilyn and see when she's available, and we can spend a different weekend together. One where the entire country isn't rushing off for a turkey dinner."

"Let's not forget football," Peter added, thinking how relaxing a few days at home would be welcome. He just had to figure out how to break the news to his family.

Amy stood and stepped in front of the whiteboard. She erased the notes from Boston to New Jersey, and drew a fresh line from Boston to Norwich, Connecticut. Peter gave her the thumbs-up.

"To recap," Peter said in his best accountant voice, "we'll be staying home for Thanksgiving. You and Marilyn will be off to the Greek islands for the Christmas and New Year's holidays. You will speak with Marilyn so the four of us can plan a weekend together. Sound good?"

"Sounds excellent. Thanks, Peter, for helping to streamline the most wonderfully stressful time of the year!"

"And I helped." Amy was grinning from ear to ear.

"Okay, kids. Time for me to start dinner," Willie B. announced. "Ever since we met Giovanni, he's snookered me into watching his cooking demos."

Amy was over the moon. The cruise had turned everyone's life around in the best possible way. "What are you working on tonight?"

"Rigatoni Bolognese. Three different kinds of meat: pork, beef, veal. Served with a dollop of whipped ricotta."

"Sounds delish!" Amy smacked her lips.

"I hope so!" Willie B. replied.

"Talk soon. Love you!" Amy signed off.

"Love you more," her father said, and ended the call.

Suddenly Amy's mood shifted.

"What is it?" Peter asked with concern.

"My mother! Yikes! She will have a hissy fit if we don't do what she wants us to do."

"Can you talk to Lloyd? He's come through many times before," Peter suggested.

Amy twisted her mouth. "I'll call him to see what my mother has been up to, but I'll text him first. Just in case she's hovering."

Amy tapped out a quick text to Lloyd:

Hi. Do you have a private minute to talk?

A few seconds went by, and he replied:

Everything alright?

Amy answered:

Yes. Want to discuss the holidaze.

Lloyd sent back a smiley face and:

Want to talk now?

Amy hit the phone icon on her mobile.

"Hey, Amy. What's on your mind?" Lloyd asked. The families stayed in constant contact, usually by text or email. Phone calls were reserved for holidays, birthdays, and special occasions.

"Peter and I are trying to plan, and I wanted to know what you and my mother had going on."

"Funny you should ask. My daughter moved to South Carolina and is expecting another baby, so it's going to be difficult for her to travel. Your mother and I discussed going down there, but she was concerned that you'd be offended."

"Another baby? How wonderful!" Amy exclaimed, then continued. "Offended? How could I be? That's a wonderful reason to visit them." This time it was her turn to give the thumbs-up. "How about we plan a weekend before the holidays? Say, mid-December before everything spins out of control."

"That sounds like an excellent idea," Lloyd replied. "Let me run it past your mother."

"Oh, don't tell her we spoke. You know how paranoid she can get."

Lloyd chuckled. "Leave it to me. I'll suggest we get tickets for Radio City and invite you and Peter, and we can have our holiday before the holiday."

"You're a genius," Amy said. "My dad is going to Greece, so Peter and I were going to plan a weekend with them, so maybe we can combine our merrymaking?"

"Excellent idea, Amy. No wonder they call you a whiz kid."

Chapter 5

Kathryn—The Sisterhood

Cross Country

The holidays were a few short weeks away. Kathryn had to finish this run, and then one more for Annie. She passed several trucks carrying hundreds upon hundreds of Christmas trees to their final destinations. She glanced over at her big German shepherd sitting in the passenger seat, strapped in with his special seat belt. She asked, "Did you know there are somewhere between twenty-five and thirty million trees sold every year?" The dog yawned. "But did you also know it takes almost seven years for a tree to grow between six and seven feet?" Murphy sputtered. "One more factoid, and I'll change the subject," Kathryn said and continued, "There are sixteen types of Christmas trees, but the balsam fir is the most popular and smells the best." Murphy expressed his boredom with another yawn.

"Well, you never know when you'll be in a trivia game." Kathryn tried to remember the last time she played a trivia game. It had been years. Many, many years.

Kathryn considered how quickly time had blown past her, and she began to ruminate about her life. It had been several years since Kathryn's husband passed away from MS. Most patients can survive for many years with proper treatment, but she honestly believed that being forced to watch her get raped is what really killed him. It was devastating. All of it. The joy of Christmas had been lost. Year after year, she would climb deeper into her fortress of solitude, pushing any semblance of holiday spirit as far back as possible, until it was over and a new year was upon her. But what did that mean, exactly? A *new* year? Had it become the same old year, year after year, as the calendar ticked by?

"I think I might have to make a few adjustments," she said to Murphy. Then, "I might be getting road weary."

Murphy let out a big dog yawn.

"Yeah, me too," Kathryn said with a sigh.

She continued her somewhat one-way conversation with her travel companion. "Ya know, it's not like I want another person in my life. I tried with Bert, but he wanted to get married, and I did not. Then there was Jack Sparrow. Nice guy, but I wasn't ready."

She tooted her horn at one of her fellow road warriors as he passed her in the left lane.

"I don't know if I can ever be in love again, but I am beginning to feel as if something is missing."

Her pooch let out another yawn. This time it had a little *woof* to it.

"Ah, so you agree?"

He let out another *woof*.

"I thought so," she continued to think out loud. "Maybe I've been so absorbed separating myself from most things that I haven't taken a better look at what I *do* have. Friendship, for one. And of course, you for another." She pursed her lips. "Maybe it's time to focus on the blessings I have."

Another *woof* of approval from her canine buddy, Murphy.

"I suspect I've been clinging to the bitterness. I got my revenge, for sure, but I suppose it didn't fill the black hole in my heart. I really hate the expression 'move on.' I'll never move on from how much I loved that man, but maybe I can open myself up and embrace the wonderful things that I've gained as a result of that horrible experience."

Murphy let out a soft groan.

"Exactly," Kathryn said, agreeing with her dog. "Well, I'm glad Annie and Myra are doing something for kids this year, and I am happy to help."

Murphy bobbed his head in approval.

"You really are beginning to understand me." Kathryn laughed.

The dog looked at her straight in the eye and *woof*ed again.

Kathryn laughed again. "Maybe I should spend more time with humans. No offense, but if I told people my dog and I have conversations, they'd lock me up in a loony bin."

Murphy bobbed his head again.

Kathryn was heading west, and then south to New Mexico. Once she delivered her load she planned to dead-head it back to Virginia. Kathryn was proud of the way she handled an eighteen-wheeler. She was also proud of the fact that she was part of an elite group of road warriors. Less than six percent of them were women, and all of them were highly respected.

Kathryn had mastered her daily driving routine: Up at six in the morning. Shower at the truck stop. Eat breakfast. Do a pre-trip safety check, then cover close to 500 miles of road in a day. At the end of the day, she'd find a spot at a stop and pull in for the night. After sitting for hours upon hours behind the wheel, she'd take Murphy for a walk and stretch her legs. If the diner was empty, they would occasionally allow Murphy to join her for dinner. Otherwise, she'd tie him to the post just outside the front door, where they could keep an eye on each other. Once that ritual was complete, Kathryn and Murphy returned to the cab and got the bunk ready for the rest of the evening. The next step was to open her laptop and notify the dispatcher she was in "sleeper mode." After she got the confirmation that her message had been received, she'd find a movie before Murphy had a chance to horn in on her small space. It never failed; by the next morning, the big hairy dog would be right up against her back.

Kathryn still had many more miles to cover before she could head in for the night. And with so many hours on the road, she had ample time to think about how she could start opening herself up to life. Normally she spent Thanksgiving alone, but this year, she decided to accept Myra and Annie's invitation to spend it with them. One thing she could not resist was one of Charles's fabulous meals.

She pressed the Bluetooth button on her steering wheel and spoke into the voice control, "Call Myra." A disembodied voice replied, "Calling Myra on kitchen phone."

Two rings later, Myra answered. She noticed Kathryn's name on the caller ID. "Everything alright, dear?"

"Yep," Kathryn replied. "If it's not too late, I would like to take you up on your offer for Thanksgiving."

"That's wonderful, Kathryn. I am so happy you changed your mind."

"Truth be told, it was Murphy."

"Oh?" Myra was a bit taken aback. It was true Myra spoke to her dogs as if they were human, as did most of the Sisters with their pets, but this was the first time she'd heard Kathryn speak about it.

"I know. I must sound like a loon."

"Not at all. I do it all the time. You know that." Myra's voice was calm and comforting.

"Yeah, well, I supposed this is the first time I've admitted my conversations with my German shepherd to anyone."

"You're talking to the right gal," Myra said, chuckling.

"I've been doing a lot of introspection," Kathryn said, and

sighed. "After losing two friends over the past two years, it made me realize how precious life is. I know I felt that way when Alan died, but having two of my fellow road warriors pass brought things into focus again."

"Oh, dear. I know how painful it is to lose someone you love."

"I know you do. And I also know how you picked yourself up and found a purpose. I, for one, was one of them. Anyhoo, I decided it was time for me to climb out of my cocoon. Again."

Myra listened intently. These are the words she had hoped to hear from Kathryn. It had been a long time coming.

Kathryn continued, "The first two attempts were a bust, but I think that's because I was still too raw from losing Alan, and I was never really present. I was living in the past. And in my grief."

"That is perfectly understandable, Kathryn," Myra said with warmth.

"I knew you would get it." Kathryn had a smile on her face.

"I do, indeed," Myra said. She knew Kathryn was on speakerphone and added, "Murphy is also invited to dinner."

A loud *woof* echoed through the cab of the truck.

"Hey Murphy!" Myra called to the dog. "You and Lady and her pups will have a grand time."

The dog responded with a yowl.

"See, I told you he talks to me!" Kathryn said, and chuckled.

"I didn't doubt you for a minute," Myra said, and smiled.

Kathryn held out her hand, and Murphy gave it a nudge. "Good boy."

"This is extremely exciting, Kathryn. I have some additional news, and I hope you will find it appealing."

"Do tell." Traffic was light, so Kathryn continued the conversation. She turned off Interstate 80 onto Interstate 25 South.

"Annie wants to have a block party for New Year's Eve."

"Block party?" Kathryn asked. Her curiosity was piqued.

"Whose block?"

"East Thirty-fifth Street."

"In the city?"

"Yes. She's a few doors down from Sniffen Court, where Camille lives."

"Are you going to spend the entire week there?"

"No. We'll go up for the event, come home, and spend Christmas here. Then we'll fly back up on the thirtieth. I hope you'll join us. And for Christmas," Myra offered.

"Won't you be sick of me by then?" Kathryn said, and chuckled.

"Doubtful," Myra replied. "It will be great fun, especially if Annie is planning the party."

"That's for sure. But a block party? How is she going to get the city of New York to shut down her street?" Kathryn said, then paused. "Right. It's Annie!"

"Exactly!" Myra replied. "Kathryn, you know we love you, and I am very happy to hear a new tone in your voice."

"A tone? In my voice?" Kathryn asked.

"Yes. I should say I *feel* the tone," Myra said reassuringly.

"I'm feeling it, too," Kathryn responded. "I better jump off the call. Traffic is picking up. I should be back in Virginia in three days. I'll give you a shout as soon as I get in."

"Wonderful!" Myra exclaimed. "Be safe. You take good care of your mommy, Murphy."

Murphy responded with another *woof*.

Kathryn felt lighter. More relaxed. She knew Alan would want her to enjoy life. She deserved it. Now she finally believed it.

The following morning, her alarm went off at six, and the rest of the day would be an iteration of the day before. It was a sunny day with clear blue skies and a few puffy clouds.

"Beautiful, eh, pal?" she said to her travel companion.

Murphy yelped in agreement. Another truckload of Christmas trees passed in the opposite direction. "I think I'm going to enjoy the holidays this year," she said, and then smiled to herself. Then suddenly a jarring thought occurred to her. "Oh, geez! I hope I don't have to wear a dress for New Year's!"

Murphy howled in agreement.

Chapter 6

Nina—Santa's Crew

Milan, Italy

Nina and her producing partner, Jordan, were going over the notes the film's director requested.

"Do you think this movie will really happen?" Nina asked, and stretched.

It had been an extraordinarily long week. The two had been working on the treatment for the film for almost a year. There were meetings after meetings with prospective investors, producers, and talent. An up-and-coming director was eager to work with them and signed on right away. The rest of their pursuits were not as easy, with the exception of one actress that Nina was thrilled to get on board. It was Gail Edwards, who once starred in the sitcoms *Blossom* and *Full House*, guest starred in *M*A*S*H, Taxi,* and *Happy Days,* and was directed by Spielberg in his foray into television. But what Nina appreciated the most was her timing and great comedic flare.

"Granted she is older now, but that makes her more seasoned. More believable," Nina continued. "She could easily play the mother of a young woman determined to marry a man no one knew anything about."

It didn't take much convincing on anyone's part. Jordan knew Gail was the perfect fit, but there was something weighing heavily on his mind. "Darling, I think we should consider pitching this as a series."

Nina's head jolted. "Really? Why?"

"Because that's where the money is now."

Nina thought about what he said. "Then that's where we need to go. Where the money is."

"I am happy to hear you say that. I know you were counting on doing a film, but think of this as a film divided into eight parts."

"Well, duh," she replied, and shot a sideways look. "How long have you been thinking about this?"

"Since the first pitch meeting."

"Six months ago?" Nina said with a gasp.

"I was hoping we could move the needle, but all signs are pointing to streaming services."

"I totally get that, and I'm fine with it. I just wish you would have mentioned it sooner. I would have taken a different approach." Nina wasn't angry. Just frustrated. And tired.

"You are an amazing writer, Nina. You can develop the script into eight parts. Easy."

"Easy for you to say," Nina said, and smirked.

"Do not underestimate your talent, young lady."

"Such a sweet talker," Nina replied.

Jordan was very budget-conscious. In order to get financial backing, you either needed a huge checkbook with a big name whether they could really act or not or something a little quirky with interesting characters, intriguing storylines, and a good setting. Jordan wanted to spend the money on the location. In his mind, the location was also one of the stars of the movie. It wasn't simply about the scenery. It was the history, the people, and the ability to almost smell the sea air, or the bakery, or the sour beer in the pub. He had several locations in mind. One was Cornwall, at the southwest tip of England. It formed a peninsula with cliffs on the north and sandy beaches on the south. Many referred to that area as "The Cornish Riviera."

Jordan walked over to the whiteboard and continued to explain his idea further. "If we do eight episodes, each one can be in a different location. We know there are millions of Anglophiles who cannot get enough of the British culture. Look how far entertainment has come from *Fawlty Towers* in the seventies, to *Downton Abbey*, then *Bridgerton* in the past few years. It's no accident that BritBox and Acorn are so popular." He wrote the prospective locations on the board. Cornwall, Cambridge, Oxford, the Cotswolds, Stonehenge, the Lake District, Kent, East Sussex, and Norwich.

"I am getting the picture. No pun intended," Nina said, grinning. "Actually, I think it's a brilliant idea!" She let out a big sigh. "I feel much better now about the project." She could feel the tension in her shoulders release.

Jordan was thankful the conversation went in a positive direction. He thought Nina had her heart set on a feature-length film, but the new suggestion was met with enthusiasm. "We can tackle this when we get back to the States."

"Now that sounds like an excellent plan," Nina replied.

"Speaking of plans, what are your plans for the holidays?"

"I haven't made any so far. Still trying to figure out Richard's schedule. He has a few holiday events he needs to attend, both in Philly and New York."

"What about your family?"

"They're all over the place. The Caribbean, Mexico, Florida, and everywhere in between."

"Sounds like they are enjoying retirement."

"That's for sure. And I am enjoying their retirement, as well. I've had the entire house to myself for a year."

"Speaking of the holidays, I'll be spending some of it with Randy," Jordan announced.

"That's great! I am so happy the two of you hit it off."

Jordan paused. "Well, I don't think your friend Rachael is too thrilled about it."

Nina wasn't surprised at Jordan's assessment but had to ask, "Why do you say that?"

"Apparently she gave him a hard time about New Year's Eve."

"We sort of started a tradition and have been spending it together for the past three years."

"There's no reason why we can't celebrate together this year, is there?" Jordan asked curiously. "Provided we don't spend it on the rooftop of a jail." Jordan recalled the previous year when he met the gang for New Year's Eve. It was supposed to be a party at Giovanni's family home in Salerno, but due to a curve in the road, the venue was moved to a jail on the Amalfi Coast. Fortunately, a local judge intervened, and the party went on as planned on the roof of the local police station.

Nina laughed out loud. "Good point—which reminds me, I have to contact Frankie, our pushy-planner-lady."

"Do you think I should reach out to Rachael?" Jordan asked.

"Nah. It will just create more drama," Nina said as she considered the irony: Nina was the actress of the group. "And from what Frankie told me, Rachael is in fury overdrive."

"Not because of me, is it?" Jordan asked. He was truly taken aback.

"You're only half of the problem," Nina said, and kicked off her shoes. She settled into the cushions of the sofa. "I know I am not telling tales out of school. Her boyfriend, Salvatore, is going to Italy for the holidays. You met him last year."

"Yes. Nice fellow. Why doesn't she go with him?"

"Because he didn't ask her." Nina rolled her eyes.

"Well, that's not very nice," Jordan said, and frowned. "Do they live together?"

"No, not that either of them asked the other." Nina paused. "It's no surprise that she is frustrated, but when Frankie encouraged Rachael to have a 'sit-down' with Salvatore, Rachael said that if he wanted a commitment, then he should bring it up."

"Oh, I know that situation all too well. You hesitate to bring up the subject because you think you will be kicked in the gut."

"Precisely. But wouldn't you rather know? I sure would. It's hard to live your life if you're waiting for someone else to make a move."

"Fear," Jordan said, and paused. "It holds the strongest influence on us. We often do things out of fear, or we don't do them for fear of the outcome."

"I think I'm long past that. At least I hope I am. Being secure with yourself is important. But I don't have to tell you how Hollywood can turn you into the most insecure person on the planet. Rejection stinks."

Jordan laughed out loud. "It does, indeed. Thank goodness we've grown a second skin. I try to let things bounce off me and go with my gut."

"That's one of the things I most admire about you, Jordan. You take a deep breath and jump, and not out of fear. It's out of curiosity. What will this leap of faith bring?"

"Nina, you surely have grown to know me."

"I wouldn't have been paying much attention if I didn't," Nina said, and winked. "Don't misunderstand me. You're an open book, but without being predictable. I suppose what I am trying to say is there will always be a story on the page."

"What a lovely thing to say," Jordan replied, smiling.

" 'Tis true! You have a free and creative soul, and I am flattered that you have included me in your endeavor."

"Likewise. I wasn't sure a young writer would want to collaborate with an old fossil like me."

Nina roared. "You're ten years older than me! That would make me a younger old fossil!"

"Okay, younger old fossil, what shall we do about dinner?"

"You know my fav is chicken Milanese."

"I think you must eat it four times a week, if not more."

"When in Milan. . . ." Her voice trailed off.

Jordan walked over to the iron coat rack that stood in the corner near the door. When there wasn't an article of outerwear hanging on it, it looked like a piece of sculpture. He grabbed their jackets. *"Andiamo!"* He said in Italian.

They linked arms and walked down the cobblestone street of his neighborhood.

"This is a captivating place," Nina said as she marveled at the pristine, historic landmarks. "I wish I could be here to see the Christmas decorations, the market, and all the wonderful holiday magic with the festive decorations, the stunning dome in the Galleria Vittorio Emanuele II, and the Christmas tree in Piazza del Duomo." She took in a deep breath of the cool evening air. "I'm glad I got to see it last year."

"So, let's plan some holiday magic for next year."

"That would be nice."

"Christmas season officially starts on December seventh."

"I shall mark it in my calendar," Nina replied.

"Excellent. And if Randy is a good boy, we'll invite him, too. Of course you must include Richard."

"Of course," Nina said, and gave him a nudge. Thinking about their earlier conversation about Rachael and Salvatore, Nina was taken aback at the idea that she and Richard never had "the talk," either. Was it fear? She wondered.

Jordan could feel Nina become tense. "Everything alright?"

"Yes, but it occurred to me that Richard and I haven't had that awkward conversation, either."

"Fear?"

"I don't think so." She ruminated for a few seconds. "I suppose we've been going with the flow for almost three years."

"That's a good way to move through life, provided it's not a symptom of being lazy, which you are not."

"Maybe he and I have been wrapped up in our careers and our routines. We spend weekends together, and he stays with me when he's working in the city."

Jordan lifted Nina's hand. "Hmm. Empty."

Nina jerked her hand back. "I didn't say I wanted to get married, Jordan."

"I didn't say you did. It was more of an observation as to whether or not you want to be in a committed relationship."

"I thought I was. I mean, I'm quite sure I am. Neither of us are spending time with anyone else."

"Do you want to? Spend time with anyone else?"

"No," Nina said decisively.

"Do you love Richard?" Jordan asked plainly.

"Yes. Very much. He's kind, witty, and generous." She paused, and then hooted, "Plus he has a job!"

Jordan laughed, as well. "I'm sorry if I've been prying into your personal life."

"Geez. You and I are almost married," Nina scoffed.

"Wrong team, sweetheart."

Nina began to pull Jordan along. "I'm hungry. We can continue this conversation over dinner. Or not."

Chapter 7

Pinewood

A Few Days Later

Myra could hear the popping of gravel being turned up by Annie's arrival. Lady gave a *woof* of acknowledgment. As per her usual entrance, Annie bounced through the door with greetings, hugs, and kisses, and not necessarily in that order. Fergus followed behind with his hands in his pockets, getting ready for Lady and her pups and their expectations of treats.

"Hello, dear!" Charles said, chopping something on the butcher block. Annie pecked him on the cheek and sniffed the pot on the stove. He shooed her away. "Your cohort is in the atrium." He looked up at Fergus, who was doling out doggie morsels. "Hello, mate. Ready to get your apron on?"

"Why is it that every time I walk into this kitchen, I become the sous chef?" he said, and snickered.

"Because you are," Charles replied. He nodded to an apron that hung on the knob of the large walk-in pantry.

"What's on the menu today?" Fergus asked, as he tied the fresh apron strings around his waist.

"Something from the homeland," Charles said, winking.

"I thought you were going to cook real food," Fergus said, and grimaced.

"Steady on, mate. I put my own spin on this stew."

"Do tell," Fergus urged.

"If I tell you, I'll have to kill you," Charles joked, although in the past that could have been a real possibility. Thirty years later, not so much.

Fergus eyed the twenty-five-year-aged bottle of Modena balsamic vinegar behind one of the colanders. "No worries, mate." He slapped his friend on the shoulder.

"We have about a half hour to kill. What you say we watch some football?" Charles offered.

"Football as in the American version? Or real football as in soccer?"

"Good one, but I still have trouble using the word *soccer* when referring to the game." Charles handed Fergus a clean towel. "Let's clean up first."

"Fair enough." Fergus wiped the sauté pan until it was shining. Within a few minutes, the two men retreated into the den opposite the atrium.

"We'll be in here, love." Charles gave the women a nod.

Myra waved back. "Have fun."

The two women were sitting at the long wooden table in Myra's atrium. They had their laptops in front of them, each contacting the vendors who promised donations of toys.

"This is really coming together," Annie said gleefully. "So far we have over two hundred toys coming in."

Myra turned to her friend. "And I have another three."

"Hundred?" Annie's eyes went wide.

"Yes!" She and Annie did a high five. "You said your goal was to get a thousand, correct?"

"That is correct!" Annie said, grinning from ear to ear.

"Do you have any idea of how many pallets that will be? Do you think Kathryn will be able to manage it?"

"We'll get the cubic footage of the pallets and let Kathryn figure out what size truck she will need."

Another high five slapped between them.

"Speaking of Kathryn, she will be joining us for all of our holiday festivities from Thanksgiving to New Year's! Isn't that wonderful?"

"Wow! How did you manage to talk her into it?"

"I didn't, really. She phoned while she was driving and said she was having some introspection, or at least that's what it sounded like."

"Oh?" Annie said, peering over her reading glasses.

"It seems as if she wants to get back into the land of the living, and not just on the highways and byways of the country."

"It's not as if she hadn't tried to make a connection in the past."

"True. But I think it was too soon. She had so much grief to deal with. Her ordeal with those horrid men was more than enough to shut down any normal person, but then the mess with Alan, being forced to watch. And then losing him. I remember what it was like after Barbara. I was out of it for months," Myra said, reminding her friend of the darkest days of her life after her daughter was killed.

"Yes, you were buried deep in that black hole. I worried you would never come out of it. You became so frail. Unresponsive."

Myra sighed. "I know I put everyone through a lot of angst, but look how far we've come!" she said, then held up her hand for a fist bump.

"You ain't kiddin'," Annie said, and grinned.

They were busy logging the promised loot onto a spreadsheet when another email dinged. Myra squinted at the email address. It was from Silly Socks. "Do you know anyone at Silly Socks?"

"No. Why?"

"Because they said they heard about our toy drive and are offering to donate fun holiday socks for the kids," Myra shared.

"Terrific! Who doesn't need a pair of fun socks?" Annie asked rhetorically.

"You surely don't." Myra faced her friend. "How many pairs do you think you have?"

Annie tilted her head from side to side. "Fifty, maybe?"

"I think that's an underestimation."

Annie snickered and replied, "I suppose you're right."

"So, who should we hit up for the other five hundred toys?" Myra asked.

Annie laughed, then said, "Definitely respond to Silly Socks and let them know we would be thrilled to accept their offer." She paused and sniffed the air. A delicious aroma was emanating from the kitchen. "What do you suppose is going on in there?" she asked.

"Let's find out," Myra replied.

Before they had a chance to get out of their seats, Charles and Fergus appeared from the den. Apparently, they could smell Charles's latest creation, as well, and Charles had the good sense to carry a kitchen timer with him just in case they got lost in the sporting event.

"How is the game?" Myra asked as the four traipsed into the kitchen.

"Someone is winning," Charles said.

"Well, duh. Do you know who?" Annie asked.

"It's one of them," Charles said, and sighed.

"Must be Madrid," Myra said. "Charles never likes to admit when his team is losing."

"They're not losing, Myra," Charles corrected her. "They simply haven't caught up yet."

Everyone laughed out loud. Besides his love for cooking, Charles had a penchant for his home team.

"Charles is making some kind of stew," Myra said.

"It's a miracle none of us have gained a ton of weight," Annie said, then chuckled.

"I know. I keep saying that to Charles, but he insists his food is nutritious, and I have to admit, it is, more often than not."

Annie added, "It's those popovers that'll get you every time."

"Especially if you eat them by the dozen like I do!" Myra said as she followed the men into the kitchen, where Charles and Fergus began sampling the goods.

"Gotcha!" Annie yelped.

"We want to be sure it's fit for you lovely ladies," Charles teased. He blew on the spoon of savory delights and put it in front of Myra's mouth.

She opened wide and accepted the scrumptious mix of meat, vegetables, and potatoes. Charles handed her a napkin to wipe the gravy that escaped her lips.

"Me too! Me too!" Annie bounced up and down.

Fergus rolled his eyes, pulled out a large wooden spoon, and scooped some into a small bowl.

Charles nudged everyone aside. "Cook coming through." He pulled a tray out of the oven that contained the dreaded popovers.

"Oh no, Charles! I was just telling Annie that these are dangerous to my hips!"

He checked the rack of puffy Yorkshire pudding the name the Brits call the soft, flaky pastry. Myra's nose followed the tray of buttery delights to the area where Charles placed them on the counter. Before Charles had a chance to turn around, Myra and Annie were practically on top of the fluffy treats.

Charles let out one of his loud whistles. "Ladies! Please! Some decorum, if you do not mind."

"Ha! Yes, we do mind!" Annie shoved another piece into her mouth. "Don't get your knickers in a snit," she cracked between the bites.

Charles shook his head and looked at Fergus. "I don't know how you put up with her," he said, and grinned.

Myra got busy pulling out bowls and flatware while Charles ladled the steaming stew into a terrine. Annie flipped the popovers into a basket, and Fergus brought glasses and napkins to the table. They sat two by two, said grace, and began to enjoy Charles's latest creation.

Annie began the conversation. "Myra and I have five hundred toys promised to us for the event!"

"Bloody impressive!" Fergus raved.

After she finished chewing, Annie said, "I'm looking for another five hundred to make it a nice even one thousand."

"Sounds like you're on your way," Charles added.

"We are going to work on the rest of the plans this afternoon," Myra said. "Oh, and Kathryn will be spending the holidays with us. Isn't that wonderful?"

"I'm chuffed to bits!" Charles used one of his favorite British expressions. "I'll have to come up with something special for Thanksgiving."

"Oh, Charles, you always come up with something special," Annie said as she waved her half-eaten popover around the table.

Charles laughed. "It's not as if we Anglos are thrilled with the idea of Thanksgiving, considering its historical roots."

"Good point," Annie said, and dunked her pastry puff into the gravy at the bottom of her bowl. "I was going to ask you how you celebrate it on the other side of the pond, but duh, I suppose you don't!" She snorted.

"That is correct." Charles had a deadpan expression, then said, "I think I shall make a crown roast."

Annie howled again. "Brilliant! Crown roast! Love it!"

"We must have a turkey," Myra said, placing her hand on Charles's arm.

"Of course! And, as you say, 'and all the fixins'!' " Charles answered cheerfully.

"Charles, we'll leave the menu up to you for Thanksgiving and Christmas. Myra and I will figure out New Year's Eve. We'll even give you the night off!"

"Bloody brilliant!" Charles gave the heavy wooden table two taps. "But I still plan to visit my idea of an amusement park for foodies!"

"Of course, we *will* expect something gastronomically fantastic at least one night while we are in the city," Annie advised.

"No worries," Charles reassured them. "Especially with my sous chef to lend a hand."

Fergus humbly bowed his head. "Indeed."

After they cleared the table, Myra and Annie retreated to the other large wooden table in the atrium where they had been working earlier. Both women always started a project or a mission using pens and lined paper pads. They didn't care that it was considered "old school." What they did care about is the underlying slur that often accompanied the remark. Annie once said, "I prefer to call it 'smart school.' "

"One thing for sure, the Gen X, Y, Z, or whatever letter of the alphabet, they tend to underestimate us." Myra winked.

"You got that right. Technology is great when used properly. Don't get me wrong; I love my phone. But I also hate it. It can be very intrusive. Annoying."

"You won't get an argument from me," Myra said in agreement. "And now they're finding many examples of social awkwardness when people actually meet in person."

Myra sighed. "Remember the days when we would run around the farm all afternoon? We'd make up games."

"Climb trees," Annie waxed nostalgically. "Lay on the

roof of one of the barns and pick out faces and shapes in the clouds."

"I sometimes feel sorry for kids today. On the one hand, they have access to almost any piece of information they could want or need," Myra replied.

"But that's part of the problem," Annie said, and then frowned. "Nobody knows what's real or not." She softly pinched Myra's wrist.

"What was that for?" It didn't hurt but was clearly unexpected.

"Just making sure you're real." Annie chortled.

Myra placed a large calendar on an easel. "Let's mark up the days."

Annie began to rattle off dates and items. She started backwards. "Toys delivered to the hotel by December nineteenth, which means they have to be unloaded and repacked on the seventeenth for transferring the pallets to smaller trucks." Then she marked the 15th for Kathryn to pick the toys up from Pinewood.

"I'll ask Charles to make sure the barn off the main road is ready. We recently had the interior floor refurbished with cement."

"Oh, a dance floor? For pole dancing, perhaps?" Annie said with a twinkle in her eye.

"Calm down, girl," Myra joked. "It was either refurbishing it or tearing it down. For sentimental reasons, I decided to refurbish it." She paused. "It's a reminder of what you just said a few moments ago. Climbing into the loft and then sneaking onto the roof to watch the sky, although I'm not sure I'd do that now."

"Don't be ridiculous. You are as spry as ever. I've seen you in that ninja outfit, climbing through a few windows."

Myra laughed and said, "I think my alter ego takes over. When I think about some of the shenanigans we've pulled, I cannot imagine I was in my right mind."

Annie laughed, too. "You are never in your wrong mind, my friend. But I'll make a deal with you. If you're willing to climb up to the top, I'll be right behind you."

"Oh, Annie. I appreciate the offer, but let's wait until it's warmer weather. There could be ice up there, and I don't want to end up on my keister."

"We'll go down together! Sisters in crime," Annie hooted.

"Sounds more like punishment," Myra said, and chuckled.

"What are you going to do with it after the holidays?" Annie asked, while tapping her pen on the pad.

"I haven't decided. We thought about turning it into a studio apartment for guests."

"That's a great idea. Close but not too close."

"My thoughts exactly. But meanwhile, it will be our staging area for the toys and the socks."

"Sounds like we have the beginning of an exceptional plan."

"We do!" Myra offered her hand for another high five.

Chapter 8

Frankie—Santa's Crew

New York City
Mid-November

The massive tree usually arrives between two and three on a Saturday morning in mid-November. After working at Grand Marshall for a few years, Frankie created her own tradition of watching the FDNY hoist the famous Norwegian spruce during the early hours, but not too early. The entire process could take anywhere from twenty-four to thirty-six hours, not counting the days it took to decorate. She set her alarm for six o'clock and planned to arrive by seven. This would be her fifth year.

The management of raising the tree didn't draw a big crowd, at least not yet. She feared someone would make this awe-inspiring ritual a "thing," and turn it into a big commercial megillah. But over the years, she recognized a few of the same people were always milling about. Frankie decided it was time for everyone to formally meet. On her way uptown, she stopped at Magnolia Bakery and bought two dozen cupcakes to give to the firemen and the crew, who were diligently working to make the season merry and bright. She also came prepared with a box of muffins and five cups of coffee for her fellow tree-hoisting spectators.

As she approached a recognizable foursome, she said, "If you're lactose intolerant, I apologize," and held out the carboard tray of caffeine.

The two couples acknowledged the gesture with nods and thanks.

"That is so thoughtful," one of the women remarked. "And I like everything dairy! I'm Judith, by the way, and this is my husband, Victor."

"Nice to meet you, Judith, and Victor. I'm Frankie."

Frankie passed the box to Victor. "Can you hold this for a sec?"

"I might run away with it," he replied with a devilish grin.

"Not if I catch you!" Judith remarked.

The second couple spoke up next. "I'm Leonora, and this is Marvin."

"Greetings!" Frankie chimed in. "Give me a second. I'll be right back, and Victor, you better not disappear with our goodies!"

"Not to worry. I'll tackle him before he can get to the curb," Judith added, and gave her husband a gentle elbow in the gut.

Frankie carried the two dozen cupcakes over to the barricades set up near the tree. Standing on the side was Captain Dag Dorph of Engine 54/Ladder 4/Battalion 9, FDNY Station. Frankie nodded, smiled, and held up the box of cupcakes. He flagged her past the barriers. "Good morning, young lady. It's alright if I call you a 'young lady?'" he asked awkwardly.

"Better than a few other names I've been called," Frankie said, chuckling. She handed over the treats. "I thought your crew could use a sugar rush."

"Thank you so much." He graciously accepted the token of appreciation. "I'm sure my guys will be incredibly grateful. They've been here since midnight, waiting for the flatbed."

"So, I heard it can take somewhere around thirty-six hours to get that baby secured?" Frankie wanted to confirm what she had read.

"Sometimes more, depending on the trunk, if it's crooked or not. They usually check that in advance, but you never know when you start trimming the bottom." The sound of electric saws drowned out any further conversation.

Before she turned to leave, she shouted, "Enjoy! And thanks for all you do for the city!" Frankie held out her hand, and got a firm shake from the fire captain.

When Frankie returned to her newfound friends, Judith proceeded to explain that they were retired and lived in Staten Island. Leonora followed, saying she and Marvin lived in Queens.

"So, how do you know each other?" Frankie asked.

"From that." Victor pointed to the tree with his free hand. "We've been coming for almost fifteen years and spotted these two awhile back. It's become a tradition now. We meet for breakfast at Andrew's Diner and walk up Fifth."

"That is so cool," Frankie said. "People think New Yorkers are not very friendly, but I've seen plenty of interaction to contradict that notion."

"So true," Judith said. "One time I was carrying a shopping bag that was a bit too heavy for its contents. Well, the handles broke and all my shoes went flying all over the sidewalk."

"How many pairs of shoes did you have?" Frankie asked as she wrapped her hands around the warm cup of coffee.

"At least a dozen. I was clearing out the collection from under my desk," Judith explained. "I wasn't going to wear my Charles Jourdan pumps on the subway, so I decided to keep my work shoes at work. One night we were going out, and I was looking for a specific pair, and then I realized that most of my shoe wardrobe was tucked away in my office. That's when I decided to bring them home. Anyway, it was raining, there were delays on the subway, the bag got soaked and the handles broke, and several hundred dollars' worth of shoes were strewn all over the sidewalk. I was ready to cry, but a few people stopped to help me. Someone went inside the store and came out with a few bags, and they helped me rescue my footwear." She turned to the group. "Now wasn't that nice?"

"Sure was," Frankie said, and nodded. "I love to hear stories like that. I know this city can be less than paradise sometimes, but the people are basically kind. As they say, we are more alike than we are different."

"I'll drink to that." Victor reached into a pocket on his jacket and produced a flask. "Anybody care for a warmer-upper?"

Frankie checked her watch. It wasn't even nine in the morning, but no judgment. She simply wasn't ready for a jolt. "Thanks, but I'm the designated driver."

"Oh? You have a car here?" Leonora asked.

Frankie chuckled and said, "No, but I have a lot of turf to cover, meaning making plans for my peeps. I've gotta be sober for the rest of the day."

"Too bad. This is some rather good bourbon." Victor put a small splash into everyone else's cup. "Maybe next year," he said to Frankie.

"I'll be sure to have all my plans nailed down before this beauty stands tall."

"What are you planning?" Judith asked casually.

"My boyfriend and his brother own a restaurant near the Flatiron Building, and their mother and aunt are going to be visiting from Italy."

"Have they been here before?" Victor asked.

"Giovanni's mother used to live here when the boys were

growing up, but she moved back a few years ago to be with her sister-in-law."

"Whereabouts do they live?" Marvin asked between pulls of his morning wake-up beverage.

"Salerno."

"Lovely area," Leonora said. "We took a vacation on the Amalfi Coast. It was glorious."

"Yes, it is. A bunch of us went there last year to celebrate New Year's Eve."

"That must have been very exciting!" Judith chimed in.

Frankie thought back to the night when they had to rescue Randy and Rachael from the local *polizia*. The memory brought a smile to her face.

"Care to share?" Judith asked.

"We had a rather raucous celebration."

"Isn't that what New Year's Eve is for? Although I barely make it past eleven," Victor joined in.

"We were waiting for two friends who had decided to rent a Vespa and tour Mt. Vesuvius. Unfortunately, they were run off the road. Thankfully, no one was hurt, but when the police arrived, Rachael didn't have her passport, and the police officer thought she and Randy were in the wrong. Anyway, it took several hours before we found out where they were. In jail. We knew there was no way they were going to make it out of the slammer that night, so we packed up the food and wine and headed to the tiny police station in Albori. The officer was so kind and let us set up tables on the roof. I suppose he appreciated the change of pace for what would have most likely been a very boring evening. Plus, he couldn't resist our invitation to share our food. Then, at midnight, we experienced the most spectacular pyrotechnics display I have ever seen. The fireworks reflected off the sea. It was truly magical."

"That doesn't sound too bad, actually." Victor added, "How did you get your friends out of there?"

"Giovanni's mother and aunt were at a party where the brother of the host happened to be a judge. It was way past midnight when Giovanni was able to contact his mother, but she got the judge and his brother to drive to Albori and bail out the wrongfully accused." Frankie took a beat, then continued, "Although I have to say, Rachael is more than capable of ending up in jail on her own." Frankie's face was beaming as she recalled the situation.

"That sounds like a hoot!" Leonora roared.

"It was, but not without a bunch of angst and quick thinking," Frankie said.

"Sounds like you have a fun bunch of friends," Judith replied.

"Yes, I do. And it's those same friends who I'm doing the planning for this year. Again."

"Are you going someplace special?" Leonora asked.

"Yep. Right here. I cannot think of anywhere else that is as festive as New York during Christmas. Don't get me wrong. Italy is very festive, but New York is something quite different."

"Agreed!" Victor held up his bourbon-laced coffee.

Frankie's story of the previous year piqued Judith's curiosity. "So, what do you have planned for your friends? And how many are you?"

"There are four of us from high school. We reconnected at a class reunion a few years ago and decided to go on a singles' cruise." Frankie shuddered. "We were all apprehensive, but agreed the worst thing that could happen was that we would have a good time island-hopping in the Caribbean."

"Couldn't be too bad," Leonora said.

"And much to our surprise, each of us ended up with a significant other."

"You met your boyfriend on the cruise?" Judith asked.

"No. I knew him before I left. I went to their restaurant at least once a week, and if I was too pooped, Giovanni delivered dinner. So, when I was going on the cruise, I needed someone to take care of my kitty, Bandit, and he agreed."

"So, you were dating him before the cruise?"

"No. He was engaged to a woman in Italy. Some kind of family thing. While I was away, they broke up, and when I got back, he invited me to dinner at the restaurant. I thought it was going to be a regular night at Marco's, but it turned out it was a date in disguise."

"How romantic!" Judith exclaimed.

Frankie didn't want to get into the nitty-gritty about her former insecurities and happily agreed. "Italians and romance are inseparable." Frankie felt a rush of heat crawl up her face. When it came to Giovanni, she was always filled with warmth, and often jelly legs. He was the epitome of a handsome Italian with the movie-star looks of Raoul Bova, the actor who played Marcello in *Under the Tuscan Sun*. It took a while for Frankie to separate Giovanni's similar looks of black wavy hair and steel blue eyes from the Marcello character in the movie. In Frankie's eyes, the actor was a bit of a cad, but she learned in real life Bova was not only known for his acting, but he was also nominated as a Goodwill Ambassador for the United Nations. She had to admit he and Giovanni had a lot in common and both could break the thermostat with their warmth, not to mention their charm.

"You're blushing!" Judith whooped.

"It happens a lot," Frankie confessed.

"That's very sweet." Leonora put her two cents in.

"Where's the restaurant?" Victor asked. "I can always go for a good Italian dinner."

"You can go for any kind of dinner," Judith said, poking him in the stomach again.

"Hey. That's my love bulge." Victor patted his slightly protruding paunch.

"It's some kind of bulge," Judith proclaimed.

"It's your delicious cooking, my dear." Victor figured it was a good save.

Judith rolled her eyes. "If you say so. But I'm not the one who serves you donuts and Big Macs."

Victor shrugged. "Guilty as charged."

Leonora addressed Frankie. "Do you come here to watch the tree lighting?"

"I work in that building." She pointed up toward the windows of her office. "Fourteenth floor."

"You get to see the tree every day, then," Marvin spoke.

"I do, but I avoid the spectacle. Don't get me wrong. I think it's great that people are out and about celebrating the holidays, but I can get a little woozy in big crowds. And I live in New York. Who would have thought? But you learn how to navigate. So rather than being smushed in a bunch of merry-goers, I have a small party for my staff, and we watch it from my office. It's not the best view, but it gets you in the mood."

"That sounds like a great plan," Leonora replied.

"I order the food from Patsy's, and everyone gets to enjoy the festivities and eat scrumptious food at the same time."

"So, what do you do in that building?" Victor was curious about his new friend.

"I'm a cookbook editor," Frankie replied.

"No wonder you've got a penchant for food," Judith said with admiration. "Who is your favorite chef?"

"Besides Giovanni and his brother?" Frankie said, and chuckled. "I have to say Mateo Castillo. Not only is he a wonderful chef, but a great humanitarian."

"I think I saw him on the TV the other day," Milton noted. "Some kind of community food thing?"

"Yes. It's called Share a Meal. He was a rising star in the culinary world and was inspired by José Andrés and the World

Central Kitchen. Mateo's group travels around the country to small communities and teaches them how to prepare healthy food for the food underprivileged. They'll hold an event at a local school or church, cook, teach, and serve."

"That's wonderful," Judith proclaimed.

"My entire line of cookbooks are with celebrities who donate a part of the proceeds to their favorite charities. We call it Cooking for a Cause."

"What a fabulous idea," Leonora declared.

"So far we've raised over a million dollars," Frankie said proudly.

Milton added his thoughts: "Wow. Impressive."

"Who else do you publish?" Leonora asked.

Frankie ticked off the half dozen chefs who currently had books on sale. "You'll see them on the morning shows between now and Christmas."

"I'll surely buy a few. Great holiday gifts."

"In more ways than one." Frankie beamed.

The fivesome looked on as the tree was now vertical and secured.

Frankie began her impromptu lecture. "The first tree was in 1931 and was just under twenty feet high. It was adorned with homemade decorations from the staff. Today the tree is eighty feet high and decked with five miles of lights." She paused. "The star has three million Swarovski crystals."

"I wonder how much it weighs?" Victor ruminated.

"Nine hundred pounds, and is worth one-point-five million dollars," Frankie replied, as if she had just finished doing a term paper on the subject.

"You're a wealth of information, dear," Leonora said.

"I'm a bit of a nerd when it comes to the holiday decorations." She took a sip of her coffee. "But I am really bummed that Saks will *not* be installing their decorations this year."

"Really? Why not?" Leonora asked with dismay.

"Cost cutting," Frankie said, and patted her lips with a small napkin. "It is going to be sorely missed. It made this section of Fifth Avenue and Rock Center so, so festive."

"At least they're not eliminating the tree or the angels," Judith said with a sigh.

Turning the conversation to what they could actually enjoy, Frankie continued her speech. "Speaking of angels, there will be twelve eight-foot luminous, haloed angels on the promenade; each will hold a six-foot golden trumpet."

"Interesting. I've seen them year after year, but never bothered to count them," Victor said. "You learn something new every day."

"You'll note, each angel will be slightly angled toward the tree." Frankie decided it was enough morning trivia. "That concludes our Rockefeller Center lesson."

"Another bit of information we can share with the grandkids when we bring them here. They just love all the lights," Judith cooed.

"Indeed. It's quite spectacular up and down the avenue with the luminous miniature white lights wrapped around the bare tree limbs. Whoever thought of that was a genius."

"You seem to be a pretty smart cookie yourself," Victor added.

Frankie took a bow. "Thank you, ladies and gentlemen." She let out a long, deep breath. "It was lovely meeting you. Enjoy the holidays. See you next year!"

"Nice meeting you also, Frankie." Each bid a fond adieu.

Frankie worked her way to her office building, where she was going to start her holiday project for Giovanni's mother. She wanted to put together a memory book starting with Rosevita's wedding photos and pictures of Marco and Giovanni from childhood up to last Christmas. She knew she was going to have to enlist the aid of Lucia, but she was still unsure how to achieve that goal. She picked up the phone and called Giovanni.

"*Ciao tesoro!*" he said when he answered the phone. "Did you enjoy the Christmas tree erection?"

Frankie burst out laughing.

"What's so funny?" Then he realized his brain didn't quite translate the situation the way he meant it. "Sorry. So sorry."

Frankie was howling. "I never thought of it that way, and now I shall never be able to think of it any other way."

Giovanni couldn't help but laugh, as well. "*Scusa.* I apologize."

Frankie was still chuckling. She finally caught her breath. "I want to make a memory book for your mother for Christmas."

"She is gonna love it. How can I help?"

"I want to get in touch with Lucia and see if she has some photos from when your parents were first married, or anything that might be fun to include. Ribbons, postcards, tickets. Did your mother collect those sorts of things?"

"I'm-a sure there is molto remembrances. I can ask Marco. He should have something. Also, I think there is a box of things she didn't bring back to Italy. I will check the apartment."

"You are a gem!" Frankie sighed.

"Even if sometimes my translation is not so good?"

"Even if your translation is hilarious," she said, and chuckled. "Can you send me Lucia's phone number and email? I'll text her and let her know about my idea."

"She will like that you are including her."

"Now I have to think of something for her."

"You gave her a beautiful shawl last year. She liked it very much."

"I'll try to come up with something, but in the meantime, what do you think about getting them tickets for Radio City?"

"I think they will enjoy it very much. I don't believe Aunt Lucia has ever been to a show there."

"Excellent. Let me know when they will be arriving, and I will get the tickets. Any other shows they might enjoy?"

"They arrive on the fifteenth. If Andrea Bocelli is in town, I am sure they will be thrilled to see him."

"Okay. Get me their travel plans, and I'll figure out a schedule for them. Will they be staying at Marco's or the apartment?"

"Ah. Good question. Maybe Marco's. They will spend more time with the children."

"Good. I'll arrange for a car service for them for the show, as well. And we should take them to dinner."

"Why? My food not good enough for them?" he said, half-teasing.

Frankie laughed, then said, "You are very funny, but maybe a great steak dinner? Keens Steakhouse?"

"That's a very nice steak dinner." Giovanni's mouth was watering at the thought of their rib eye.

"Alrighty. You get the travel plans, and I'll take care of the rest."

"You are my special Bossy Pants," Giovanni said, and chuckled.

"Oh, now you're calling me that, too?" Frankie remarked. "Just remember, I am not bossy. I just have better ideas."

"Very true, *cara*. You always have good ideas, except when you go shoe snowing."

"You mean snowshoeing?" she corrected him.

"Either way, you promised you will never do it again." Giovanni reminded her of the fiasco in Lake Tahoe when she went snowshoeing alone, got lost, dropped her phone, and twisted her ankle. "You had me so worried when we could not find you."

"I know, and I am sorry. Believe me, I do not want to repeat anything like that again."

"*Molto bene!* I don't want to repeat that also."

"You have your instructions, Signor Lombardi?"

"*Assolutamente, pantaloni prepotenti!* Yes, Bossy Pants!"

"You really like that nickname, don't you?" Frankie said and smiled.

"*Si, cara mia,*" Giovanni answered in his native tongue.

"I prefer *cara mia* better."

"And you are. My dear one." This time he answered in English.

"Okay. I've gotta get going. I have a few things I have to do here. What time do you get off work tonight?"

"The usual. Eleven."

"Ok. I'll see you at the restaurant. Eight o'clock, okay?"

"*Si. Ciao, bella!*"

"*Ciao,* Giovanni." Frankie ended the call. Never in a million years would she have guessed she could find someone as loving, kind, generous, responsible, and loyal. It was usually *Pick one. Two if you're lucky. If you get three, you live a magical life.* She honestly believed she was blessed. She also believed, in some karmic way, she'd earned it. She didn't like the word *soulmates.* It was terribly overused, and not fully accurate, for the most part. She preferred to think they were soul travelers on a loving journey together.

Frankie spent an hour drawing a layout of what she hoped would become Rosevita's memory book. Finding the pieces would be the challenge. She checked the time. It was almost eleven, which meant it was seven in the evening in Salerno. She wondered if Lucia and Rosevita were together and hesitated to reach out to her at that moment. She had another idea: call Giovanni and ask him to call his mother. This way, she would be distracted, and Lucia could read Frankie's text without having to explain why her nephew's girlfriend was contacting her.

Frankie hit the redial button. "Gio, can you call your mother now?"

"Now? *Perché?*"

"So I can text Lucia, just in case they are together. This way your mother will be on the phone with you. *Capisce?*"

"Ah. *Capisce!* I'll do it right now. *Ciao!*"

Frankie waited for about a minute and then sent a text to Lucia and explained her idea and asked if she could help. Another minute went by, and she got a reply telling Frankie to call her in an hour.

Capisce! Frankie texted back.

Frankie began making a list, one of many. This was for Thanksgiving. She offered to make Thanksgiving dinner for her parents, Giovanni, and any orphans from her gang. She planned to commandeer her mother's kitchen. Nina was going to be in town and offered to help. Richard was still on the fence about where he should go. His brother was going to be in town, and they hadn't seen each other in almost two years. Regardless of the number of guests, there would always be more food than anyone could consume. This year she planned on getting some takeaway containers from the restaurant so everyone could go home with leftovers.

She decided to check in with her pal. The last time they spoke, Nina was feeling a little glum about the project with Jordan. Frankie hoped things were moving ahead.

Nina answered on the first ring. "Babycakes!" Regardless of her mood, Nina always sounded cheerful. Frankie attributed it to her acting ability, but Frankie could tell when Nina wasn't as bubbly as she appeared.

"Alright. Spill. What is going on?" Frankie urged her friend.

"Oh, the usual stops and starts. We got a commitment from a young, talented director, and Gail Edwards is on board. It's the financing part that is still nebulous. And now Jordan thinks we should break it up into episodes and pitch it as a series."

"That sound like a great idea, actually. And it's exciting

you have Gail. She is really talented," Frankie said, then paused. "I remember you both played sisters in both of your sitcoms. That was pretty cool. How did all that come about?" "We were both pulling into the studio lot and parked next to each other. We had never met before, so we both did a double take at the resemblance. Must have been the hair that convinced the show runners," Nina said, and then chuckled. Both women were known for their full, curly locks, which Nina often tied back with a bandanna.

"Ha. I think it had to do with talent," Frankie replied.

"You can be rather sweet when you're not being bossy," Nina said, teasing.

"Nina Hunter! You must stop turning compliments into something self-effacing."

"Stop using big words," Nina said, and cackled. "You know I can't manage more than three syllables at a time."

"There you go again. You're an accomplished writer," Frankie said, then sighed.

"I do it because I know you'll always have something nice to say."

"You sound a bit insecure. What's up?" Frankie had good instincts when it came to reading people's feelings, even if it was over the phone.

"Oh, Jordan mentioned my relationship with Richard. Well, he didn't actually bring it up, but when we started talking about the holidays, it took a left turn into 'did I love him? Are we committed?'"

"Whoa. Heavy," Frankie replied.

"Yep. So, I guess I have that cranking in the back of my head."

"I take it you haven't had *the talk?*"

"Correct. Let me ask you something. Does every couple have to have *the talk?* If things feel good and are working well, why does there need to be *the talk?*"

"You have a point. I suppose it's some unwritten rule that couples need to have a set of rules to follow, maybe?"

"What about you and Giovanni?" Nina paused, then said, "Have the two of you had *the talk*?"

"Not exactly."

"See? Nobody wants to do it."

"I am happy to say, Gio has expressed his love for me, especially when I went missing in Tahoe. I can't think of any ex-boyfriend who would have done what he did."

"That's true. He went straight to the airport and hopped on Mateo's air-share," Nina said in agreement. "I laugh every time I picture Giovanni traipsing through the slush in his beautiful Italian leather shoes."

Frankie snickered. "That must have been a sight. But listen, Richard caught up with him in Denver. It has to mean something, Nina. It was quite a team effort trying to figure out what happened to me."

"Don't remind me. I was petrified."

"So was I, but it all ended well. For everyone."

"It did, and in spite of the angst, the storm, the power failure, and the assortment of people stranded at the hotel, it turned out to be fun," Nina said, as she reflected on the trip from two years before.

"Before we go too far down memory lane, tell me more about the project and Gail."

"Yes, and she and I were faced with the same ageism junk. She walked away from it and moved to Sedona, but I thought she would be good for the part."

"Mother-daughter thing?" Frankie was trying to remember the synopsis.

"Yeah. And I think it will work. Jordan's spin is that it takes place in various parts of England, with each episode in a different town."

"Sounds like it could be a hit, Nina."

"From your mouth to God's ears," she replied. "When Jordan first mentioned it, I was almost sick to my stomach, but when he explained it further and how the location is part of each episode, I got psyched. So, that will be my homework assignment over the holidays: breaking the script into eight parts."

"If anyone can craft it, it's you, honey pie," Frankie said reassuringly. "Speaking of the holidays. What's the plan?"

"I'm flying back next week. Still not sure what Richard will be doing for turkey day, but it's really fine. I know he's missed his brother, and it will be nice for the two of them to spend time together."

"Is his brother married?" Frankie asked.

"Divorced."

"Ooh. A playmate for Rachael? Not that she needs another one."

"Another one? What about Salvatore?"

Frankie proceeded to explain Rachael's disappointment. "But of course she met someone in the parking lot at the senior center."

Nina burst out laughing. "How does that girl do it?"

"She's a dude magnet," Frankie said, chortling. "I had a 'sit-down' conversation with her the other night. I told her to try a different approach with Salvatore. Instead of giving him a hard time, wish him well. Tell him to have fun. At first, she vehemently protested, but I urged her to try it. She had nothing to lose."

"And did she?" Nina asked, but was skeptical.

"Yes, she did. I explained my mother's words of wisdom."

"You mean the ones we never followed?" Nina asked.

"Yep. Make them run after you. Be blasé."

Nina began to laugh. "Rachael? Blasé? That would be something for the books."

"Right? But after she tried it, she told me it was empowering."

"Exactly. Why do we have trouble pulling up our big-girl pants to stand in our own power?"

"Because we're not supposed to. Remember, strong women get accused of being bitchy, while men are rewarded with words like *powerful. Dynamic.*"

"So true. I'm glad we've pushed past that."

"Me too. But why did it take us so long?" Frankie asked rhetorically.

"It must have been the sea air," Nina mused.

"True. The cruise was a turning point in all of our lives."

"Thankfully, in a good way," Nina replied.

"That's because we had positive attitudes, with little expectations. I know that sounds like a contradiction, but think about it. If you have an intention but don't attach yourself to the outcome, then you can enjoy the experience. A positive outcome is gravy."

"Speaking of gravy . . . what time do you want me at your folks' place?"

"Early-ish. Like ten? I'm getting a ten-pound turkey that will take about three hours."

"What else is on the menu?"

"We have to have pasta. You know my father is not a fan of turkey. Give him the stuffing, mashed potatoes, and gravy, and he'll skip the bird."

"I'm with him, unless you make turkey grilled cheese sandwiches," Nina suggested lightly.

"That sounds like a good idea for leftovers." Frankie jotted down a note to include extra cheese on her shopping list. "What kind of bread?"

"I happen to like grilled Swiss, turkey, and bacon on rye."

"That sounds delish. You're making me hungry." Frankie's stomach growled in agreement.

"Do you need help shopping?" Nina offered.

"I might. I hope to take the week off."

"When have you ever done that, except for our excursions?"

"Like never. But it's time to start paying more attention to the things that bring me joy."

"Doesn't your work bring you joy?" Nina asked. She was puzzled.

"Yes. I created something, and it's working well."

"So, what's the problem?"

"I feel like my job is done. It can continue without me."

"What on earth are you talking about?" Nina said. She was surprised to hear her friend speak like this.

"It's routine now. It was exciting creating the imprint, curating books. Now it's about finding chefs with a favorite charity. Not that it's a bad thing, but the hard part is essentially over. I accomplished what I set out to do."

"Well, of course you did. You always do," Nina said reassuringly.

"Now I feel as if I need to find another project. Something to stimulate my creativity."

"I totally get that. We must feed our souls," Nina waxed philosophically.

"Indeed, we do, girlfriend. Moving on to fun stuff. Got any ideas about New Year's Eve?" Frankie was at a loss.

"Well, it's going to be hard to top the past three years."

"Yes. No twisted ankles, no jailbirds," Frankie said.

"At least we didn't do too much damage on the cruise."

"That's because we kept Rachael on a leash," Frankie said, and giggled.

"I don't think the ship's captain would agree." Nina recalled Rachael planting mistletoe in a number of places on the boat.

"We were lucky he was good-natured and didn't toss us overboard," Frankie added.

"So true."

"Giovanni's mother and aunt are coming into town, and I have to make some plans for them."

"Are they coming with those fine gentlemen we met? The two Parisi brothers?"

"Good question. I'm waiting for Giovanni to let me know what the travel plans are, so I can't do much planning until I get the info."

"I'm sure it will all come together with you at the helm," Nina said.

"By the way, Giovanni is now referring to me as *pantaloni prepotenti.*"

"That's adorable!" Nina yelped.

"Yeah. Now I'm 'bossy pants' in two languages." Frankie smiled to herself.

"I can always come up with a French version."

"Thank you. No," Frankie answered. "I told Giovanni that I'm not bossy. I just have better ideas."

Nina chuckled and said, "Well, that much is true."

"Okay, honey pie. I've gotta get out of here. When are you getting back?"

"Next week."

"Okay. Safe travels, and let me know when you land."

"Will do. Love you, babycakes."

"Love you too!"

When the conversation was over, Frankie asked herself, *What will we do for New Year's Eve?*

Frankie stretched her arms over her head and began to play with her long, dark ponytail, curling her locks around her finger. It was something she did when she was deep in thought, something she had been doing since she was a kid. It was her father that was the first to comment. "What are you thinking about, Francesca?" he had asked.

"Huh? What do you mean?" she had answered.

"I noticed that you play with your hair when you are mulling something over," he said, and smiled.

"Oh." Frankie had been oblivious to this habit. She immediately came back with, "It helps me think, Daddy."

He couldn't argue with that, especially when it came from a five-year-old.

The more Frankie thought, the more she spun her hair, contemplating all the people and all the festivities coming up. Then she chuckled to herself. "I guess I'm swapping my fancy holiday anxieties for my normal ones." She flicked her ponytail back, stood, smoothed her tunic sweater. It was time to clear her head and take a walk.

She took the elevator to the lobby, said goodbye to the security guard, walked through the revolving doors, and stepped into the cool, crisp air. Firemen and construction workers were in the process of securing the tree to the scaffold that would remain until all the decorating was finished. Frankie calculated it would be another week or so.

She headed toward Sixth Avenue and then two blocks north to Radio City Music Hall. She could have easily looked up the information online, but there was something special about the box office and the façade of the famous hall.

Frankie approached the historical building that began construction in 1932. It was known as The Great Stage, and six bronze plaques graced the façade representing dance, drama, and song. A wraparound marquee featured its name in neon with reddish pink and yellow art deco lettering. Beneath the marquee, the iconic scroll boasted the performances of the RADIO CITY CHRISTMAS SPECTACULAR STARRING THE RADIO CITY ROCKETTES. Frankie got the chills as she looked up at the words moving across the front and sides of the building.

The annual show started running the week before, and she knew it would be a sold-out venue if she didn't purchase tickets soon. She decided to grab six tickets for December 18th. Even though she didn't have all the details, she knew Lucia and Rosevita were arriving on the 15th and were going to spend three weeks in the states. The 18th was a safe bet. On second thought, she decided to purchase eight tickets, just in case the Parisi brothers were tagging along with Rosevita and

Lucia. The other four would go to Marco, Anita, and their two children. If the Parisi brothers did not join their female companions, Frankie and Giovanni would use the tickets and go with the gang. There were a few people ahead of her in line, and as she was waiting, she heard a voice she recognized call out, "Hey girlie!" She turned quickly to see Randy Wheeler heading in her direction.

"Hey!" She gave him a big hug. "Rehearsal?"

"Yes! And you?"

"Tickets for Giovanni's family."

Randy gave her a subtle nod. "Follow me." He led her to the side door where a security guard was standing. "Hello, Rupert! This is my friend Frankie."

"You work at Seventy-five Rock," he said pointedly.

Frankie was startled. "Yes. Yes, I do."

"You gave us a box of cupcakes last year when we were stationed at the tree." He grinned. "This year I have door duty."

"Nice to meet you. Again." Frankie was moved that he remembered this small act of kindness. Not that she was doing it for the thanks. She did kind things out of the goodness of her heart. Not for anything except the satisfaction she was spreading some kind of love, whether it was accepted or not. "Just put it out there," she would often say. And she didn't expect people to feel obliged to reciprocate. It wasn't that she didn't have standards for other people to follow. She certainly had expectations, particularly when people promised to do something. *Say what you mean, mean what you say, and do what you say you are going to do. And if you can't, let someone know if you need help.* Those words hung in a frame in her office. One coworker once accused Frankie of having high standards. "You say that as if it's a bad thing," Frankie had responded, and smiled. She wasn't sure how that landed, but that particular coworker was never late with any of her work after that encounter.

"Well, Rupert, had I known you would be here, I would have saved one for you. The guys working on the tree inhaled them."

"I don't doubt it. You know, most people don't go out of their way for other people," Rupert said, and gave her a wide smile.

"We just need to keep on keeping on, and maybe it will rub off. You never know how you can touch someone else's life. Even if it's paying a total stranger a compliment. I mean, as long as it's not creepy," she said, and chuckled.

Randy interrupted; he agreed with everything Frankie was saying, but it was a little too kumbaya for him. "I want to give Frankie a tour before the massive crowds gather." He looked at her. "You do want a tour, do you not?"

"I most certainly do," Frankie said with a huge smile on her face.

"Follow me, dearie." He made a crook of his arm, and Frankie threaded hers through it.

"Nice seeing you again, Rupert," Frankie called as they walked toward the magnificent lobby.

"Nice to see you. Save a cupcake for me next year."

As they entered the grand lobby, Frankie froze and gasped. "This is magnificent."

"You've been here before," Randy said plainly.

"Yes, but never when it's been decorated, and with nobody else around. It's hard to take it all in when there are a few hundred people milling about." She gazed at the enormous chandelier decorated with lights in the shape of a Christmas tree. Large green wreaths wrapped in lights hung on the red marble walls between the fifty-feet-high mirrors. A forty-foot-high mural called *The Fountain of Youth* by Ezra Winter served as the backdrop for the grand staircase that led to the mezzanine level. It was the quintessential example of opulence and grandeur.

"The mural was painted in a tennis court near Winter's

studio and then transported here. But the mural had to be restored after someone covered it in polyurethane. I guess they thought they were preserving it." Randy *tsk*ed.

"Wow." Frankie didn't know what else to say, so she said it again. "Wow. I never had the opportunity to view it without a bunch of heads in the way. Winter was known for the deep rich colors he used. The golden tones, lush greens, and deep reds. I believe it was an Oregon Indian legend that was the inspiration."

"Well, aren't you Miss Smarty-Pants?" Randy teased.

"That's 'Smarty, Bossy Pants' to you, buster," Frankie countered his remark.

"You've seen the *Crouching Panther* in the ladies lounge on the third floor, haven't you?" he asked.

"Yes! I want that in my apartment!" Frankie exclaimed. "And what were you doing in the ladies lounge, I might ask."

Randy *tsk*ed again. "Darling, it's part of the history of this magnificent building. It's rather spectacular, isn't it?" Randy said, and sighed.

"Maybe that's why they call it the Radio City Christmas Spectacular?" Frankie said, grinning.

"Nothing gets past you, does it," Randy said with bent elbows, placing his index finger on his cheek.

"Only when you and Rachael get past me," Frankie nudged him.

"You are never going to let us forget that side trip, are you?" Randy said, and then rolled his eyes.

"You are correct. How many people do you know that went for a spin around Mt. Vesuvius in a Vespa?"

"I'm sure there are plenty," Randy said defensively.

"And how many of them end up in jail?"

"Detail, details," he huffed. "Come. Follow me." Randy sashayed his way toward the main entrance of the theatre. "Ta-da! It is gorgeous, isn't it?"

"Wow." Once again Frankie was reduced to a monosyllabic response. Randy went on to give her additional lesser-known facts of the venue.

"The stage is comprised of four elevators, and boy, you gotta be quick and get out of the way when they're changing scenes." He then looked up and pointed. "The ceiling is eighty-four feet high." He stopped to take a breath. "And did you know that thirty-six Rockettes can fit across the stage?"

"Funny. I never counted."

"There's also a secret apartment."

"Have you considered becoming a tour guide?" Frankie asked with a grin.

"Funny-Smarty-Bossy-Pants." He turned and then asked, "Are you coming to see the show?"

"Are you one of the Rockettes?" Frankie asked with a grin.

"Listen, missy, I can kick as good as the rest of them."

"I have no doubt," Frankie replied. "What is your part, exactly?"

"I'm doing a few introductions, a little tap, bow, and thank you." Randy made an exaggerated curtsy.

Frankie checked her watch. "I have to get going. Need to buy tickets for the matinee on the eighteenth."

"Come. I know a few people," he said, and wiggled his eyebrows.

The two went back through the grand lobby, and Randy knocked on the ticket booth door. A round woman with bright pink cheeks opened the door. A pair of glasses on a pearl chain dangled from her neck. "Randy. What do you want now?" she asked, with one hand on her hip.

"This is my friend Frankie. She needs to buy tickets."

The woman smiled, exited the booth, and clicked the numerical pad lock. "Hello, Frankie. Give me a sec. I don't want people to start bashing in the window."

"I can wait," Frankie was quick to acquiesce.

"How many and for which show?" the woman asked kindly.

"Eight for the eighteenth matinee," Frankie answered.

"Do you know where you want to sit?"

"My boyfriend's family is visiting from Italy. I'd like the best seats available, please."

"Let me have your credit card, and I'll ring it up for you," the woman said.

Frankie dug into her purse and handed her card to the woman.

"Quick, Randy. Let's go shopping," the woman hooted.

"You won't get too far with that one," Frankie said, smiling.

"Don't believe her," Randy objected. "She's a bigshot at Grand Marshall Publishing."

Frankie twisted her mouth and rolled her eyes. "He exaggerates."

"Oh, fiddle-lee-dee," Randy said with his arms akimbo.

"Be back in a jiffy." She leaned in and said, "Don't worry, honey, there's no way I can get out of that booth. And don't think I haven't tried." The woman went back to the booth, shut the door, and locked it. A few minutes later, she reappeared with an envelope containing the tickets for the front center row of the mezzanine. "Don't faint when you look at the receipt." The woman raised her eyebrows.

Frankie calculated the cost would be upwards of 2,000 dollars, and she wasn't far off. It was steep, but the memories would live throughout Giovanni's lifetime. Giovanni told her he would pay for the tickets, but Frankie decided it was going to be her Christmas present to his family. But she still wanted to make the memory book for Rosevita, and perhaps another scarf for Lucia. She'd check her bank account later. For now, she was getting into the Christmas spirit and decided to look at the charge after she got home.

She and Randy linked arms again as Randy walked her toward the door, and out the side entrance. Frankie's concern over Rachael's moodiness prompted her to stick her nose in her business. "Randy? Can I ask you something serious?"

"Uh-oh," Randy said, stopped abruptly, and disengaged his arm from Frankie's.

"I'd say it's none of my business, but my friends are my business, including you."

Randy anticipated a *but*, so said it before Frankie had the opportunity to do so: "But?"

"But Rachael is feeling rather abandoned this year. I know you and Jordan don't get a lot of time together, but with Salvatore going to Italy and . . ."

Randy interrupted with, "And he didn't discuss it with her. Yes, I got the whole enchilada. With hot sauce."

"I had a tête-à-tête with her," Frankie said, and moved out of the way of people bustling along the sidewalk. "I suggested she back off and give Salvatore some space. Play nice."

Randy snorted. "I love Rachael, but I'm not sure if she knows how to play nice."

Frankie gave him a backhanded swat on the arm. "She can. When she wants to. My point is, she needs a little TLC right now."

Randy rolled his eyes. "Ugh. Please don't try to make me feel guilty. Rachael already had her go at it with me."

"What I was trying to say is that I think my conversation with her might have struck a chord. A good one," she said, and paused.

"But?" Randy anticipated another one.

"This may sound mean, but, if her good behavior gets rewarded, perhaps she may continue on a more chill path."

Randy squinted. "What do you mean?"

"Have the two of you kissed and made up?"

"Not exactly. She's giving me the cold shoulder," Randy said, and feigned a shiver.

"All I am saying is to go easy on her. Make a plan. It doesn't have to be when Jordan is here."

"But I have eight shows a week between now and Christmas," Randy whined.

"Invite her to one. Give her a tour. A little kindness can go a long way, especially since she's feeling a little wounded."

Randy cocked his head. "You are a genius! We have family day when the cast can bring a guest to a performance. I don't know why I hadn't thought of that!"

"There's a reason why we bumped into each other today," Frankie said, and smiled.

"Speaking of today. Isn't it your day off?"

"It's supposed to be, but I started my own tradition watching the FDNY secure the tree."

"Ah, the cupcake thingy," Randy said, nodding.

"I thought I'd get a jump on a few things in the office. I want to make a memory book for Giovanni's mother."

"That's so sweet," Randy said, and sighed. "Sometimes I wish I had kept track of all my meanderings, but then again, it would be an X-rated book!" He snorted.

"You are such a card," Frankie said, grinning.

"The Queen of Hearts," Randy said, and batted his eyes.

"And a wit." Frankie laughed. "I better get moving. I have to place my orders for Thanksgiving. I'm cooking. I figured I'd give Giovanni a break. Marco, Anita, and the kids are going to her parents' in Westchester."

"Are they closing the restaurant?" Randy asked.

"They decided to let the sous chef and the staff decide. They settled on a prix fixe menu from noon until three. This way, they could still get home to be with family."

"That sounds nice," Randy mused.

"I'm glad the two brothers are managing their time between work and play."

"And what about you, missy?" Randy said, eyeing her curiously.

"What about me?" Frankie asked innocently.

"Puh-lease, girlfriend. You are a workaholic." Randy shook his finger at her. "You need to downshift."

"Yeah, yeah," Frankie said. "I'm learning. I know it's about balancing your life. Funny thing, their culture seems to be able to do it better than us, but now that Marco and Giovanni have been ensconced in New York, they're in overdrive a lot of the time."

"Running a business in New York can be excruciating, especially the restaurant business."

"That's for sure. But I think they've developed a good staff and a good rhythm. Ever since Anita had the kids, and they moved to Tenafly, Marco has been doing a much better job with his balancing act."

"And I am sure you have been a big influence on Giovanni."

"We're working on it. We're both a bit obsessive."

"That's an understatement," Randy said, and laughed out loud.

"Okay, Mr. Wise Guy. You need to get to work, and I need to work on one of my many lists," Frankie said, smiling.

"See? You always have a list," Randy scolded her.

"Blah. Blah. Blah," Frankie said, and then stuck out her tongue. "Okay, champ. You have your marching orders! We'll chat soon!" Frankie gave Randy a big hug.

"Tootles!" Randy said, and hugged her back.

Frankie decided to walk back to Rock Center and then stroll down Fifth Avenue. As she entered the promenade area, she peered over the marble walls that surrounded the famous ice-skating rink. That, too, was in the process of being adorned in holiday décor.

Located on the lower level of the center, the gilded bronze statue of Prometheus glistened in the sunlight, overseeing the rink below. Frankie recalled one of her art history classes where she learned the great statue was created by the sculptor Paul Manship and was installed during the Great Depression. The heroic Greek figure represented the advancement of knowledge and human resilience.

As she made her way toward the promenade between the

rink and the avenue, she noticed two women dressed in the traditional Salvation Army uniforms standing on the promenade. Frankie recognized them from the year before, and the year before that. She wondered if everyone had a permanent spot from one Christmas to the next. She decided she would ask them when she went back to work on Monday. Meanwhile, she was on her way to Albanese Meats & Poultry to order her turkey. She insisted that she do all the planning, ordering, and cooking so Giovanni could focus on the restaurant. It was her turn to nourish the people she loved.

Chapter 9

Pinewood

Thanksgiving

The aroma of roasts in the oven and fragrant pies cooling on racks filled Myra's kitchen. Charles had started at dawn to prepare a feast for the Sisters. When the Sisters completed a mission, it became a tradition for Charles to show off his culinary skills, and holidays were no exception.

Myra was busy getting the long, polished dining room table ready for the "good dishes and glassware," a total departure from the mismatched plates and mugs they used every day. She carefully inspected each piece of the Royal Doulton dinnerware that had been in her family since she was a child. She was pleased that every piece was still in mint condition. The Waterford Crystal glasses would sparkle once she wiped them down. It had been over a year since she'd used them. She pulled white linen tablecloths and napkins from the sideboard and waited for Yoko to bring a masterful centerpiece.

Several minutes later, Lady announced Yoko's arrival with

a familiar *woof*. Myra could swear her pooch had an individual bark for everyone. Myra heard Charles's voice greeting Yoko and directing her to the dining room.

Myra caught her breath at the autumnal-themed flower arrangement. "That is absolutely gorgeous!" she said as she stared at the vibrant orange-tinted hydrangeas, burnt-orange roses, tall black willows, and long cornstalks, all surrounded by lance leaf and sycamore pods.

"This is for the sideboard," Yoko announced. "I'll get the rest."

Myra placed the linens on the table as Yoko scurried back to her car. She returned with a long box that contained shorter versions of the assortment of flowers. They were just high enough so as not to obscure the view across the table. Charles was following her with a second box that contained autumn leaves and gold tealights.

"Yoko, you have outdone yourself again!" Myra rejoiced at the festive transformation of the room.

"It is my passion." Yoko made a slight bow.

"It is, indeed." Myra bowed in return.

Charles quickly disappeared into the kitchen while the two women set the table, beginning with gold charger plates, then adding the rest of the dinnerware, glassware, and silverware. Myra gave each knife, fork, and spoon an extra rub before she placed them on the table. When they were finished, they stepped back to observe their creation.

A familiar voice exclaimed, "Martha Stewart would be proud." Myra and Yoko turned to see Annie standing in the archway with a bottle of Dom Pérignon champagne in her hand.

"Hello, my friend," Myra said, and gave her a hug. Yoko followed suit.

"You gals have been busy little beavers!" Annie exclaimed. "Looks spectacular."

Myra put her arm around Yoko and said, "Our master

green thumb." She then noticed a few crumbs on Annie's cheek. "What are you eating?"

"I stopped by Charles's family kitchen and swiped one of the popovers he was experimenting with."

It took Yoko a beat to realize Annie meant the farmhouse kitchen. "Do you think he could spare another one?" she asked.

"Not if I get there first!" Myra darted past the two women and hopped over Lady, who was sunning herself between the atrium and the dining room. The dog lifted her head slightly and resumed her position.

Fergus was also in the kitchen, wearing an apron announcing SOUS CHEF on the front, the letters surrounded by flames. Myra chuckled at the sight.

"I see you are official now."

"Ah, yes. I am chuffed to bits. Always wanted one of these."

Annie stood behind Myra. "It suits you."

"We must make it more official," Charles said, and disappeared into the pantry for a split second, returning with two toques. "And Bob's your uncle," he said as he plopped the shorter version of the chef's hat on Fergus's head. The two men stood next to each other as Myra and Annie howled.

"You look like the Swedish chef on the Muppets!"

Charles lifted his forefinger and placed it under his nose to imply a mustache, then did an impersonation pretending he was speaking Swedish. *"De bonkie, boner viener, oopa snitzel."*

The women were laughing so hard, Yoko ran into the kitchen. "What am I missing?"

Charles repeated his shtick, and Fergus joined in. Tears were rolling down Myra's face.

"I sure hope you cook better than your accent!" Annie teased.

"Fer sure and do gotten!" Charles answered with more gibberish.

"Let's get serious," Myra said, and tapped her foot, feigning impatience. "Where are the popovers?"

Annie spotted the crumbled mess on the counter opposite the stove. "I call dibs!"

Myra grabbed the back of Annie's pants. "Oh, no you don't. You already had yours." The two women pretended to scuffle their way across the kitchen.

"Ladies! Ladies! A bit of civility, please," Charles said in his more sophisticated British accent.

"Steady on," Fergus added, and chuckled. "Good thing Maggie isn't here. She'd be tackling the lot of you."

"Speaking of Maggie. Where is she today? She's joining us for dinner, correct?" Myra asked Annie.

"She's scoping out the area where they plan to do the Santa Crawl this year."

"I wouldn't mind going from pub to pub," Fergus said with a grin.

"You have to dress like Santa," Annie replied.

Fergus patted his stomach. "I think after today, I might be a good candidate."

"Why would anyone want to be around a bunch of drunks dressed in costume?" Myra asked.

Fergus and Charles darted glances and began to laugh.

"Oh, right. You have Guinness for breakfast," Myra added.

"It's got lots of vitamins and minerals," Fergus defended the daily tradition in the UK.

"And calories," Annie said, and patted his stomach.

Yoko leaned against the doorjamb with her arms folded. "This is quite entertaining, but I believe I should also have the pleasure of one of these fine treats, albeit a bit of a mess." She nodded toward the mess of broken pastry.

Myra pulled Annie aside. "She has a point. Let's behave and share," she said, grinning.

Fergus pulled a plate from the cabinet and placed the disheveled remains of Charles's experiment on top of it. He handed it to Annie with a few napkins.

"You ladies go back inside and play nice." Fergus gave Annie a pat on the fanny.

"Sounds like a good plan," Yoko said, nodding. "Thank you."

Just as they were about to return to the atrium, Yoko mentioned, "I see you are taking good care of the plants." She nodded to Myra.

"How could I not? You did such a beautiful job with this indoor garden. Besides, you would flip me over with one of your martial arts moves, sensei."

Yoko raised her eyebrows. "You know from where you speak."

"Yes, and you taught me well." Myra was referring to the weekend retreat Yoko hosted to teach the Sisters basic karate and judo. "I'm still unsure if I want to experiment with parkour, with all that running and jumping."

Annie elbowed her friend and said, "It's easy-peasy."

"Easy-peasy for someone who practices pole dancing at home."

"Oh, dear Myra. A few lessons from me and you'll be wrapping your legs around a pole and hanging upside down." She turned to Charles. "Wouldn't you like to see that?"

Charles hesitated. "I shall remain civil and maintain decorum," he said with a straight face, and then winked at his wife. The two had a very passionate relationship, but Myra kept that side of herself, to herself. She began to fidget with her pearls.

Annie spotted Myra's tell. "Oh, Myra. What are you keeping from us?" she said, raising an eyebrow.

"I am not keeping anything that isn't none of your business," Myra replied with a stern look, but the blush on her cheeks said otherwise. She jerked Annie's arm and led her into the atrium, where the sun filtered through the vaulted sky-lights.

"Myra's got a secret," Annie taunted her friend.

"Put a lid on it, will you, please?" Myra said, with a little more vigor this time.

"Okay, okay. Don't be so touchy." Annie pinched Myra's cheek. "I love it when you get all embarrassed."

Myra was now clutching her pearls and lowered her voice. "You may know your way around a pole, but I know my way around Charles."

Annie hooted, "You are too much, my friend. After all these years I've known you!"

"You utter another word, and I shall have to kill you."

Yoko watched the two women banter back and forth. "And this is why I find our group so interesting. You never know what is going to come out of a conversation."

"Martial arts master or not, don't make me hurt you," Myra jested, and feigned a karate chop.

"What else do we have to do for dinner?" Annie asked.

"Nothing, really. The table is set; Charles and Fergus are cooking up a storm."

"Excellent." Annie moved over to the sideboard, where she'd left the bottle of champagne. She held it against her cheek. "Still chilled. What do you say?"

"I say, here's to the bubbly!" Myra exclaimed.

"I am going to have to take a rain check," Yoko said. "I need to get back to the shop. There are over a dozen people who will be breaking down the door to get their holiday arrangements."

"I'd say we'll save you some, but. . . ." Annie smirked.

"We shall replenish your supply." Yoko referred to her husband Harry. She turned and made a slight bow. "We will see you in a few hours."

"Okey dokey!" Annie said as she popped the cork. She

turned to Myra. "The parade! We have to watch the Macy's Day Parade!"

"We do!" The two women moved into the living room, plopped on the couch with their champagne flutes, and kicked off their shoes.

Myra clicked the remote, and they became part of an audience of fifty million people watching helium-filled balloons some as much as sixty feet high move across their television screen. The colorful characters bobbed their heads at the onlookers who lined the streets of New York City. Fifty-feet-long floats rose two stories high, each filled with more characters, celebrities, sports figures, and cast members from Broadway musicals. Eleven marching bands from across the country provided the audio for the cadence, and other entertainers appeared on a performance stage. It was three hours of sheer entertainment and had become part of the annual tradition: parade, eat, football, nap, leftovers.

Approximately 250 miles northeast of Pinewood, Frankie and Nina were in similar motion in Ridgewood. Nina arrived at the Cappellas' house carrying several canvas shopping bags and several bouquets of flowers.

Nina leaned in and gave Frankie a kiss on the cheek. "What's that you're working on?"

"A turducken. I know the name sounds a little gross, but it's a deboned chicken, stuffed inside a deboned duck, stuffed inside a deboned turkey. Supposed to be the 'ultimate' poultry dish," she said, using air quotes.

"Sounds interesting, but complicated."

"Trust me. I didn't do any of the deboning. That part of cooking creeps me out. Did you know I became a vegetarian for a while?"

"You did? Why?" Nina asked with surprise.

"I opened a package of chicken one night and I gagged.

Not for any particular reason. The chicken was fine. Sorta. Anyway, I went for about six months without eating meat, but I was also traveling across the country, and it was much harder ten years ago to find delicious vegetarian dishes. And then I began to feel wimpy. Sluggish. So, I went to the doc, and it turned out I was seriously anemic."

"Then what?" Nina asked.

"He wrote me a prescription for steak," Frankie said, chuckling.

"He did not," Nina replied emphatically, referring to the physician who'd served their families since they were kids.

"No, he did not, but I do like my red meat! But seriously, I started to eat good cuts of beef once a week, plus my green leaves, and a month later I was feeling much better. I think it goes back to my childhood."

"Doesn't everything?" Nina said, and squinted with one eye.

"Ha ha. Seriously, it started when I was a kid. When my mother would get home from the butcher shop with freshly ground beef, and I'd grab a spoonful and lock myself in the bathroom," Frankie said.

"Why the bathroom? Did you think it was going to make you sick?" Nina asked curiously.

"No. I didn't want anyone to take it away from me."

"Geez. Raw meat? You sound like *Rosemary's Baby*," Nina said, and grunted.

"I know. Right? So, she took me to Dr. Movva to see if there was anything wrong with me," Frankie said, while making a circling motion next to her temple with her forefinger.

Nina chuckled. "Well, we know you're not right in the head."

"Stop," Frankie fussed. "Anyway, they determined I was going through a phase, and as long as it didn't make me physically ill, and I wasn't growing fangs, or horns, then I was fine."

Santa's Holiday Spectacular 105

"How did I not know this about you?" Nina leaned her back against the counter and folded her arms.

"I guess I never thought it was worth mentioning. You've seen me order steak tartare, have you not?" Frankie said, raising an eyebrow.

Nina chuckled and shook her head.

Frankie clapped her hands together. "Alright, enough of this chatter. We have to get busy."

"What do you want me to do?" Nina asked, then pulled an apron from a hook inside the pantry door.

"Do you want to do the flowers first?" Frankie asked as she donned a pair of cooking safety gloves.

"Good idea. Vases in the garage?"

"Yes. On the shelves to the left."

Frankie perused the ingredients list and double-checked that everything was lined up on the counter in proper order. She reread the instructions for the third time. "This might be a bit more complicated than I thought," she muttered.

"I am sure it will be fine," Nina said cheerfully.

"Well, just in case it isn't?" Frankie walked over to the double-door refrigerator and pointed to several trays covered in foil.

"Let me guess. Lasagna. Eggplant rollatini, fixings for an antipasto, chicken cutlets for Milanese."

"You know me well. And yes, the Milanese is especially for you. I can't guarantee it will taste as good as it does in Italy, but Gio gave me a recipe he said would make you incredibly happy."

"Frankie, if I know you, which I think I do, you were planning on serving all that food anyway, were you not?"

"Guilty. I can't help it. It's in my DNA," Frankie said, and her eyes went wide.

Nina brought the flowers out to the laundry room behind the garage and proceeded to create a centerpiece. Earlier that morning, she'd taken her dog Winston for their routine walk through the woods. The big Bernese mountain dog had no idea how big and powerful he was. It took a lot of woman-handling power to keep him tethered to a leash when a squirrel would scurry past them on the forested path. Nina claimed it was her daily workout. Before they left the house, Nina found a cutting basket in her parents' shed. It was the perfect accessory for gathering natural elements for her planned display. She had collected a variety of leaves and pine cones.

When she finished tweaking the stems and was satisfied with the condition of her collection, she piled them on a clear tray to be scattered down the middle of the table. Her plan was to create a replica of a forest floor with greens, leaves, and pine cones. She was careful not to include any types of berries, because they can be poisonous to pets and children. Nina had only discovered that tidbit when someone had given her a mistletoe ball. A small note sat at the bottom of the box it had been shipped in warning to "keep from pets and children." That's when she decided she should bone up on the types of poisonous plants. There were the basics such as poison ivy, sumac, and oak, as well as foxglove, but she was surprised to discover that lilies were also dangerous. She had been living in Los Angeles at the time and ripped out her entire garden of tiger lilies. She was sad to see them go, and Winston had never shown any interest in them, but it was better to be safe than sorry.

She opened a box which contained a dozen low clear bowls and planned to float flowers and candles in them.

Nina continued to fuss with the flora when she heard Frankie call to her.

"Coming!" Nina moved quickly to the kitchen. "What's going on?"

Frankie pointed to a large pot. "Look."

Nina stared into the large saucepan. "It looks like oatmeal."

"The bag broke while I was trying to poach it, and the stuffing escaped from the chicken."

"Now what are you going to do?" Nina was well versed in culinary skills.

Frankie thought for a moment, then said, "Put the colander in the sink." She picked up the pot with the soupy mess and dumped it into the vessel waiting for its contents. Frankie squeezed and scraped everything from the bag, then tossed it into the trash. Then she scooped the mess into a food processor. She hit the button, and a minute later, she inspected the contents. "We now have chicken stuffing instead of a stuffed chicken."

"Girl, you are brilliant." Nina placed her hand on her pal's shoulder.

"How about I toss in some pancetta?" Frankie asked as she stared at the mush.

"Bacon? Nah. How about more celery, leeks, and carrots?"

"Yeah, you're probably right. And a lot more seasoning."

"So, I guess we can't call it turducken." Nina sighed.

"Nope. Besides, I didn't like the first syllable of the word, anyway," Frankie said, grimacing.

Nina was about to say it and then it finally hit her. "Oh, yeah."

Frankie snapped her fingers and said, "How about turkey canard farci au poulet?"

"Aren't you fancy? What does it mean?" Nina asked.

"Turkey with duck stuffed with chicken," Frankie said, and chuckled.

"You're not a cookbook publisher for nothin'!" Nina said, snorting.

Frankie chuckled. "And what have you created, my creative friend?"

"I was waiting for you to put the tablecloth down."

"Well, then let's do that right now. The turkey canard farci au poulet will take three hours."

"Thanks for inviting Richard's brother. I can't imagine the two of them sitting in a diner eating hot turkey sandwiches."

"I'm glad they're coming. Watching Rachael in action will be a great sideshow."

"I already warned Richard," Nina said, and snickered.

"So why isn't Salvatore coming for dinner?"

"Rachael told him she had plans for Thanksgiving."

"Oh? How did that go over?"

"She said he was taken aback, but she said she was very sweet about it."

"Ah, giving him a shot of his own medicine?"

"Yep, with candy," Frankie said, and raised her eyebrows.

"So, you really think she's taking a new tactic about not being so needy?"

"I wouldn't go that far, but at least she's trying a new approach."

Nina placed her hands on her hips. "I love Rachael, and I'm glad she's trying to downshift. Sometimes she is her own worst enemy."

"That is for sure. But aren't we all?" Frankie said, then raised her eyebrows. "By the way, I ran into Randy the week before last, and we discussed Rachael's ire with him. I suggested he invite her to a performance, which he should have by now. He thought it was a brilliant idea."

"Aren't most of yours? Brilliant, I mean," Nina teased as she spied the cornucopia of delights. "So how many are we today?" she asked as she began to take the Lenox china from the breakfront cabinet.

Frankie began to count, "You, me, Richard, his brother Robert, Giovanni, Mom and Dad, and Rachael. That makes eight."

"And of course you're cooking for what, eighteen?"

"Naturally," Frankie said, and gave a wide smile.

* * *

Back at Pinewood, Charles was readying the ingredients for his famous Yorkshire pudding, or as Americans call them, *popovers*, but there is a slight difference in preparation. The English version uses gravy drippings, while the American version uses butter. Americans will eat them for breakfast, and the Brits have them with their roasts. Either way, the Sisters gorge on them, so Charles always makes several batches. He looked over at his mate and said, "Sometimes I think I should simply make several dozen of these and skip the rest of the meal."

"And then I'd throttle you," Fergus responded, holding up a rolling pin.

"No weaponry allowed. Need I remind you we have regulations?" Charles said, referring to the rules the Sisters agreed on many years before. No guns or extreme implements of destruction. They could only formulate the punishment from what was on hand, like the time they put the illegal construction materials' company managers up to their waists in cement. But it was the holidays, there were no missions to contend with, and all was good. At least for now.

"I hear Kathryn is going to join us today," Fergus remarked as he snipped the ends of the green beans.

"Yes. Myra was beginning to worry about her. They had a conversation the other day where Kathryn seemed to be going through some kind of transformation."

"A good one or bad?" Fergus asked as he adjusted his torque.

"Myra said Kathryn sounded reticent, but in a more thoughtful manner," Charles said as he checked the roasts in the ovens.

"I can imagine it must get lonely out there."

"I think it was something she felt she needed to do. To process everything. Plus, none of us are getting any younger," he said as he breathed in the fine aroma of his basting.

"I prefer that we refer to it as becoming more seasoned," Fergus added.

"Bloody good analogy, mate!" Charles said, shut the oven, and patted his friend on the back. "I could always depend on you to put a good spin on things."

"Indeed."

A few hours later, the guests began to arrive, with shouts, cheers, hugs, and kisses, including from all the dogs: Lady and her pups; Kathryn's dog Murphy; and Maggie's new mutt, Walter, whom she'd named after Walter Cronkite. Maggie spent many days and nights on stakeouts, sitting alone in her car. She really hated it and decided she needed some company. She went to the local shelter and rescued a schnoodle, a cross between a poodle and a schnauzer. He was just under a year old and was surrendered by a family that was leaving the country. Maggie thought it might be challenging to get the dog to adapt to his new name, but he was quite the smarty-pants and responded immediately. He knew what hand was feeding him.

"Maggie and a dog, in a car, with a bag of junk food. What could possibly go wrong?" Fergus mused, as he directed his comment to the bubbly, curly, redhead as she bounced into the room.

"As long as she doesn't feed the pooch beef jerky, the air should remain relatively pure," Charles said, and chuckled.

"I've given up beef jerky," Maggie announced, and gave the two chefs pecks on the cheek. "Smells divine in here." She squatted down and called her new family member closer. "Walter, meet Charles and Fergus." The dog sat and lifted one of his paws.

"Bright little fella." Fergus wiped his hands on a towel and shook hands with the pooch. Charles was next with a welcome.

"Alright?" Charles said as he looked into the sweet dog's

face. Walter went down on all four paws and smushed his nose between them. "Bashful?"

Myra and Annie scampered into the kitchen, which was alive with noise.

"What a sweetie," Myra said, and crouched down to greet the new family member. She patted him on the head. "He's so cute!"

Maggie's face was flush and freckled. "I don't know what took me so long to figure this out."

"You kept saying you couldn't have a dog because of your work. I kept saying, yes you can, and here you are," Annie said, grinning.

Walter was already fitting in with the crowd of friends and the fur family.

"Shall we let them run for a while so we're not tripping all over them?" Charles suggested.

"I shut the gate behind me, and I think everyone is here," Nikki said, and walked to the butler pantry where the wine refrigerator was located. "I brought some chard, Sancerre, and rosé."

"I have two cabs, a pinot noir, and a merlot." Kathryn held up her bag.

"More champagne, as promised," Yoko said.

"We shall be pissed and stuffed by the end of the day," Fergus joked.

"Now everyone, get out of the kitchen so I can finish my creations. Go. Scoot!" Charles fanned them toward the atrium. "Dinner will be ready in a few minutes."

With the exception of Charles and Fergus, the group moved out of the way. Exclamations of delight and awe were uttered when everyone got a glimpse of the dining room table.

"Gorgeous!" Nikki whooped.

"Wowie!" Kathryn roared. "Yoko, you are brilliant, and the tableware is beautiful."

Myra and Yoko took bows. "Let's crack open one of those bottles of bubbly and sit in here." Myra gestured to the long U-shaped sofa that was surrounded by luscious plants.

"Everything looks stunning," Maggie said. "The plants have really thrived."

"That's because I wouldn't let you near them," Myra teased.

"Not everyone can have a green thumb, ya know," Maggie said defensively.

"True. Everyone has their own talent." Annie added.

"Speaking of talent, what does Charles have in store for us today?" Kathryn asked, "because whatever it is, smells delish."

"Charles's protest to the colonization was to prepare a crown roast," Myra said.

Everyone laughed, and Maggie hooted. "That's brilliant! But does that mean we don't get turkey and all the fixins?"

"Don't be silly. I would never let that happen." Myra winked while Annie filled champagne glasses.

"I'll bring two out to Charles and Fergus," Maggie offered.

"You're just going in there to swipe whatever isn't nailed down to the counter," Annie joked.

"Ha. So what if I am?" She took the glasses from Annie, spun on her heels, and retreated to the gastronomical headquarters led by Charles and Fergus.

Shortly thereafter, Charles appeared with a platter of carved turkey, followed by Fergus and the crown roast. Maggie was hauling a tray of side dishes. "There's more." She nodded toward the kitchen.

"I'll help," Kathryn offered.

"Please, everyone take a seat. You will find your names on the lovely cards that are wrapped with wheat, courtesy of Nikki."

Everyone checked for their assigned places. "Cute idea." Kathryn nodded at the place settings. "Everything is so pretty."

"It'll be prettier with food on it," Maggie said, and grinned. Once everyone was seated, they held hands and said grace, with a special nod from Myra to Kathryn. "I am so happy you decided to join us today."

"What? And miss this feast?" Kathryn lifted her glass. "To all of you. Your support, your friendship, and your love." She got slightly choked up and then regained her composure. "And of course to our celebrated chef and sous chef!"

A resounding "Here! Here!" filled the room as the lavish platters of food were passed around the table.

Two hundred and fifty miles away, a similar but smaller gathering was forming. Frankie's parents were about to return from visiting a few friends in the neighborhood; Nina was upstairs changing her clothes. Giovanni was assigned the wine, and Rachael had been charged with dessert. Richard and Robert were only a few minutes away, picking up cognac, Strega, and sambuca for after-dinner digestive aids.

Nina bounced down the stairs with her hair wrapped in a scarf adorned with the colors of autumn; her cashmere track suit was burgundy. She could have been in an ad for a holiday magazine.

"You look spectacular!" Frankie said as she finished drying the pots that were sitting in the rack.

"Oh, good. I haven't seen Richard since I've been back, and I wanted to wow him."

"Oh, he'll be wowed alright," Frankie said, and tossed the towel to Nina. "I have to do a presto-change-o. I'll be right back."

"I'll put the tablescape together," Nina called out, as Frankie took the steps two at a time.

"Glassware and dishes are on the sideboard. Silverware in the chest," Frankie shouted back.

Nina went into the laundry room, where her pieces were waiting. First, she spread the twigs and branches from one end of the table to the other. She interspersed the forest floor with clear bowls of water and floated red-colored peonies and burnt-orange tea roses in half of them. Three-inch-high glass vessels had pinecones adorned with gold glitter at the bottom with gold candles floating above. It would be dazzling when the candles were lit. At least that was her plan. *It worked at home*, she thought to herself. As she inspected her workmanship, Giovanni entered the kitchen from the back door.

"*Felice Ringraziamento!*" he called out. "Smells *molto bene*!"

"Hey, Gio!" Nina said as she returned to the cooking hub. He kissed her on both cheeks. "Happy Thanksgiving!"

"You look *bellissima*!" Gio exclaimed.

Nina felt the blush rush over her cheeks. "*Grazie*! You look rather handsome yourself." Nina noted his Luca Faloni half-zip cashmere sweater. She fingered the fabric. "Very nice!" Under the sweater, a crisp white shirt collar peeked out.

He rubbed her sleeve with the back of his hand. "*Anche tu!*"

"Frankie should be down in a minute," she said. "Here, let me help you with those bottles." Nina cleared a space on the counter on the far side of the kitchen.

"I need to put the white and rosé in the refrigerator."

"I think the one in the garage has room." Nina tilted her head in the direction of the laundry room. "You know the way? Through that door and then to the left."

"*Sì*. Yes. I'll be right back. Meanwhile, can you decant the Montepulciano? It should rest for at least twenty minutes."

"There might not be any left in twenty minutes," Nina said with a devilish grin. She was well aware that particular bottle cost nearly one hundred dollars in the store. Then she noticed a second bottle in the box. Giovanni was as generous as he was handsome and kind. Nina rejoiced in how she and Frankie lucked out finding two very decent and desirable men—emphasis on the word *desirable*. Yes, there were decent men out there, but you didn't necessarily want to kiss many of them. *Everyone has a level of standards*, she thought to herself. She was glad she had raised hers after her last relationship debacle. And the debacle before that, and the one before that. *Who knew a singles' cruise could be so fruitful?* The women had expected disastrous results, but they knew they would have fun trying.

Rachael was still the only one who was out on a limb, jumping into relationships and then jumping out as fast. Nina hoped Frankie's advice would take hold and Rachael could calm down when it came to men. Then she thought about Robert and shuddered. *What did she sign him up for? At least there isn't any mistletoe around!*

Just as Frankie came down the stairs, her parents returned from their visit with friends. "Hello Mom! Pappy!" Frankie called out. She bounced down the flight wearing a rust-colored V-neck tunic sweater, leggings, and knee-high boots. She called it her "uniform." Her long black hair was pulled into the usual ponytail, exposing the gold and diamond huggie earrings that Giovanni gave to her for her last birthday. The previous Christmas, he bedazzled her with emerald and diamond cluster earrings. Besides her cats, Bandit and Sweet P, diamonds were beginning to become her best friend, too. When she reached the bottom of the stairs, she wrapped her arms around both of parents and gave them a huge squeeze.

"Something smells delicious!" her mother exclaimed.

"And it's not the house burning down!" her father joked.

"Very funny. Ha ha," Frankie responded.

Nina and Giovanni entered the foyer, and everyone greeted one another with kisses and handshakes. Giovanni helped Frankie's mother, Bianca, with her coat. "It's so nice to have someone take care of everything," she exclaimed.

"Let me have that," Frankie said, gesturing to her father's coat.

"Wow. Do we still live here?" he joked again.

"Dad, did I ever tell you that you should be a comedian?"

"Not that I can recall," he said with a squint.

"Good. Because I never will," Frankie lobbed one right back at him.

Giovanni stood with a wide grin on his face. He was incredibly happy Frankie's parents embraced him into the family. If they had any qualms about the two of them sharing a bedroom, they never mentioned it. Besides, both William and Bianca thought it was just a matter of time before Giovanni popped the question.

William rubbed his hands together. "So, when do we eat?"

"In about a half hour. We're waiting for Richard and his brother Robert, and the usually late Rachael. She always has to make a grand appearance."

"Ah, yes, part of her quirky charm," her father said with a smile.

Giovanni excused himself, took Frankie's arm, and ushered them into the kitchen. "Now I told you that I was going to do everything, so please step aside."

Giovanni took both of her hands. "I just wanted a minute with you to tell you how beautiful you look."

Frankie blushed. "Even with an apron on?"

"Even without one." Giovanni wiggled his eyebrows.

She gently brushed him away. "Go play with my father."

Giovanni gave her an odd look. "Play what?"

"Watch a game. Keep him occupied. Pour some prosecco. Just get out of the way, please!" She was practically whining. "If I need anything, I will let you know. Now go!" She flung her arm in the direction of the living room.

Giovanni shot Nina with a questioning look. She shrugged in return and nodded for him to skedaddle. "Ok, but let me pour something for everyone to drink." He went back to the garage and returned with two bottles of Starfield sparkling brut rosé. Nina followed him to the living room, carrying a tray of champagne flutes.

"I think you will like this," Giovanni said as he peeled the foil, pulled off the cage, and popped the cork. "It's from the El Dorado AVA region."

William watched the bubbles rise to the top of the glass of pink wine. "AVA?"

"It's a designated wine-grape growing region where specific grapes are grown. Grapes have quite different characteristics, and the water and soil is everything, and of course the weather."

"Interesting," William remarked.

"People ask me, what is the best wine? And I tell them, 'It's the one you like.'" Giovanni smiled and began to pour. "Nina, please ask Frankie to join us for one minute."

Nina dashed into the kitchen and pulled Frankie away from the broccoli rabe she was sautéing. "What?" Frankie tugged in the opposite direction.

"Your presence is requested. For one minute."

Frankie threw the kitchen towel over her shoulder and reluctantly followed Nina.

When she entered the room, Giovanni leaned over and kissed her, then handed her a glass. "Here is to family and friends! Cin cin!"

The small group clinked glasses, then Frankie made a beeline back to her greens that were waiting in garlic, olive oil, and Parmigiano Reggiano.

"I better see that she doesn't set anything on fire," Nina said, took a sip, and padded back to the aroma-filled kitchen.

"What do you suppose she has going on in there?" Bianca asked.

"She did not tell me, and I decided it was better not to ask," Giovanni said, and raised his eyebrows.

"I see you are getting to know my daughter well," William responded.

Giovanni thought he might just blush.

A few minutes later, the doorbell rang, with petite Rachael

holding several boxes of pastries that came up to her nose. "Greetings and salutations!" She practically danced her way into the room.

"Rachael! So nice to see you. It's been ages!" Bianca said, giving her a kiss.

"Indeed." William followed with a peck.

Then came Nina.

"*Hola, chica!*" Rachael yelped and handed the boxes over to Giovanni. "Been way too long!"

"Yes, it has." Nina wrapped her arms around her friend and spun her around.

Giovanni helped Rachael with her coat and gave her a kiss on each cheek. "Hello, handsome." Rachael batted her eyelashes at him.

Moments later, the doorbell rang again. It was Richard and Robert. Nina held her breath for what felt like an eternity. *What would Rachael do?* she asked herself. Much to her surprise, Rachael was much more retiring than Nina ever remembered. Nina introduced everyone, and Rachael smiled and shook hands. No flirtation, no coochie-cooing. *Maybe Frankie was right.*

William and Giovanni helped the newly arrived guests with their coats and the after-dinner liquor they had brought; then Giovanni poured each of them a glass of the sparkling wine.

Nina went back to the kitchen to check on Frankie. It was way too quiet in there. At least there weren't flames shooting out of the doorway. "How's it going, babycakes?"

"I think I've got everything under control." Frankie gestured to the lavish antipasto platter. "Round up the troops and bring this out, will ya?"

"Aye aye, captain!" Nina saluted and followed her orders.

The group made their way into the dining room, with everyone commenting on the tablescape. "Very creative!" Bianca said, and then turned to Nina: "Is this your handiwork?"

"It is. Thank you." She looked over at Richard, who showed an enormously proud expression on his face. Richard moved over to where Nina was standing. "Is it assigned seating?" He looked for place cards. "No. I figured we could wing it," Nina replied, waiting for Rachael to make a cutesy comeback. Nothing. Nina suspected Rachael had eaten a gummy or taken a sedative, but that wasn't Rachael's style. *Frankie's heart-to-heart obviously made an impression.* But just to be sure, Nina whispered in Rachael's ear, "Are you okay?"

"Couldn't be better," Rachael replied with a big grin.

Nina decided to let the chips fall where they may and suggested they sit boy-girl-boy-girl. Clearly William would sit at one end of the table, but what about Giovanni? William cleared that up in a second. "Giovanni, since you are our sommelier, please have a seat across from me," he said, and gestured to the other end of the table. Frankie understood how important that signal meant to her father, and to Giovanni.

"Let me pour the wine first." Giovanni opened a bottle of Sancerre, circled the table, and gave a brief explanation. "It comes from a small region in France and is made from the sauvignon grape in the Loire Valley. Sancerre is an area, also known as an appellation, which indicates where the grapes are produced. Sancerre is approximately six thousand acres in the middle of the country. It is believed that it was initially cultivated by the Romans during the first century. I will not bore you with any further details, but it has become immensely popular."

William raised his glass. "Today we witness the true meaning of the word *Thanksgiving*. I am thankful for everyone at this table. Each of us is a gift to each other."

Frankie's eyes teared up. She truly had much to be thankful for, especially her turkey canard farci au poulet.

Chapter 10

New York

Early December

Frankie was busy at her desk when her phone rang.

"Hey, babycakes! Bravo on Thanksgiving dinner! Everything was absolutely delicious, including your not-so-turducken," Nina complimented.

"Yeah. That turned out quite well," Frankie said with a huge sigh of relief.

"And everything else you prepared. Richard and Robert were moaning and groaning when we got back to my parents' house."

"Did they enjoy themselves?"

"Absolutely! I have to say, Robert was quite taken by Rachael."

Frankie let out a yelp. "Ha! I knew she could get results if she downshifted."

"And get this. They are going to a play this weekend."

"Whoa. How long is Robert in town?"

"He and Richard have been discussing forming a partnership. Richard wants to find a better solution than trapsing back and forth to Philly."

"Oh?" Frankie was intrigued.

"He said he wanted to spend more time with me. Can you believe it?"

"Yes, I can. Why wouldn't he? How did you manage to pry that out of him?"

"I didn't have to." Nina recounted the conversation. "When we got back to my place, he told me he was getting weary of all the travel. He said watching you and Giovanni together in a normal setting made him think. He's been commuting back and forth for nearly three years, and I've been on the other side of the world for one third of it. He went on to say that he appreciates how important it is to have quality time with someone. Kiddo, he is thoroughly impressed with the relationship you've developed with Gio."

"Heck, even I'm impressed with the relationship I have with Gio!" Frankie snorted.

Nina continued, "I explained that I still have a lot of work to do on the script, but I think I'll be able to convince Jordan that I can do most of that from here."

"You mean you won't be jumping the pond every other month?"

"That's my plan," Nina said.

"Fantastic!" Frankie cried. "It will be so nice to have you close by, and in the same time zone."

"Richard said the same thing."

"So, if Jordan asks you again, will you tell him you are in a committed relationship?"

"I'll tell him that if I don't stay put, I will never be in one," she said, and chuckled. "I know he can understand that. I've put my career choices before my personal life for too long."

"I hear ya," Frankie mused. "Does that mean we're getting old?"

"No, honey bunch. We are getting wise. Seasoned," Nina replied.

"I like that. Seasoned," Frankie said in agreement. "So, tell me more about this partnership with Richard and Robert."

Nina shared what little she knew, including the thought that her life was moving in a calmer, more fulfilling direction. How? That remained to be seen, but Nina was up for the adventure.

Matt knocked on the doorjamb of Frankie's office.

"Honey pie, I have to go. My watchdog is hovering," Frankie joked, smiling at Matt.

"Okay, babycakes. To be continued," Nina said as she ended the call.

"Watchdog?" Matt said, smirking.

"You no-likey?" Frankie said with a grin.

"Do I growl when I see you?"

"Not usually, but that doesn't mean you aren't growling behind my back."

"I only growl when you are late for a meeting and my phone is blowing up, or when you are working too late."

"See? My watchdog." Frankie flagged him in. "What's up?"

"Just going over the last-minute details for the tree lighting gorge-o-thon." He flopped into one of the seats across from her desk. He had his tablet and a notepad with him. Frankie was a bit "old-school" when it came to taking notes. Paper first, check, recheck, then input. Check and recheck again. Frankie discovered that having backup notes that were not under the influence of power outages, computer crashes, hacking, or just dumb deletions was the smart way to go. She learned the hard way. And always use a thumb drive or external hard drive to save your work.

"Okay. Let's have the bad news first," Frankie said, as she leaned on her forearms.

"What makes you think there's bad news?" Matt said, and gave her a sideways glance.

"You're right. I should not presume there is bad news."

"Everything is coming together. The only hitch is that the conference room isn't going to be available until five."

"But we reserved it," Frankie whined.

"I know, but Mr. Big Cheese usurped your reservation. He is having a meeting with a big agent."

"Aren't they all big agents?" Frankie said, and smirked. "Why does he have to be a show-off on such a big day? Can't he use the executive conference room? His own office?"

"Those are for his private party."

"Oh, the one he has while we're having ours?" Frankie said with a touch of annoyance. The CEO knew that an office party had become a little tradition in the editorial offices, but he declined to attend.

"Of course. He realized what a fabulous idea you had and decided to copy it. Besides, the view from his office is much better than yours."

"Oh, phooey," Frankie muttered. "When does he go to St. Barth's?"

"Not soon enough. His executive assistant is about to pull all her hair out."

"And who is catering his soiree?" Frankie asked, folding her arms across her chest.

"Per Se."

"Of course. The most expensive restaurant in New York." Frankie heaved a huge sigh. "And I am sure he is going to put it on his expense account."

"I am sure. But. . . ." Matt paused.

"But what?" Frankie could not imagine what else could possibly annoy her at that point.

"But when I was in the facilities offices, I ran into Mike Winslow."

"The CFO?"

"Yes."

"And so?"

"And so, I asked him what forms you should fill out for reimbursement for the party."

Frankie blinked several times, then said, "You asked him what?"

"I asked him which forms we needed to submit. It was worth a shot."

"Well, what did he say?" Frankie was once again leaning forward on her desk.

"He said that since this is considered a company function, you should fill this out." Matt was about to hand her the form. "I mean I should fill it out."

"They are going to reimburse me?" Frankie was stunned.

"I played a little dumb. I asked him if he was planning to attend."

"What did he say?"

"He said he didn't get an invitation. I told him that it must have gone into his junk folder."

"Matt, you are brilliant!" Frankie exclaimed. "I could kiss you!"

"Ew. Cooties," he said, and pretended to flag her away. "Anyway, he said he would be delighted to attend."

"Even better. Maybe after a glass of wine, he'll be amenable to reconsidering my idea of moving the office party here and make it a combo celebration."

"I'll be hot on the trail with whatever he's drinking," Matt said in a conspiratorial whisper.

"You are a man of many talents, but I didn't realize stalking was one of them."

"Only when necessary," Matt said, and rolled his eyes.

"Say no more. They can't get any information out of me if I don't know anything," Frankie said, chuckling. "Everything else good?"

"Perfect. I'll get a few people to hustle after Mr. Big Cheese is finished with his meeting. And if he isn't, I'll just have to put a few trays on the conference table and light the chafing canisters. I'll function as if no one else is in the room."

"You are the best," Frankie said, and smiled. She knew Matt was not kidding about ignoring everyone else in the room.

Two days later, the halls of the editorial offices were decked out with garlands, long streams of stars, candy canes, and holly. As promised, Matt stood in the doorway of the conference room with his arms folded and was giving the agent the stink eye. Matt wasn't too concerned. He sensed the agent couldn't wait to get out of the room. He, too, knew it would be a madhouse at the plaza below. The agent stood and shook Mr. Big Cheese's hand. "We'll talk," he said over his shoulder as he inched past Matt.

"Oh, Mr. Snyder. My apologies. I didn't realize you were in a meeting," Matt said as he glided into the room.

"No worries, Mike." Snyder picked up his two cell phones and pushed himself away from the marble table. "I have to run. Excuse me."

"It's Matt, you knucklehead," Matt muttered to himself when Snyder was no longer in earshot. "How long have I been working here?" he said in a slightly louder voice. Rosie from the art department walked in to give him a hand.

"Do you always talk to yourself, Matt?"

"Matt? Oh, is that my name?"

"Er, yes."

"Tell that to Mr. Big Cheese."

Rosie burst out laughing. "He thinks my name is Rita."

Several other people stopped in to help, and within a half hour, the room went from stodgy conference room to holiday magic. The menorah, tree, and Kwanzaa candles were proudly displayed down the center of the table, surrounded by the catering trays. By six o'clock, the party was on a roll, with a lot of rollatini.

By eight o'clock, most people were stuffed, and restless. Frankie decided to make an announcement.

"Hi, everyone! I hope you've enjoyed the festivities. I know it's been a long day, and we still have a lot of holiday merriment over the next couple of weeks. Please do not feel compelled to hang around until ten. The lights will be on for the next four weeks, so you will surely have an opportunity to see them. I am sure you have plenty to do."

"Are you tossing us out?" a voice called from the back of the room.

"Not at all. But if you want to head out, please do. I'd say take whatever food is left over, but we seemed to have cleaned our plates. Now shoo. Get home to your families—fur, people, or otherwise. Be safe out there, and we'll see you in the morning."

Matt moved next to her. "Are you really throwing everyone out?"

"Look at them. They are tired. I don't want to be that boss who insists people hang around until the fat lady sings."

"I think she's singing now," Matt said about one of the performers below.

"Ha! It seems everyone enjoyed the food and the camaraderie. That was really the point. Like I said, they'll see that tree every day for the next four weeks. Now help me clean up, and then you can vamoose," Frankie stated.

"I could kiss you!"

"Ew. Cooties," Frankie said, and chuckled.

Pinewood

Myra and Annie were in the renovated barn with their clipboards, taking inventory of the toys that had been delivered. There were dozens of shrink-wrapped pallets containing toys ranging from toddler learning games to handheld video games.

"Wow. How much do you think all of this is worth?" Annie asked.

Myra flipped through the bills of lading. "I am going to need a calculator."

Annie handed Myra her phone. "There's one on here." Myra pulled up the app. "I suppose we should use the retail prices of everything."

"Yes. I am going to have the load insured. Can you give me your best guess?"

"Guessing is not very accurate, my friend." Myra peered over her reading glasses. "Here." She handed Annie her phone. "I'll call out the numbers, and you can do the math."

It took the better part of the morning to determine a retail sales figure. It was in the neighborhood of 15,000 dollars.

"That is quite a haul," Myra exclaimed. "And it doesn't include the socks. Better add another two grand to the total."

"Let's just round it up to twenty thousand. I'll call my insurance agent when we get back to the house," Annie offered.

"Perfect. Kathryn said she'll swing by later to eyeball everything so she'll have the right truck."

"Looks like it could be one of her regular trailers."

"It does." Myra put her arm around Annie. "We done good, girl."

"By the way, Kathryn seemed much more relaxed at Thanksgiving."

"Yes, she did. More comfortable." Myra nodded.

"Do you think she'll end the feud with Pearl?"

"One could hope. I can't even remember what it was all about."

"Neither can I," Annie said in agreement. "But one step at a time. She's coming out of her self-imposed isolation."

"If it weren't for our missions, I really don't know what kind of interaction she would have with other people. I mean, besides the people she meets at the truck stops."

"And there's no guarantee she'll see the same people more than once or twice a year," Annie said.

"Ah, but that is probably why she felt comfortable. She didn't have to interact with them on a regular basis."

"Good point," Annie responded. "So, what do you say we grab something for lunch? Let's see what the boys are up to."

"Isn't there some kind of soccer or football something going on this week?" Myra said, and placed her reading glasses in her vest pocket.

"Isn't there always? It seems like the season never ends," Annie said, and chuckled. "Come on." Annie gestured for Myra to get into the passenger side of the golf cart.

Myra took a deep breath, strapped herself in, and prepared herself for her lead-footed friend to hit the accelerator and kick up the gravel. As they sped toward the farmhouse, Myra grabbed the frame of the cart to steady herself. "Glad you got the windshield fixed."

"And check out the new steering wheel cover."

Myra looked at the customized leather and chuckled. "You have all the Sisters' names on it."

"Yeah. A tribute to our team."

Annie made a quick turn, throwing Myra off balance. Annie grabbed her by the sleeve.

"We may not have a team if you keep driving like this!" Myra dreaded every time she got into a vehicle with Annie behind the wheel. "Why do you always drive as if you are in some kind of race?"

"For fun?" Annie asked rhetorically.

"Maybe for you, but not for me." Myra held her breath for the next few minutes until they came to a jolting stop. "I shall never get used to this," she said as she unbuckled her seat belt and jumped from the cart.

Annie wrapped her arm around Myra's shoulders. "We weren't even going over thirty-five miles per hour."

"Huh. You sure could have fooled me."

The women entered through the rear kitchen door, where Lady and her pups stood waiting. Annie and Myra stopped to give the dogs pets and smooches on their heads. "Where's Daddy?" Myra asked. Lady gave a soft *woof* and led them to the den, where Charles and Fergus were watching a soccer match.

"See? I told you!" Annie exclaimed.

"Hello, love." Charles stood and kissed his wife. Annie leaned over the sofa where Fergus had situated himself and gave him a peck on the cheek.

"What's for lunch?" Annie asked.

The two men looked at each other. "We weren't expecting you back so soon."

"I take it the answer is 'nothing yet'?" Annie grumbled.

"Are you hangry?" asked Fergus.

"No, but I will be if you don't get your fanny into the kitchen and whip something up for us. We've been working in the barn for hours," Annie joked.

"Right-o!" Charles stood and motioned for Fergus to follow. "I think we can cobble a few grilled cheese sandwiches together, eh, mate?"

"Make mine with tomato and bacon, on rye. Please," Annie said demurely.

"Your wish is my command," Fergus said with a straight face, following Charles into the kitchen.

Myra and Annie plopped down where the men were sitting, grabbed the remote, and changed it to one of the shopping channels. Annie rested her head on Myra's shoulder. "Why do we watch this stuff?"

"To see if there is something we have absolutely no need for but buy anyway?" Myra answered. "At least we donate most of it."

"Very true. We have good intentions." Annie sat upright as the current items were being hawked by the hosts. "Look. It's a dancing ballerina inside a bottle of water that lights up."

"Let's buy a dozen," Myra said jokingly.

"Only twelve dollars with six flex-pays. What a bargain," Annie said, and laughed. "Imagine someone spending seventy-two dollars on that?"

"When I was a little girl, there was a company that made anisette. Inside the bottle was a ballerina sealed inside a glass dome that also housed a music box. I don't remember the tune, but I enjoyed watching her spin around." Myra sighed. "Unless that bottle on the shopping channel contains a delicious digestif, it's not worth the money."

Annie smiled to herself and made a mental note to order one as a gag gift for Myra, but then it occurred to her to check eBay. They might have one exactly like Myra described, probably without the liquor, but they could remedy that.

A few minutes later, the aroma of bacon wafted into the room. "I think we should give them a hand." Myra elbowed Annie. "Or at least pretend," she said, and chuckled.

Chapter 11

New York

Mid-December

Frankie and Matt were going over some of the BLADS (basic layout and design) for one of the cookbooks that was being published the following year. "Do you think Moroccan food is going to be popular?" Matt asked.

"The publicity department is going to have to work on that angle, although my gut is telling me yes. No pun intended." Frankie made a few notes in the margins of the pages.

"Are you ready for SantaCon this year?" Matt asked offhandedly.

Frankie groaned. "Another extravaganza where drunk people roam the streets of New York."

"Doesn't that happen every day?" Matt asked sarcastically.

"Yes, but this is filled with people dressed like Santa, elves, and fairies."

"Aw, come on. Don't be a Grinch," Matt shot back.

"I'm not, but why does everything have to turn into an event? It's no wonder some people think the holidays are too commercial."

"Funny you should mention that, Boss Lady," Matt said. "Did you know that it started in San Fransisco in 1994, when it was originally called *Santarchy*, as a rebuke of all the commercialism surrounding the holidays?"

"No, I did not know that. Why didn't I know that?" Frankie said, smirking. "I thought I knew everything."

"But now it has spun itself around to be a celebration."

"Is that what you call it?" Frankie said, and twisted her mouth.

"What's gotten into you lately? You tossed people out of the tree-lighting party, and now you are poo-pooing SantaCon."

Frankie wrinkled her brow. "Huh. You're right. I've been feeling a bit cranky lately."

"It's not like you're not under any pressure, or anything," Matt said sardonically.

Frankie was pensive for a few minutes, then said, "I think I'm in over my head."

Matt leaned forward and lowered his voice. "Whatever you need, you know you can ask for my help."

"I appreciate that, but it's more about Giovanni's mother and aunt coming. I want to show them a good time while they're here."

"I am sure you will," Matt said reassuringly. "You've planned all the holiday trips the last few years, and everything was a success."

"Yes, but not without trauma and drama," Frankie said, and sighed. "I guess I just want things to go smoothly for a change, and everyone can enjoy being together. But I still haven't figured out what to do about New Year's Eve."

"A house party is always good. You can drink and not drive."

"I don't want to put my parents through that."

"It's not like you're a teenager and are going to go wild and set the sofa on fire."

"Have you met Rachael?" Frankie chortled. "I'm being mean. She's never set anything on fire. Not that I know of."

"How about reserving something at Del Frisco's Grille? It will be like a private party. It's festive and you don't have to do anything."

Frankie tapped her pen on her desk. "That actually sounds like a good idea. I'll run it past Giovanni and see what he thinks. His mother and aunt invited their *fidanzatos* to join them."

"Finn what?"

"Boyfriends. Two brothers for two sisters-in-law."

"Aw. That's kind of sweet."

Frankie finally smiled. "It is." She then told him the story of the makeover she and Nina accomplished with the two women, who had been wearing black, blacker, and blackest for several years.

"So, they really do that? Do they roll down their stockings and wear black shoes?"

Frankie burst out laughing. "Yes. It reminded me of my grandmother and her sisters. But Nina and I convinced Rosevita and Lucia that they should return to the land of the living, and we colored their hair and decked them out. Giovanni didn't even recognize his mother. The ladies went to a party, met the Parisi brothers, and the rest is *amore*."

"Wow. That's such a nice story," Matt said, and smiled. "But Frankie, I don't know what you are worried about. Can't you make a few plans and then let them go wild on their own?"

Frankie laughed. "Ha! Who knows what kind of trouble they could get themselves into! But I did buy tickets to the Christmas Spectacular at Radio City, and we have plans to take them to Keens Steakhouse."

"Didn't you tell me that Giovanni's mother lived in New York for a long time?"

"Yes, she did."

"So? I don't think she'll need a chaperone during her entire stay here. You know, you can't boss everybody around all the time."

"I can't? Wait a minute. I think I have a certificate somewhere in my drawer," Frankie joked.

"Look, why don't you focus on the memory book, talk to Giovanni, and then sketch out a plan. Then you can let Giovanni's mom decide what *she* wants to do," Matt suggested.

"You're right. I've been stressing about things I shouldn't worry about, and I should be taking care of the things that I can actually do."

"See? Am I not the best assistant you ever had?"

"You are! I could kiss you!"

"Ew, cooties!" they said in unison.

PART II

Chapter 12

Mid-December

Vinny "The Mooch" Massella and his goofy pal, Jimmy "The Snitch" O'Mara, were walking through downtown Brooklyn, heading to the pizzeria. But they weren't going to get a slice. In fact, the pizza at this joint was barely edible. But the clientele wasn't interested in pie. They were there to place bets or wash money. Nothing violent. That is, unless you didn't pay your debt, and today was a day of reckoning for Vinny. All he needed was a couple more weeks, and he'd be able to pay the full tab of 20,000 dollars. He hoped Bucky would show him some mercy.

"How'd ya get into such a mess?" Jimmy asked, as he wiped his nose on his sleeve.

Vinny looked at him in disgust. "Didn't anybody ever tell you to use a Kleenex or something?"

"Yeah, but it was running, and I don't have one."

"Whatever," Vinny huffed at his childhood friend.

The two had lived on the same street in Brooklyn when

they were kids, almost forty years ago. Both had spent their youth hanging around the pizzeria, doing odd jobs for the owner at the time. Vinny would mop the floors, and Jimmy would clean the counters. The place was immaculate, assuring they would get an "A" rating from the Board of Health. They only failed once, when someone left an "occupied" rat trap in the back room.

Everyone lived in fear of the proprietor, Louis Amato. When he was informed the restaurant had failed the health inspection, he demanded to know who was responsible. Nobody wanted to be a snitch, but Jimmy's eyes darted in Vinny's direction. Amato caught Jimmy's glance and fired Vinny on the spot. That's how Jimmy became known as "Jimmy the Snitch." Later that day and every day after, Jimmy argued, "I ain't said nothin' to nobody," which was true, but everyone knew Jimmy had a terrible poker face.

Vinny knew Jimmy was just a simple soul and had no inclinations toward malice, so kept him under his wing. However, his wing was about to be broken unless he could convince Bucky, the current owner of the pizzeria, to give him more time and figure out a way to raise some serious cash.

Several years earlier, Louis retired and sold his "business" to a musclehead named Bucky Barflow. He was scarier than Louis. Much scarier.

"I miss the old days," Jimmy said with a touch of melancholy. "The Amato family had principles, ya know? I mean, they would cut you some slack if you were loyal. Now, these guys—from somewhere I never heard of and can't pronounce—they got no manners."

Vinny had to chuckle at that. Manners wasn't exactly what was missing. Human decency was terribly lacking. It had been replaced with depraved indifference.

At fifty-two, Vinny was still living rent-free in the upstairs apartment of his mother's two-family home, hence the name "Vinny the Mooch." His mother didn't mind. She had her boy around. He helped with the laundry and bought groceries, and they watched professional wrestling together on Friday nights. His mother would howl at the grown men bouncing each other around and curse at them in Italian.

There was a time that Vinny lived the high life. He had a solid union job and made good money. But he never could hold on to the cash. He liked the ladies and enjoyed showering them with gifts. He also liked the ponies. Not the kind at a county fair, but the ones at the racetrack. It didn't take long for him to rack up some serious debt. Like many other gamblers, he was constantly going for "the big win" or "the sure thing." As the money began to thin, so did his stable of female companions. There was little interest in a chump who was down on his luck and had a gambling problem.

Vinny's life had become a boring routine, until now. Now, his well-being was in danger of not being well.

In the past, he was able to cover his bets, but lately his luck seemed to have run out. He recently borrowed 10,000 dollars from his mother, using the story that he needed a down payment on a new car. When she asked to see it, he told her it was being shipped from Florida. Six weeks had passed, yet no car. She stopped asking. He was feeling quite downtrodden. His life was an embarrassment.

"So how come you're in this pickle?" Jimmy pressed the issue that Vinny clearly did not want to discuss.

"Somebody gave me a tip for the Belmont Stakes. It was going to pay thirty-six to one. So, I placed ten clams with Bucky."

"Ten thousand? Wow. Did it win?" Jimmy asked innocently.

"What do *you* think? I wouldn't be in this mess if it did."

"Wait. I'm no mathematical genius, so how did it double? Was it the vig?" Jimmy was referring to the interest on an unsecured loan from an unauthorized "lending institution."

"Yep."

"Whoa. Isn't that like loan sharking?"

Vinny looked up at the heavens and placed his hand on Jimmy's shoulder. "Bucky isn't really running a pizzeria."

"Right. Right. Right. Right. Right." The connection had sunk in. "So whaddya gonna do?"

"I have an idea."

"Cool. Like what?"

"Let's see if Bucky will give me a two-, three-week stretch. Then I'll tell you, cause if he don't, I'm probably gonna be laid up with casts on both my legs."

Jimmy winced at the idea of Vinny getting his kneecaps slammed. "Can't you work it off?"

"What, with minimum wage?"

Jimmy nodded as they shuffled their way to Vinny's fate.

When they got to the shop, a few regulars were sitting inside at a small table. Bucky was perched on a stool, wearing a tank top which exposed tattoos from head to toe. Vinny didn't want to think about the ones that weren't visible. Not that he ever saw Bucky naked, but in the summer his body art was on full display, covering his calves and thighs. Bucky's big, chunky gold chains hung from his inked neck. The nose ring reminded Vinny of a bull, not that it took a fertile imagination to consider the similarity. Bucky nodded in Vinny's direction, then jerked his head, indicating to follow him to the back room. Vinny was silently praying he would be able to walk out the door on his own two feet.

Bucky folded his arms and leaned against the puke-green-colored cinderblocks. It occurred to Vinny that the place hadn't been painted in an exceedingly long time, but that wasn't a pressing issue at the time.

"Whaddya got for me?" Bucky seemed to increase in size, like an inflated cartoon character, with his facial tattoos growing exponentially.

Vinny took a deep breath. "It's like this." He paused, waiting for Bucky to lift him by the shirt and throw him against the ugly cement. "I need a couple more weeks."

Bucky looked down at his prey. "You know the rules, Vin."

"Yes, yes, I do, but I can pay you in full, and then some. If I have it calculated right, it'll pay five times what I owe you. I have a deal in the works."

"Yeah? What kind of deal?" Bucky shifted the toothpick from one side of his mouth to the other.

Vinny began to explain his plan, while Bucky listened intently.

"You got two weeks," Bucky relented. "But if you don't deliver, it's going to cost you an extra twenty grand."

Vinny was so relieved, he thought he was going to wet his pants, and scurried past the looming Bucky to relieve himself. His hands were shaking so badly, he could barely manage his zipper. He swiped his hands under the faucet, shook them dry, and quickly exited the bathroom. He nodded toward Bucky, then nudged Jimmy and half-bolted out the door.

Jimmy was almost as winded as Vinny. "What happened back there?" He scanned Vinny for any marks or bruises on his face.

"He gave me two weeks." Vinny leaned over the nearest trash can and let go of the breakfast that was churning in his stomach. He reached over to Jimmy's shirttails and wiped his mouth.

"Hey! Whaddya doin'?" Jimmy jerked away.

"Giving your mucus some company."

"That's disgusting," Jimmy scowled.

"You're one to talk."

As the two ambled down the broken sidewalk, Vinny knew he needed Jimmy's help and began to tell him the plan. "There's a hundred thousand dollars' worth of goods rolling in."

"Yeah? So?" Jimmy had no idea where the conversation was going.

"So, I got a lead on where and when." Vinny kept looking around to see if anyone was following them. Even though Bucky gave him some extra time, it didn't mean he wasn't going to get smacked around.

"No foolin'?" Jimmy asked. There was excitement in his voice. "How'd you find out?"

"Let's not get into too much detail for the moment." Vinny stopped walking and nodded for them to move closer to the building. "I cannot divulge my source; however, it's an exceptionally good source. A beautiful source. You could say it's a perfect source."

"Yeah? For real?" Jimmy lowered his voice. "Come on, you can tell me."

"Nah. No can do, but if you help me, I'll cut you in on the deal."

"Seriously?" Jimmy was enthralled at the idea of pulling a caper with Vinny. It had been a long time since they did a few "shakedowns" for Louis when people owed him money. It usually consisted of a punch in the gut, or a serious smack in the face, with a stern warning that more or worse would follow. Jimmy was secretly happy he never had to inflict serious bodily harm on anyone. For Louis's customers, a stern warning was enough for them to mortgage their house or sell the family's silver cutlery in order to cough up the cash. Bucky preferred harsher "incentives," which often required the use of a steel bar or similar leaden instruments.

Jimmy was content driving a delivery truck for his Uncle Frank's liquor store. He got paid in cash and had a fair "allowance" to the inventory, but a little extra "green" was always welcome. "So, when is this going down?"

"Maybe the week after Thanksgiving, or the week after that. I'm waiting for the final details."

"Whaddya want me to do?"

Vinny laid out a rough plan and what Jimmy's responsibilities would be.

"Got it, boss." Jimmy was flattered that his best friend and hero wanted him back on the job.

Kathryn pulled into Pinewood to survey the haul from Myra and Annie's toy drive. The three met at the barn.

"Thanks again for a great dinner. I'm glad I came."

"We're glad you joined us," Myra said.

"Charles really knows how to work magic in the kitchen," Kathryn noted.

Annie couldn't help herself. "Rumor has it he's rather magical in a lot of places."

Myra turned abruptly, then stopped. "He is. Especially when it comes to electronics," she said with a sly smile.

Annie wasn't sure how to interpret that comment, but she had to agree; when it came to technology, he was aces.

Kathryn seemed unfazed by their exchange. She was appraising the incredible number of toys the Sisters had collected. "This can fit into an intermodal-size trailer," Kathryn said.

"You are the professional. Get whatever you need and put it on the company card." Annie was referring to a special credit card from a shell company that Annie managed. In order for the Sisters to operate remotely, they would often need access to cash or use a credit card. The card was issued through a bank in Nebraska, where Annie had a business account in the name of "For Barbara," a company dedicated to helping women. It wasn't quite a lie, even if their means were slightly outside the law. As long as they maintained a balance in the account and the credit card bill was paid every month, there was no reason for anyone to want to audit their books.

"Roger that. When do you want me to pick it up?" Kathryn asked.

"Whenever you want," Annie said. "I just have to let the hotel know in advance when we will be delivering the goods."

"I can probably get to it day after tomorrow, transfer to box trucks, and deliver to the hotel in three days."

"Perfect. It will be a little ahead of schedule, but the hotel promised it wouldn't be a problem," Annie said.

"And I'd feel more comfortable knowing everything arrived and the only thing we need to think about is what we're wearing," Myra said as she stroked her pearls.

"Okay! We have a plan!" Annie hooted and gave the other two women a high five.

"You have someone to help you, I assume?" Myra asked.

"Yes. Two other drivers are going to meet me at the distribution center. We should be able to do it in one trip with three small trucks."

"Well that certainly sounds easier than trying to figure out how to get a semi down Fifth Avenue," Myra said.

"Or trying to get a permit," Kathryn added.

"Imagine dealing with New York City bureaucracy?" Myra retorted.

"No, I cannot," Annie added.

"Okay, dear friends, I shall see you tomorrow morning. I'll plan on getting here around nine once the commuter traffic dies down."

"Okey dokey," Annie said, and waved as Kathryn hopped into her SUV.

Myra watched as Kathryn maneuvered her vehicle down the rocky path. "Must seem like driving a kiddie car after being in her truck all week."

"I never thought of that!" Annie said, and grinned.

New York City was being overrun by drunken Santas, boozy elves, and ossified angels. The dreaded SantaCon had begun.

Frankie was leaving the building when she saw one of the Salvation Army ladies speaking to a police officer. The woman looked very distraught. Frankie's people-caring side immediately kicked in, and she moved closer to where the woman was standing. She could hear the officer repeating what the woman had just told him.

"A drunken Santa knocked you over. By the time you were able to regroup, you noticed all the money in your bucket was missing. Is that right?"

The woman was clearly shaken. "Y-y-yes. In all my years, nothing like this has ever happened."

The officer continued to write in his notebook. "You're sure it was a Santa who stole the money?"

"Everything happened so fast. He rammed into me and knocked everything over. Besides, they all looked alike, except he was a little skinnier than the others."

The officer sighed. He knew it was going to be impossible to find the culprit among the hundreds of other Santas staggering along the sidewalk. "Do you think he did this alone, or did you notice anyone helping him?"

"Like I said, I was so stunned, I couldn't tell."

The policeman flipped his notebook shut. "Okay, Ms. Duncraft. If anything turns up on our end, I'll be in touch. Meanwhile, if you think of anything else, please give us a call." He knew there would be no further communication on the subject. Finding a criminal Santa in New York City would be a major undertaking, especially with the extra millions of tourists visiting Midtown Manhattan during the holidays.

After the police left, Frankie went over to the woman. "Is there anything I can do?" She dug into her tote bag, produced a handkerchief, and gave it to the woman. "Can I buy you a cup of coffee? Tea?"

"Thank you, but no. I have to report this to the office." She began to gather her things, picked up the red bucket, and then began to cry. "I lost a lot of money today. Enough to feed a family of four for a week."

Frankie bent over and picked up the woman's bell that was lying on the sidewalk. "Let me help you."

The woman looked up into Frankie's eyes. "You are very kind."

"And you are very brave," Frankie replied, and then she spotted a glove on the ground next to where the woman had fallen. She picked it up and wondered if it belonged to the scallywag who'd mugged the volunteer. She was about to ask when she noticed a slip of paper stuffed in the glove. "Do you think he was wearing this?" she asked the woman.

"He was wearing a black glove, but I don't know if that belonged to him. Like I said, it happened so fast."

The crinkled paper had an address in Brooklyn, and Frankie got a bit of a jolt. Something told her that little piece of paper might hold the answer to who the thug was. She knew the police wouldn't follow up on it, but she might be able to talk her friend Nina into helping her do a little detective work on their own. She knew it was a crazy idea, but crazy ideas weren't new to Frankie.

Just as the woman was about to walk away, Frankie placed her hand on the woman's sleeve. "Do you have an extra minute?"

The woman looked perplexed. "I must report this."

"I know. But if you can humor me for a few minutes, I would appreciate it. My name is Frankie, by the way. I've seen you here for the past several years."

"I'm Carol. Yes, eighteen years to be exact."

"Well, Carol, I'm sorry we had to be introduced like this, but would you accompany me across the street?"

Carol still had no idea what Frankie was getting at. "But I really must get going."

"Please? I promise it won't take more than ten minutes. Here, let me carry that for you." Frankie gestured to the frame for the sign and the kettle.

"Oh, it's no bother," Carol replied.

"Please?" Frankie said with wide puppy-dog eyes. She placed her hand under the woman's elbow. "Come."

The woman resigned herself to the fact that this "helpful young woman" was going to help her, whether she wanted the help or not. They waited at the crosswalk until the little person in the box lit up to signify it was safe to cross—although one still had to be mindful of speeding taxis. They passed the front of Saks and then crossed 50th Street and walked one block north. Frankie continued to guide the woman toward the famous building with two Gothic spires, and beautifully sculpted, bronze doors. Frankie stepped aside so Carol could enter first. They were now two of the five million annual visitors of St. Patrick's Cathedral.

Carol gulped back more tears and whispered, "Today I needed an angel, and you came along and brought me here."

Frankie took Carol's equipment for lack of a better word and asked one of the security guards if she could leave it near their desk. She explained the woman had just been mugged. For managing as many visitors as they do every day, the guards were patient and kind. "You take your time," one of the older gentlemen said to Frankie.

The marble steps to the sanctuary were filled with hundreds of red poinsettias. Dozens upon dozens graced the perimeter's many altars honoring different saints, where people could light tealight candles and pray to their patron saint.

Carol was not Catholic but appreciated the feeling of peace that filled the sacred space. Regardless of one's religion, everyone could use a sense of peace. Carol sat in a pew while Frankie lit a candle near the statue of Saint Jude, also known as Thaddaeus, the patron saint of lost causes. Frankie thought it fitting for the situation. As she walked toward Carol, Frankie noticed the expression on her face. It was calmer than it had been fifteen minutes ago. She slid next to Carol as they sat in silence for a few more minutes. Frankie gave Carol the nod that they should be on their way. For someone who had been in such a hurry, Carol was less anxious and more stable.

Frankie retrieved Carol's red kettle and frame and thanked the guards. When they got outside, Frankie flagged down a cab for Carol, reached into her wallet, and handed Carol a fifty-dollar bill. "I hope this helps."

Once again, Carol's eyes filled with tears. But this time, they were tears of gratitude. "You really have been my guardian angel today."

"I am happy to be able to help," Frankie said, as the driver loaded Carol's things into the back of the SUV. "Have a good night," she said, and gave the woman a hug.

As Frankie watched the cab navigate through the traffic, she pulled the piece of paper from her pocket and decided to check it out later. For now, she still had a lot of preparation to do. Giovanni's mother and aunt were due to arrive the next day.

When Frankie got back to her apartment, her fur-babies were eagerly waiting for her near the door. Frankie was always astonished at how they situated themselves right in the entryway. There was no time for them to get to that particular spot at the click of the lock. Or maybe they were quicker than she imagined. But it was as if they sensed her walking into the lobby of her building and got ready to greet her. She scooped Bandit in her arms, something he was only willing to tolerate for a minute—max. He was a cuddle bug but not comfortable being raised off the ground by a human. Sweet P was no different. She scooted out of Frankie's arms as quickly as Frankie picked her up. Yet she, too, was a cuddle bug. Both on their own terms.

Frankie hung her coat as the cats paraded toward the kitchen. Frankie pulled her phone out of the same pocket where she stashed the piece of paper. She called Giovanni to let him know she was home and would meet him at the restaurant within the hour. She needed to feed the kitties, change her clothes, and process what she experienced an hour earlier, but she was immediately distracted with the almost complete memory book that was sitting on her dining table. She was just waiting for Lucia to bring a few pins and ribbons. When Frankie approached Lucia about being her "secret helper," Lucia was thrilled to be included in the preparations. Her son, Dominic, scanned all the photos Lucia could find. There were close to one hundred. Frankie was grateful that Giovanni was able to help edit them. Through her contacts with the art department, she was able to get the pages with photos printed ahead of time. There were placeholders for Lucia's final contributions with captions, ready to go.

Frankie was psyched at how beautiful the memory book turned out. It was a twelve-by-twelve-inch tanned-leather book with a wraparound binding. Leather strips on each side fastened together in a gold ring. There was a three-ring binder inside, to give more space between pages for the ribbons Marco and Giovanni won when they were on the high-school football/soccer team. Her plans for the final touches were dried sunflowers, wrapped in a newsprint copy of the day Rosevita and her husband were married and tied to the front with another leather strip, with Italian lira coins and U.S. coins hanging from the top and bottom of the strip. She got goosebumps.

The cats were beginning to pace.

"Okay. Okay. Keep your mittens on. I'm coming." Frankie laughed. As with every meal, they skirted between her ankles. "Stop messing with me, please. You don't want mommy to trip."

Bandit looked up at her as if to say, "Let's get crackin', lady." Frankie swore if Bandit wore a watch, he would tap it impatiently with his other paw. Frankie often anthropomorphized animals and inanimate objects, giving them human attributes. She would say "excuse me" if she bumped into a chair. She got over worrying about what other people would think or say. It amused her, and who couldn't use a little amusement in their life?

Once the fur-babies were busy with their dinner, Frankie freshened up and slipped into a fresh pair of leggings and sweater. No boots this time. It was black athletic shoes.

When she arrived at the restaurant, the aroma from the kitchen was comforting and stimulating at the same time. She didn't have to see the menu. She must have eaten her way from antipasto to dolce over a hundred times. Most of the time, she let either Marco or Giovanni choose for her. They knew exactly what was going on in the kitchen.

Giovanni greeted her in the usual fashion: a kiss on each cheek, with one extra. Her usual seat at her usual table was awaiting her arrival. It felt like home. In many ways, it was. It was where Giovanni and Marco grew up and worked in the family business all their lives. They were raised in the apartments on the second floor, above the restaurant. Giovanni still maintained an apartment there, but spent the nights at Frankie's. It was actually a good setup. Giovanni and Frankie had coffee together in the morning; then he would go back to his apartment to shower and get ready for work. It was like having two separate bathrooms, except they were five blocks apart. It suited Frankie fine. Giovanni often got off work at eleven at night, so Frankie could still have some "alone time" with her cats, reading a good book, or a watching a murder mystery show.

Giovanni brought two glasses of wine over to Frankie's table and pulled out a chair. "May I?" he asked. Frankie was never quite sure if he was teasing, or if it was something in-grained. *Manners.* Yep, that's what it was.

"Please," she said, and smiled into his deep blue eyes. *Damn, he is good looking,* she thought to herself and began to blush. Frankie knew that he knew what he was doing: turning her into mush. But then again, Giovanni wasn't a player, a flirt, a manipulator. He was genuine. Not perfect by any means, but a good man with good intentions. Frankie counted her blessings every day.

The two proceeded to discuss their day, including the incident with Carol from the Salvation Army. Giovanni took Frankie's hand. "You are an angel. *Bellissima angela.*" Frankie chuckled.

"What's so funny?" Giovanni asked.

"I was thinking about how lucky I am, and you are just so, so . . . you! My life couldn't get any more like a Hallmark movie if I wrote it myself!"

Giovanni cocked his head. "Hallmark?"

"It's a movie channel and production company. They make romantic movies and play them on their network. I mean networks, plural." She realized the conversation wasn't going anywhere and decided to change it. "I'm almost finished with the memory book. Just waiting for Aunt Lucia to deliver the last odds and ends tomorrow."

"I am sending a car to pick them up from the airport. They're arriving in Newark, so they'll go to Marco's."

"Excellent. This way, Lucia can hand over the goods."

Giovanni chuckled, then said, "I will bring the—what you call—goodies. I am going to Marco's house to greet them. Say hello and then come back here, so Marco can help them get settled."

"Good idea!" Frankie said, and smiled.

"So, tell me more about this poor woman today. You helped her, yes?"

"Yes, and then I forced her to go to St. Patrick's with me."

Giovanni laughed out loud. "You hijack this woman who was mugged? I am kidding. But it sounds a little funny, no? *Comical*, as you say."

"When you put it that way," Frankie said as her eyes went wide. "She must think I'm some kind of religious zealot!" Frankie's expression turned to horror; her eyes widened further.

Giovanni was still chuckling. "Can you imagine if that

woman called the police again?" At that point, his eyes were tearing from laughing so hard.

Frankie lowered her voice to impersonate a male officer, "Not your lucky day, ma'am."

They realized their joviality was spilling over to the rest of the restaurant guests, who were laughing along with them. Giovanni raised his glass. *"Cent'anni!"* Then he motioned for the server to pour the other patrons a drink of their choice.

"You are the best host," Frankie said, and placed her hand on his arm. "So, tell me, when the boyfriends arrive, where are they going to stay?" she said, and raised her eyebrows.

Giovanni grinned and shrugged. "I no ask."

"Okey dokey, then. Let's talk about New Year's Eve. I know we're a little late, but there seems to have been a lot going on with everyone. I'm not sure what will be available, but Matt suggested we make a reservation at Del Frisco's Grille. It will be like a private party but with other people that you don't know."

"Are you not tired of being around Rockefeller Center?" he asked.

"Not this time of year. Besides, I don't think Amy and Peter have seen the tree yet."

"Sounds *perfetto,*" Giovanni replied. "Will everybody be there?"

Frankie began to count. "Amy, Peter, Nina, Richard, Rachael plus someone, you, me, and your mom and Lucia, along with the Parisi brothers, if they want to come."

"Nice. Good. Who is Rachael's plus someone?" he asked.

"That remains to be seen," Frankie said, and chortled.

"As always!" Giovanni said, raising his glass.

When Frankie finished her dinner, she said goodnight to the staff and walked to her apartment. Giovanni would catch up with her after he closed. Frankie got home, changed into her pajamas, washed her face, and made a cup of tea. She padded into the living room, sat cross-legged on the floor with her back resting against the sofa. She clicked on the television and got a glimpse of the local news.

She shot upright when she heard of a second mugging of a Salvation Army collection worker. This time it was in the Bronx. She knew they had to be connected. She felt it in her gut. Two Santa thieves in one day? Was it the same person, or was it a ring of rotten Santas? The news broadcaster did not mention the one earlier. Perhaps they didn't know? The two stories had not been tied together. On the one hand, it made sense. The Manhattan division may not have entered the information into the system by the time the second robbery occurred. Frankie pulled up a map app on her phone and typed in both areas. She couldn't make a connection. Maybe it was simply a coincidence.

She thought maybe her gut was just wrong, until an hour later, when a third story appeared on a later broadcast. By that time, the three incidents were on record. Frankie added the third location to the app. She got up and went to her desk where she'd left the crumpled piece of paper. She drew a triangle connecting the three locations. Then, *bingo*. The address was right in the middle of the triangle. Should she call the police? They'd never follow up unless there was some concrete evidence. They didn't have time for a wild, unruly Santa chase.

She sent Nina a text:

What are you doing tomorrow night?

Nina replied:

No plans. What's up?

Frankie:

I'll give you a buzz in a few.

Nina sent a thumbs-up as a reply.

Frankie filled in Nina about everything that transpired and her plan to check out the clue she found in the glove. It didn't take much convincing for Nina to be on board, and the two agreed that they would meet tomorrow night after Frankie wrapped up work. Just after she ended the call, Frankie realized that she would have to make an excuse as to why she would be out tomorrow night. Not that she owed Giovanni an explanation, nor would he demand one, but she didn't want to give him a reason to worry. She sent another text to Nina:

If anyone asks, we went to listen to a new band downtown. Or a string quartet.

Nina:

Ok. But who?

Frankie:

Make something up. You're the writer.

Nina:

The Vienna String Ensemble at the Morgan Library.

Frankie:

Perfect. I'll find some string ensemble music to listen to. ♥

Francesca didn't want to lie to Giovanni, but she knew he would not stand for her putting herself in a vulnerable situation, even though she had no intention of confronting anyone. It was just a little stakeout. She loved solving mysteries.

Kathryn pulled the rig onto the Pinewood property. Myra and Annie were waiting near the barn.

"Now that looks more normal to me," Annie said, and nodded to the cab of the truck.

Kathryn jumped out. "Good morning, ladies."

"Good morning to you. Such a beautiful, crisp autumn day," Myra said, fiddling with her pearls. Something didn't feel right. "Kathryn, I know you know exactly what you are doing, but I'm getting a little tingly."

Annie grimaced and turned her head toward Myra. "You okay?"

"Fine, but I just worry about my Sisters, I suppose."

"Myra, I've been doing this for years now. Hundreds of thousands of miles have passed beneath my wheels. I've checked over the rig. All is in good working order. Not to worry." Kathryn placed her long, strong arms around Myra's shoulders. "Let's get this baby loaded."

Kathryn gave the rear panel a push, and it rolled upwards. Then she lowered the mechanical lift gate. Annie powered up the forklift and began steering the machine with the big, long, steel metal forks. Myra held her breath.

Ever since the barn renovation, and the restored forklift, Annie had practiced driving and managing the monster truck. *Fast cars and heavy machinery. Go figure for someone who is a countess,* Myra thought to herself and smiled. That was her longest, dearest, and "bestest" friend commandeering the beast.

Annie managed to get the forks under one of the pallets but couldn't coordinate the hydraulic lift well enough.

Kathryn walked over and jerked her thumb. "Off, lady. We don't have all day," she said, grinning.

Within twenty minutes, Kathryn had all the pallets neatly piled and secured. She rolled down the door, pushed the liftgate button, and then jumped off the short ladder. "Ready to roll!"

Myra clapped her hands. "This is exciting. Thanks for doing this, Kathryn."

"Are you kidding? Anything for you guys!" She flung her big arms around the two women.

"Where are you parking your rig?" Annie asked.

"I'll drop the trailer at the distro center, drive the rig to the lot where I reserved a space, and then walk to my buddy's condo. It's a few blocks away. Easy-peasy," Kathryn explained. "I'll give you a holler once I get to Jersey."

"Sounds good! Safe travels!" Myra said, and waved.

Several hours later, Kathryn pulled the big rig into the distribution center, unhitched the trailer, and went into the office to turn in her paperwork.

"Hey, G. How ya doing?"

"Kathryn Lucas. The best-looking truck driver this side of the Mississippi." George extended his callused hand.

"What about the other side of the Mississippi?" Kathryn laughed as she clasped the man's hardened grip.

"Ain't never been," he said, and returned a wide smile exposing several gold teeth.

"Really? I'm surprised," Kathryn said as she filled out the forms.

"Yeah. My wife didn't like me being out on the road for too many days, so I kept my runs to less than two nights," he explained. "Did get to see a lot of the East Coast, and some of the Midwest."

"Too bad you missed the Pacific Northwest. It's spectacular."

"Yeah. I seen videos," George answered. "So, what ya got in there?" he asked, pointing his pen toward the trailer.

"Toys for Tots," Kathryn replied. "It's for a benefit a friend of a friend is putting together. They're bringing in a bunch of kids from local orphanages and throwing them a holiday party."

George leaned past Kathryn to get a better look at the trailer. "That thing filled with toys?"

"Yep! And funny socks," Kathryn said, then signed her name to the forms and handed George the clipboard.

"Now ain't that grand? Who collected all them toys?"

"My friends Myra Rutledge, queen of confectionaries, and Annie De Silva—Countess De Silva, I should say. They hit up everyone they knew at the manufacturing companies, and Mattel was not going to be outdone by Hasbro!" Kathryn hooted. "Those two women are supreme negotiators."

"Maybe we should send them to Washington!" George snickered.

"These women get things done. They could never tolerate politics," Kathryn said, and chuckled.

George nodded. "I hear ya. Well, it was good of them to go on a mission like this."

Kathryn bit the inside of her lip. *If he only knew what kind of missions the Sisters had managed to pull off over the years.*

"They are quite a team," Kathryn said, and changed the subject. "I'll be taking my rig to the lot and leaving it there for two days. I'll be back tomorrow with two other drivers and three box trucks. We've gotta get the toys to the New York Hilton on Sixth Avenue, so box trucks are the only way we can manage."

"Gotcha. What time do you think you'll be here?"

"Is there ever a good time to try to make a delivery in Manhattan? Besides the middle of the night?"

"Not really. So why aren't you doing it in the middle of the night?"

"Unions. They get triple overtime to work the loading dock at the hotel, and the hotel doesn't want to shell out the money, and we don't want to annoy the unions, either. This way it will be like a regular delivery."

"Things are complicated these days," George replied.

"Ain't that the truth. We didn't want to attempt getting a permit to bring the rig into the city, so this was the best option. We'll get here around nine in the morning, after most of the morning rush is over."

"Sounds like you've got it covered. I'll be taking the rest of the week off after my shift today. Need to help the missus with decorating the house. Even with the kids grown and gone, she still wants lights along the roof."

"It's a nice tradition," Kathryn said.

"Tell that to my back," George laughed, and then grunted.

"Here's a tip. Take Aleve or Extra Strength Tylenol before you go to bed. Chances are you'll wake up feeling less like you got hit by a truck."

"Well, we got plenty of them around." George motioned to the lot outside which was filled with trailers. "It's the holidays for sure."

"Indeed. I better get a move on. Have a great holiday if I don't see you."

"You do the same, Kathryn. Nice to see you." George gave her a two-finger salute.

Kathryn started her engine and pulled out of the distribution hub, then made her way toward the lot where she was planning on parking her cab for the next two nights. When she arrived, it was more paperwork and a deposit on the space. "See you in two days," she said to the young man behind the desk.

Kathryn walked the seven blocks to her friend's condominium at Harbor Pointe. She announced herself to the doorman, who handed her an envelope with the keys.

It was a new complex with spacious floor plans, a clubhouse, fitness center, and pool. Her road-traveling pal, Jerry, bought the two-bedroom unit as soon as it opened. A place the same size with the same amenities would easily cost four times as much in Manhattan. Maybe more. He figured he was close enough to the lot where he could park his rig, and close enough to the ferry to get into the city if he wanted to. It was less than an hour ride to Midtown Manhattan. It was convenient and quiet. Everything a weary road warrior would want after a long haul.

Kathryn turned the dead bolt, entered the brightly lit space, and let out a low whistle. "Wow. He wasn't kidding. This place is fantastic!" She walked to the French doors that opened to a small balcony with a courtyard view. "Sure beats sleeping in the cab."

She remembered she had to call Myra and let them know she had arrived. The first thing she asked was "How's my boy?"

She was referring to her pooch, whom she'd left in the capable hands of Myra and Charles. This particular trip would be too much confusion for Murphy. Besides, he appreciated having lots of room to stretch out in front of a fireplace.

Once she was off the phone, she settled in, and with nothing else to do for the rest of the day, she started to once again contemplate her life and lifestyle. She was warming up to the idea of spending more time in the company of people, rather than simply passing them by on the highways. She looked around Jerry's luxurious apartment. She thought she could get used to an upgrade in her life. After Alan died, she sold the house and moved into a small cottage. It had enough room in the back for Murphy to scamper about, and the kid next door took care of the lawn and her mail when she was on the road.

The road. What about the road? She knew she couldn't keep up with it much longer, and perhaps it was time to consider something less taxing on her body, and Murphy's. It hadn't occurred to her how confining it must be for him. Of course he didn't complain. Not that he could, but he never put up a fuss and gladly hopped into the cab. She knew he simply wanted to be with her. Protect her. Keep her company. And the feeling was mutual.

These thoughts were racing through her head when her stomach began to growl. She had skipped lunch, and now it was almost three o'clock. She decided to take a shower and try the Portuguese restaurant Jerry recommended.

Before she left the condo, she phoned the other two drivers to confirm the time and location where they were picking up the box trucks. Satisfied that everything was running according to plan, Kathryn headed out for an early dinner. She was looking forward to some bacalhau à brás, a traditional Portuguese dish made with cod, onion, and thinly sliced potatoes. It was considered Portuguese comfort food, and Kathryn was in the right mood for comfort. She was beginning to feel more comfortable about her future, whatever it might hold.

After her delicious dinner, Kathryn strolled back to the apartment complex. People were milling about, some with glasses of wine, chatting on the patio. They greeted her with a smile and a "good evening." Yep, it was a far cry from a truck stop.

The following morning, she realized there was no food in the house, and she walked a few blocks to a small café. A television was behind the counter with the morning news. She stopped her fork in midair as she listened to the story about Salvation Army people getting mugged by people dressed like Santa. She looked over at the waitress. "That's just not right."

"What has the world come to?" the waitress said, and freshened Kathryn's coffee.

"Do they think it's a ring of rotten Santas?" Kathryn asked before she blew on her hot coffee.

"They didn't say much except it happened fast. No description except a man wearing a red suit, hat, and a mangy beard."

Kathryn finished her breakfast, paid the check, and began the five-block walk to the truck rental offices. Her other two drivers were already there. "Good morning!"

"Morning, Kathryn. You're rather chipper today," one of the men said.

"Yeah, until I heard about the Salvation Army Santa muggings."

"Ain't that a shame?" the other man said. "I don't know how they're gonna catch whoever it is."

"It's like going to Greenwich Village on Halloween. It's hard to tell the normal people from the freaks," the first man said.

"I think anyone who would want to cramp themselves into a crowd of a million people dressed in costume is *not* normal," Kathryn replied.

Both men snickered and agreed. Kathryn filled out more paperwork, produced the credit card, licenses, and insurance information. Everyone was handed a set of keys, and they drove to the lot where the trailer was parked.

As the small caravan approached the chain-link gate, Kathryn spoke into the squawk-box. "Kathryn Lucas. Picking up trailer in slot four-two-nine."

After a short pause, the disembodied voice asked, "Are you sure it's four-two-nine?"

Kathryn checked her paperwork. "Yep. That's me."

"Huh. . . ." the voice responded.

"Is there a problem?" she asked.

"Four-two-nine was picked up this morning at two a.m."

"That can't be right." Kathryn was confused. "Can you buzz me in please?"

"Sure." The buzzer sounded, and the gates opened.

Kathryn pulled her truck in front of the office and looked toward the space where she'd left the trailer the day before. It was empty. *What in the . . . ?* She stomped into the office.

"Where's my trailer?"

"I don't know, but it was signed out, like I said."

"By whom?" she demanded.

George's substitute checked the computer. "Says here, Patrick Falcone."

"Who?" Kathryn's voice was several decibels louder.

The kid shrugged. "Here. Look for yourself."

Kathryn's mouth fell open. "Who in the heck is Patrick Falcone?"

"The guy who signed it out." The kid had no other explanation.

"Do you have a copy of his ID? Phone number? He obviously picked up the wrong load."

"I guess." The kid was not going out of his way to be helpful, which was making Kathryn steam.

"Look, someone pulled the wrong trailer out of this lot; someone has to be responsible for this," Kathryn said as calmly as she could.

"My boss is on vacation this week."

"And? Isn't there someone who might be a little more accommodating?" Kathryn said, as she counted to ten in her head. Speaking of heads, someone's head was going to roll if she didn't get an answer ASAP. She stared him down until he feebly picked up the phone.

"Hello? Hi, this is Raymond at the lot. Someone picked up the wrong trailer, and I don't have any info." The kid continued to reply with innocuous answers. "Uh-huh. Yeah. I guess."

Kathryn was drumming her fingers on the counter. Her patience had worn thin. "Give me the phone. Please." She practically wrenched it from his hand.

"Hello. This is Kathryn Lucas. I dropped a trailer here yesterday afternoon. Yes, George was here. Yes, I know he's on vacation. But none of that is helping me find my load." She handed the phone back to the kid.

He kept nodding his head, as if the person on the other end could see his reaction. "Okay. Thanks." He checked the computer again. "There's no contact number here."

"Isn't that just swell."

"When they find out they have the wrong shipment, they'll bring it back." The kid was trying to be reassuring. "You can wait here if you want."

Kathryn knew she had to call Myra and Annie immediately. Maybe Charles and Fergus could get some traffic-cam footage to follow the route of the truck. It was a long shot, but Charles and Fergus had pulled off even longer shots in the past. Kathryn huffed her way outside, where she could have a private conversation out of earshot from the other two drivers.

Myra picked up the phone in her lyrical tone. "Hello, Kathryn. How are you today?"

Kathryn took in a deep breath. "I wish I could say I'm fine, but I am not."

"What seems to be the problem?" Myra asked with concern.

"Someone picked up my load by mistake," she said, and took another breath. "And they don't have a phone number to track the driver down."

"Surely they'll realize they have the wrong one, no?"

"Not until they get to their destination and open the trailer. It could be days," Kathryn said with much frustration. "But I have an idea."

Myra was all ears. "Shoot!"

"See if Fergus and Charles can get some of the traffic-cam footage between here and the turnpike. I can give them the plate numbers, and maybe we can figure out where that truck is headed."

"Good thinking," Myra said with a tinge of relief. "I'll get on it right away. Charles is outside chatting with Fergus. I'll grab them and call you right back."

"Okay. Good." Kathryn ended the call and went back inside to speak to the clerk.

Myra dashed out the kitchen door and began waving and yelling to the two men. "Charles! Fergus! I need your help!"

The two men ran toward her. "What is it?" Charles asked with a heavy breath.

"What's wrong?" Fergus added.

"Kathryn's trailer was loaded to someone else's rig by mistake. The guy at the distro center told Kathryn they didn't have a phone number, which I think is very odd. But that's moot."

"Is Kathryn alright?" Charles asked.

"Yes, but she is fuming," Myra said. "She asked if the two of you could get some traffic-cam footage to see if you can try to track it down. She said to check from the distro center to the turnpike entrance."

"Right-o," Charles replied.

"Roger that," Fergus added.

"Let me get her back on the phone." Myra hit the speed dial number for Kathryn and put the call on speakerphone.

"Hey," Kathryn answered, and walked back outside with

her phone. "I convinced the kid to let me see some of the security footage from last night. He wasn't very accommodating until I slid a hundred-dollar bill across the counter."

"Were you able to see anything?" Charles asked.

"Two men dressed in jeans and leather jackets. Not exactly truck-driver attire, but anything goes these days. One stood facing away from the camera, the other kept his head down."

"As if they were avoiding being recorded," Fergus surmised.

"Seemed that way, but I am so fired up right now, I'm not thinking straight," Kathryn replied.

"Kathryn, you are thinking just fine," Charles said in a calm voice. "Were you able to see a signature?"

"Nope."

"Did the drivers show ID?" Fergus asked.

"They showed something. Looked like a license."

Fergus turned toward Charles. "Those are easy to fake."

Charles continued, "Fergus and I will get right on this. You sit tight. Get some lunch. We'll get back to you ASAP."

An hour later, a tractor-trailer pulled into the empty lot of a partially abandoned warehouse in Brooklyn. Two offices in the rear were connected to a generator that provided electricity for the illicit business dealings of Bucky Barflow. That's where he would meet his "laundry clientele" and exchange dirty money for freshly cleaned, with no residue of drugs or fingerprints.

Vinny and Jimmy were standing outside, waiting to reveal the merchandise. Bucky sauntered out of the building like the thug that he was. There were no pleasantries. "Whaddya got?"

Vinny hopped on the ladder, gripped the latch, and gave the rolling door a yank. The expression on Bucky's face went from dubious to wrath when he saw a pallet containing dozens of Lego games. Next to it were boxes of socks with funny faces. "What is this?" he growled. Spit was spewing from his mouth.

Vinny looked at Jimmy, and then again at Bucky. He could barely get the words out. "I . . . I . . . I don't know what happened." He turned to Jimmy. "You've got some explaining to do."

Bucky grabbed both of them by the collar and dragged them inside the building. He shoved them into two metal folding chairs. "This is your idea of a big haul? Toys? Socks? You must think I'm some kind of an idiot." Vinny could swear steam was coming out of Bucky's pierced nose.

"No! No!" Vinny held up his hands, as if he were expecting to get smashed in the face. Again, he turned to Jimmy. "You better have a good explanation, buster."

Jimmy's hands were shaking. "Patsy Fazola and I went to the distribution center just like you said. He used his fake license to sign out the trailer. We hooked it up to the cab and drove off."

"Which trailer?"

"The one in four-two-nine," Jimmy said with a cracked voice.

"You dummy. It was space four-nine-two." Vinny lowered his head. He knew he was a dead man now.

Bucky burst out laughing, a huge departure from his normal reactions. "I would say you were messing with me, but this is even dumber than either of you could do on your own. Now bring back the kiddie toys and bring me the electronics. That's what you promised, right?" He gave Vinny a tap on his shoe.

"Yes. Okay. Okay."

"You've got two days," Bucky replied in an eerily calm voice. Vinny did not like the sound of it. "And if it doesn't happen, add an extra ten K to your tab."

The two men scrambled from the chair before Bucky had a chance to knock it out from under them, and they scooted out the door.

Vinny was beside himself with emotion. "How did this happen?"

"Patsy and I went to the yard. Patsy gave the guy his fake license, the guy pointed to the spot. We hooked up the trailer and drove out."

"But you got the wrong trailer. W-R-O-N-G." Vinny spelled it out, just in case Jimmy hadn't yet absorbed how bad the situation was.

"I know. I know. I know. So, let's bring this one back and get the right one."

"Let's hope it's still in the lot." Vinny hopped into the passenger side, and Jimmy got behind the wheel. "Do you still have the paperwork?"

Jimmy pointed to the visor above Vinny's head. "It's up there."

Vinny pulled the visor down and looked through the paperwork. "It says right here, four-nine-two."

"Well, this is the trailer the kid pointed to," Jimmy said, trying to defend himself.

"And you didn't bother to check?"

"It was dark."

Vinny shook his head. He took his cell phone from his pocket and dialed the number on the paperwork. A young voice answered.

"Hey, I got a trailer with the wrong goods. We need to bring it back and get the right one."

"Oh, yeah. A lady was here about an hour ago. I think you got her stuff by mistake."

Vinny rolled his eyes. "Yes, Einstein. We're bringing it back. We gotta get the one in four-nine-two."

"Okay." The kid hesitated. "But the trailer in four-nine-two was picked up a few minutes after the lady left."

"Say that again." Vinny was breaking out in a sweat.

"Yeah. The other trailer was picked up."

Vinny turned to Jimmy. "Stop the truck."

"How come?" Jimmy pumped the brakes just as he was turning the rig around.

"Because the trailer you were supposed to pick up actually got picked up." Vinny paused, then shouted, "By someone else!" Vinny looked down at the paperwork again. "Get out! We need to check this load again."

"Why? It's toys."

"Yeah, you knucklehead. It's Toys for Tots! Geez, we stole toys from kids." Vinny leaned his head against the back of the seat.

"Okay. Okay. Okay. Listen, I got a little stash. Maybe you can put it on the ponies?"

"You got a stash?" Vinny stared at him suspiciously.

Jimmy looked sheepish, then answered, "Yeah, I been doin' a little hustle on the side." He reached behind the seat, pulled out a duffel bag, and placed it on Vinny's lap.

"What's this?" Vinny asked.

"My stash. Look inside. A few hundred bucks."

"And where did you get this stash?" Vinny had had his fill of bad news, and the day wasn't quite over yet. He dug farther into the bag and pulled out a Santa cap. "What's this?"

"Part of my disguise."

"Your disguise for what?"

"My side hustle."

"Which is what? You working at Macy's or something?"

"Nah. Too many screaming kids and annoying parents. I knocked over a few Salvation Army kettles."

"You did *what*?" Vinny was stupefied. "You stole money from the Salvation Army?"

"Well, kinda."

"Kinda?" Vinny yelled, his voice bouncing inside the cab. "How could you do such a thing?"

"I dunno. Seemed like easy pickings."

Vinny was incredulous. "But the Salvation Army? What is wrong with you?"

"I'm sorry, boss. I figured you could use the money. Just in case."

"I can, but not like this. This is beyond criminal." Vinny was at a total loss. There they were, two grown men with a trailer of stolen toys and stolen money. "God is going to get us for this." He shook his head in shame.

"Yeah. So is Bucky." Jimmy sniffled.

Charles and Fergus were busy in the War Room in Pinewood when they hit pay dirt. The truck was caught on camera leaving the lot; then it got picked up again as it crossed the Bayonne Bridge. From there, it took Interstate 287 and reappeared crossing the Verrazzano.

"Looks like it's headed to Brooklyn," Fergus said as he looked up at the six-feet-wide monitor mounted on the wall.

Charles called Kathryn and asked, "Does the trailer have a GPS?"

"Yes, but only if it's engaged."

"Does it activate automatically when the wheels are in motion?"

"Again, only if it's engaged, but they are most of the time."

"Right. We'll keep checking camera footage." Charles and Fergus were quite handy at hacking even the most complex and secure servers. All they needed was the longitude and latitude, and they were in. They got a blip on the big screen. The truck moved for a minute, then stopped again, but now they had a confirmed location. Technology was a great tool.

They quickly informed Myra and Annie. Annie called Kathryn and said, "I'm sending Maggie later today."

"Is she alright? I caught the tail end of some news clip about SantaCon across the nation. A camera caught Maggie getting plowed over by some drunk St. Nick in D.C.," Kathryn said.

"This SantaCon thing is the equivalent of St. Patrick's Day," Annie remarked.

"A license to get rowdy," Kathryn said with a chuckle.

Annie continued. "She'll be taking the Gulfstream, so she should be arriving around two o'clock. Pick her up at Teterboro. Charles will send you the current location, and the two of you can scope it out. Just make sure that truck doesn't leave your sight."

"Got it." Kathryn was not sure what the overall plan was, but as long as Myra and Annie were at the helm, it was going to be a good one.

Chapter 13

Manhattan was buzzing with excitement. The decorations, the visitors, and the traffic added to the welcomed chaos of the holidays. The thirty-feet-high snowflake—with 16,000 crystal prisms—that hung at the intersection of Fifth Avenue and 57th Street was visible for several blocks.

Giovanni left the restaurant and drove to his brother's house to greet his mother and aunt while Frankie cleared off her desk at work. Her last task was to finish the memory book, but that would have to wait until Giovanni returned with the extra items.

In the meantime, she checked in with her gal pals to confirm New Year's Eve dinner. Amy and Peter were going to stay with her father and Marilyn in New Jersey, then take a car service to meet up with the rest of the gang for dinner. Nina and Richard were committed to the evening. They agreed to share a car service with Amy and Peter, since where they were staying was only a few miles away from one another. Rachael still had an unnamed plus-one. She'd had one date with Richard's brother Robert, and it seemed to go well. Both said they would like to do it again next time he was in town. When that would happen was still in question, and Rachael, following Frankie's advice, didn't want to be too forward. Then there was another possibility with Nicholas, the young nurse practitioner she'd had coffee with. That, too, went well, but Rachael was treading lightly. She also had to consider her current paramour, Salvatore, who was trying to appease Rachael's annoyance with his holiday plans. But he was not going to be available for the turn of the calendar. *Too many men, too little time.* She hadn't juggled this many men—all of whom were suitable relationship material—in a long time. Rachael was all atwitter at the attention she was getting, and Frankie had to gently remind her to "Think, girl, think! Big picture here. Be mindful, not reactionary."

In her heart, Rachael knew Frankie was right. Every sticky situation Rachael had gotten herself into was from jumping the gun. Immediate gratification was her modus operandi, but she began to realize that wasn't necessarily the best course of action. She was looking forward to a New Year with a new attitude, but for now, she could use Frankie's reminders.

In the end, Frankie and Giovanni decided to make plans with the three other couples, including whomever Rachael showed up with, and send Rosevita, Lucia, and their beaus to Atlantic City for a New Year's extravaganza. Frankie had worried that dinner at a restaurant wasn't special enough for their special guests, and it was Rosevita who mentioned it might be nice to go to a casino while she was visiting. Frankie made dinner reservations at Del Frisco's for her group and began the arrangements for Giovanni's mother, aunt, and the two Parisi brothers, starting with a car service to the Ocean Resort and Casino, where they would have ocean view rooms. Dinner reservations for Latin cuisine and music at Amada were also included. Fireworks on the boardwalk, barring any inclement weather, would wrap up the evening for them. The package was pricey, but Nina, Rachael, and Amy agreed to chip in to pay for the treat. It was the least they could do as a token of appreciation for rescuing them from the police station the year before.

Frankie was also able to procure tickets for Andrea Bocelli in concert between Christmas and New Year's. She wanted to give them a wonderful, exciting holiday experience. She checked off her list: Radio City, Bocelli, New Year's Eve. She provided the entertainment; the enjoyment part was up to them.

Frankie looked out her office window. It was already dark, but the lights from the giant Christmas tree lit up the promenade. She checked in with Nina, who was going to pick her up at the apartment around eight o'clock so they would begin their sleuthing. Frankie had plenty of work to keep her busy before she headed home, but her mind was on the adventure that was about to unfold.

Kathryn hadn't anticipated staying on in the metro area, so she had to rent a car. Her rig wasn't quite right for local traffic. Plus, it would be much easier to spot. After she picked up the innocuous mid-sized car, she drove to Teterboro Airport to pick up Maggie.

As far as Charles and Fergus could surmise, the trailer was still in the same place it had been in earlier that day, which became Maggie and Kathryn's target address.

Given the options of having the tar beaten out of him or taking Jimmy up on his offer, Vinny succumbed to the latter. As much as he hated the idea of using money that had been donated, he had to take a chance on a big win at the track. Obviously, they couldn't take the truck through the streets of Brooklyn without being conspicuous and subject to police intervention. That was the last thing they needed. Instead,

Vinny called Patsy and insisted he pick them up and bring them to an off-track betting facility. It was the least Patsy could do, since he was part of the major mix-up. Vinny vowed to himself, and to anyone on high who would still listen, that he would return the money to the Salvation Army—of course, after he paid off Bucky Barflow.

Patsy arrived forty minutes later and was grumbling about missing one of his "programs" on TV.

"Yeah, well, I'm gonna be missing a limb if I don't fix this mess," Vinny responded.

When they arrived at the betting window, Vinny made the sign of the cross three times and prayed to Saint Cajetan, the patron saint of gamblers and the unemployed. At that moment, Vinny was both. He placed his first bet of one hundred dollars on a long shot with twenty-to-one odds, running at a track in California. Vinny's forehead was damp with sweat as he watched the horses cross the finish line from 3,000 miles away. His hands were shaking. His legs were shaking. And when he realized he had won 2,000 dollars, he almost dropped to his knees. Jimmy was elated and started slapping Vinny on the back.

"Easy. Easy. We only got another forty-eight thousand to go. And that ain't gonna be easy."

Patsy finally had something positive to say: "Maybe if you give Bucky some of the money, he'll give you another extension."

"From your lips to God's ears," Vinny said.

Patsy looked around. "Between you and me, I don't think he's listening to either of us."

"Shut your piehole!" Vinny snapped.

Jimmy started to snicker.

"That's goes for you, too!" Vinny yapped at him.

Vinny kept his winnings in one pocket and placed another one-hundred-dollar bet on the next race. This time he gained an additional five hundred dollars. He did the same thing with his winnings and placed a third bet on the following race. Another long shot, and Vinny was another 3,000 ahead.

"Okay. That's it for tonight."

"But you're on a streak!" Jimmy protested.

"Exactly. I don't wanna jinx it. Let's go back to the warehouse, and I'll give Bucky the five grand. That should buy us another day or two to figure out this fine mess."

The three men climbed back into Patsy's Cadillac and headed back to the warehouse where Bucky spent his nights "entertaining." Vinny did not want to know what that entailed, because Bucky didn't appear to be a fun kind of guy.

Nina pulled up to Frankie's building and double-parked. She pinged Frankie to let her know she was outside. Frankie exited her apartment wearing black leggings, a black long-sleeve shirt, black vest, black gloves, and black boots. Her long black hair was stuffed into a black knitted cap.

When she opened the passenger door, Nina let out a hoot. "You look like a ninja!"

"And you look like Nina Hunter," Frankie said, and grinned. "I wanted to look the part."

"*I'm* the one who's supposed to dress the part," Nina joked.

Frankie eyed her up and down. "Dark denim is fine."

"You said we were going to surveil the situation, not get all James Bond-like," Nina said, rolling her eyes.

"Don't be a party pooper. We are simply doing some reconnaissance work. If we discover anything, we turn it over to the police."

"Right, because there is no way we are going to try a citizen's arrest."

Frankie blinked several times. "I may be kooky, but I'm not crazy."

"Good. Glad we got that clarified." Nina checked the street before she pulled away from the cars parked along the curb.

"Do you think we should put the address in the GPS?" Frankie asked.

"I'm going to want to say *no*. I don't want any evidence on record should something go awry."

"Fine. I'll use the GPS on my phone."

"Good—this way, you'll be under surveillance when the authorities realize we are interfering with police business," Nina said.

"Ah, I see your creativity is at its peak tonight."

"I can't help myself," Nina said, and grinned as they turned east to cross the Williamsburg Bridge.

On the other side of town, Kathryn and Maggie entered the Holland Tunnel and proceeded down the West Side Highway, around the Battery to the FDR Drive. They drove north and then drove east via the Brooklyn Bridge. Maggie kept an eye on the GPS on her phone and called out directions to Kathryn. As they continued, they drove past several dilapidated buildings and found themselves in an area filled with warehouses, most of which appeared to be abandoned.

Kathryn turned off the headlights and moved the car slowly down a pothole-infested road, rusty chain-link fences lining the street.

"This is kinda creepy," Maggie said as her eyes darted in all directions. Then she tapped Kathryn's arm. "Look." About a hundred yards away, a glow emitted from the lower level of one of the decrepit buildings.

Kathryn gasped. "There it is," she choked out, and pointed to the trailer.

"Are you sure that's the one?"

"Yep. See? It has a Mario Brothers sticker on the side."

"Well, that can't be a coincidence, now, can it?" Maggie said, as she plunged her hand into a bag of Cheetos.

"How can you eat that stuff?" Kathryn said, and made a sour face.

Maggie licked each of her fingers. "Yum. Want some?" she asked, jiggling the bag in front of Kathryn's nose.

"No, thank you." Kathryn suddenly noticed something and cocked her head. "Check out that car." She motioned to a vehicle parked on the same side of the street but another hundred yards from the building.

Maggie wiped the remaining orange dust from her fingers and pulled out her binoculars. "They're facing toward us, but I don't think they can see us past that telephone pole. Here, you take a look."

"Two women. One in a cap, another one with curly hair." She handed the glasses back to Maggie. "See if you can get in closer." Kathryn pushed her seat as far back as she could so Maggie could climb over her and switch places.

Maggie adjusted the settings on the binoculars. "Huh."

"What?" Kathryn asked.

"You remember that show *Family Blessings*?"

"Yeah. Used to watch it whenever I was home. Why?"

"Because the person behind the wheel looks like Nina Hunter."

"The star of the show?" Kathryn said with surprise.

"Yep." Maggie kept squinting into the lenses. "Here, take another look." The two women crawled over each other again.

Kathryn lifted the binoculars again. "Wow. She *is* the spitting image of her. How crazy is that? And what would she be doing here? And at this time of night?"

"We don't know if it's really her, but she could win a look-alike contest for sure." Maggie pulled out her phone and sent a text to Charles:

Check NJ plates PND-P23

Seconds later, Charles responded:

Car registered to Nina Hunter, Ridgewood, NJ

"Holy cow!" Maggie said in a loud whisper. "That car is registered to Nina Hunter!"

"You can't be serious!" Kathryn squinted. Just as she was

adjusting the lenses, the two women in the car in front of them ducked down behind the dashboard. "They spotted *us* spotting *them*!"

A few hundred yards away, Nina and Frankie ducked their heads. "They're on to us!" Nina hissed.

"But who are they?" Frankie asked rhetorically.

Nina climbed into the back seat. "Hand those over." She motioned for Frankie to give her the small opera glasses they had been using. "You could have bought a real pair if you were going to play Nancy Drew," Nina said and clicked her tongue. "Wait a minute. One of them looks like that reporter that got knocked over during the SantaCon in D.C."

"What is with all these bad Santas?" Frankie asked another rhetorical question.

"Yeah. It was on the news last night, but she got up and finished her story. I recognize her hair." Nina fidgeted with her curly locks. "Just like mine, but hers is ginger red."

"What do you suppose they're doing here?" Frankie asked again.

"Covering another story? Maybe they're on a stakeout?" Nina was as baffled as Frankie.

A Cadillac pulled onto the street. Both women in both cars ducked down. The Caddy stopped at the chain-link gate; then the driver pressed a button on a box, and the gate opened. Three men got out of the car while the women surreptitiously watched.

"Frankie, I don't like this. It's getting way too weird," Nina said in a hushed tone.

"You're right, but let's wait a minute before we pull away. We don't want to bring any attention to ourselves."

"You mean any more attention," Nina said, and let out a huge whoosh of air.

"Look! Look!" Frankie said in a loud whisper. "That guy is wearing a Santa cap."

" 'Tis the season," Nina quipped.

"This is too much of a coincidence."

Vinny gave Jimmy a slight slap on the back of his head. "Will you take that thing off? You look like an idiot."

"Well, my Santa stash got you some winnings. It's good luck."

"Only if Bucky doesn't break my legs."

The three men disappeared into the warehouse.

Maggie sent another text to Charles informing him that three men arrived at the warehouse. She and Kathryn were going to wait to see what their next move would be. They still didn't know what Nina Hunter and her friend were doing in a desolate warehouse area, but for now they had to keep their eyes on the trailer.

Kathryn had thought about stealing the truck back, but then again, they still didn't know if someone had made an honest mistake in hitching the wrong trailer.

Nina and Frankie were still ducking down in their car when the three men walked out of the warehouse. Two got in the cab of the truck, and the Caddy driver returned to his vehicle.

Jimmy started the engine of the big rig. "See? Bucky didn't kick your hiney. This cap is good luck."

"Shut up and drive. I still have to come up with the rest of the cash in another two days. Plus, another ten thousand. That's sixty thousand bucks!"

"Maybe more good fortune at the ponies?" Jimmy said with a wide grin.

"I am not pressing my luck. Again," Vinny said thoughtfully, which is exactly what he was doing: thinking. He snapped his fingers.

"What?" Jimmy asked.

"I have an idea."

"Yeah? What?" Jimmy asked with enthusiasm.

"Never you mind. This is something I have to take care of on my own."

"If you say so, boss, but I'm telling ya, this baby is a lucky charm," he said, as he tapped the fuzzy ball at the end of his cap.

As soon as the big rig maneuvered from the lot and was several yards down the street, Kathryn started her engine and made a K-turn with her headlights off. Thirty seconds later, Nina started her vehicle and began to crawl, keeping a distance of a few yards behind Kathryn and Maggie.

Kathryn spotted them in the rearview mirror. "Nina and her pal are following us, following the Caddy, which is following the truck. What do you suppose is going on?"

"Beats me, but we gotta keep an eye on those goods. If Nina wants to play reconnaissance, that's up to her. I don't think they're any sort of a threat to us."

Kathryn shook her head. "I don't get it."

The bizarre caravan proceeded toward the roads that allowed tractor trailers. Once they were over the Bayonne Bridge, back on the New Jersey side, Kathryn suspected they were heading toward the distro center. "Looks like they're backtracking."

"Do you think this could have been a big mistake?" Maggie asked.

"Messing with us is always a mistake," Kathryn said, while she carefully followed the car and the rig.

"So how does Nina and her friend fit in?" Maggie said curiously.

"That, I cannot figure out, either. But they are the least of our problems now," Kathryn said, as she followed the truck heading toward the exit ramp. "Until we know where these guys are going, we can't waste our time thinking about them."

"Even if they're following *us*?" Maggie asked innocently.

Kathryn glanced into her rearview mirror. "Even if."

The parade of vehicles slowed as they approached the distribution center where this whole mess began.

The rig pulled over. Two men jumped out and disconnected the cab from the trailer.

Kathryn wrenched her head to get a better view from a block away. "What are they doing?" she said with exasperation. That's when the cab juggled a U-turn and began to leave the area without the trailer. The Caddy followed.

Kathryn and Maggie watched in surprise.

"They're leaving it there? In the middle of the street?" Maggie said with disbelief.

"Looks that way," Kathryn said, trying to figure out what the plan could possibly be. Theirs and hers.

"But why?" Maggie asked.

"Who knows?" Kathryn said. "But at least we know where our toys are."

"So, what do we do now?" Maggie asked. "We can't leave the trailer unattended, and we can't let those guys get away."

"Why not? They returned it."

"Yeah, but my nose for news is tingling. Those guys were up to something."

"Okay, Lois Lane, what do you propose we do?"

"I'll stay here while you follow them."

"Follow them where?" Kathryn asked with a bit of a snip in her tone.

"Just do it. I'll ring Annie and Myra and get some advice from them, but I think we need to split up."

"Are you going to be alright?" Kathryn said as she looked around for some type of shelter. She spotted a small bus-stop shed. "There. Go huddle in that. I'll keep you posted."

Maggie held up her hand for a high five. "Whatever it

takes!" she shouted the Sisterhood motto and hopped out of the car. She noticed the other vehicle a half block away. She decided to find out exactly what Nina Hunter and her friend were doing and began to approach the car.

Nina and Frankie made a futile attempt to slide down in their seats. Maggie tapped on the window.

Nina sheepishly rolled it down. "Hey. Aren't you the reporter who got shoved by a bad Santa?"

"Hey. Aren't you Nina Hunter, star of *Family Blessings?*"

"Uh, yes. And this is my friend, Frankie Cappella."

"Nice to meet you, but before we get into the why you are following me, I mean us, I need you to drive Frankie to meet up with Kathryn. She'll ride with Kathryn, and you'll come back and sit here with me until we can suss out the rest of this caper."

Frankie jumped in, "I think the guy with the Santa cap is the one who's been mugging the Salvation Army people."

"And you tracked him down?" Maggie asked with a dubious tone.

"Yes. But that doesn't matter now. It looks like they're getting away," Frankie replied.

"Hang on," Maggie said, then pulled out her phone and called Kathryn. "Where do you think you're heading?"

"Looks like we're approaching a yard. A big rig and a few other trucks of different size."

"How far are you?" Maggie asked.

"Not far. Maybe less than two miles."

"Give me a crosswalk and Nina Hunter will hotfoot it over to you."

"Huh? To do what?" Kathryn asked curiously.

"We gotta join forces. We're the good guys," Maggie said.

"If you say so." Kathryn gave Maggie a street name and a landmark. "Tell her to get cracking."

"What's your number?" Maggie asked Nina. "I'll text you the info."

The exchange took a few seconds.

"Wish me luck!" Nina said as she put the pedal to the metal. She drove as fast as she could without breaking too many traffic safety laws. Less than five minutes later, Nina spotted Kathryn's vehicle idling along the curb, half a block away from the lot. Frankie dashed out of Nina's car, scurried to where Kathryn was waiting, and jumped in.

"Hi. I'm Frankie." She held out her hand.

Kathryn wasn't sure if she should shake it or not, but she decided to trust this smooth-moving female.

"Kathryn." She grasped Frankie's hand. Before she let go, she looked her straight in the eye. "What in the Sam Hill are you doing? Besides following us?"

Frankie's eyes widened. "We weren't following you. We were trying to track down the people who've been hitting the Salvation Army kettles."

"Wait. What?" Kathryn was perplexed. "I haven't heard of any of this."

"It was on local news the night before. I work at Rock Center and helped one of the victims—Carol. The police took a report, but there wasn't much they could do. There was a mob of people, all of them dressed like Santa. One of them knocked her over and stole the money out of the kettle."

Kathryn gripped the wheel. "I heard about this, but *you* guys are looking for *them*? *Here*?"

"Later that evening, I heard of another incident in one of the other boroughs," Frankie went on. "Then the third. I pulled out a map and did a triangulation."

"Are you an engineer?" Kathryn asked.

"Cookbook editor."

"And you do triangulations as a what? Hobby?" Kathryn asked with a tad of skepticism.

"I'm a mystery junkie. And after helping Carol, it became personal to me. That woman has been doing this for eighteen years."

Kathryn snickered. "You got a little vigilante in you, eh?"

"Huh. I hadn't looked at it that way, but I suppose under these circumstances, you may be correct. Although I had no intention of apprehending them. I simply wanted to gather information and turn it over to the police."

Kathryn snickered again. "I doubt they will do anything. They have millions of people to cover with not the biggest staff."

"I know, and I really didn't expect them to send a SWAT team, but at least I tried."

Kathryn smiled and patted Frankie's throbbing hand. "You've come to the right place. Or, I should probably say 'the right people.'"

Frankie furrowed her brow. "I don't understand."

"You will. Eventually," Kathryn replied. "If you are certain one of those guys was the culprit, we'll manage it."

"We?" Frankie looked behind her to see if there was anyone else in the car.

"Hang tight, super sleuth. It might be a long night."

Frankie's phone vibrated in her pocket. She had completely lost track of the time. It was Giovanni checking in.

Giovanni:

Cara, you okay?

Frankie:

Yes, sorry. Concert ran late and we went out to grab a nightcap.

Giovanni:

Ok. See you soon.

Frankie explained to Kathryn that it was her boyfriend, and he'd just arrived at her apartment. Frankie didn't think Kathryn was up for small talk, so she left it at that. She surmised Kathryn was the type of person who would not hesitate to ask if she wanted more details.

Kathryn and Frankie kept their eyes on their targets and saw the two men get out and hop into the Cadillac. Kathryn pressed the speed dial to Maggie. "We're on the move. They dropped the cab at a lot."

"Nina and I are getting acquainted. Did you know she is working on a project developing a series for television?"

Kathryn rolled her eyes, knowing Maggie couldn't see them, although Maggie could probably guess what she was doing. "Interesting. Sit tight. I'll phone you back and let you know where we are."

"Roger that," Maggie said, and turned to Nina. "You wouldn't have any snacks on you, would you?"

"There are some granola bars in there," Nina said, nodding to the glove compartment.

"Fannn—*tastic!*" Maggie whooped. "You gals are okay with me."

"They were Frankie's idea. She was much better prepared for a stakeout than I was."

"Well, I've been on way too many, and I can tell ya, snacks saved me." Maggie unwrapped the chocolate-almond bar.

Nina brought up the incident on the news.

"Wasn't the first time I got shoved around," Maggie said, licking the chocolate off her fingers.

"There should be napkins in there, too." Nina pointed to the glove box again.

"Thanks. Normally I come prepared, but this was a last-minute thing, and I hardly had time to grab my go-bag."

"Okay. Now it's your turn." Nina settled into the back cushion of the seat. "What are you guys doing chasing a tractor trailer?"

"It's loaded with toys. Toys for Tots. Annie, my boss, is going to a gala at the Hilton in a few days. It's for a friend who is being honored for her charity work. . . . Anyway, Annie and her friend Myra got a bunch of toy companies to donate a thousand toys."

"Wow. That's impressive," Nina said with admiration.

"Oh, and socks. They're bringing kids from orphanages to

the event to meet Santa, have some holiday cheer, and get some toys."

"Let's hope it's not a bad Santa!" Nina said, half-jokingly.

"I can tell you this much, if anyone misbehaves, Annie and Myra will give them what-for." Maggie decided to leave it at that. No need to get into their side hustle of judicial enforcement, although that may become necessary if the goofy guy in the Santa cap was culpable.

Maggie's phone rang several minutes later. It was Kathryn.

"Looks like they're heading back to the warehouse."

Frankie was getting anxious. She had to figure out how to get back to her apartment before Giovanni began to worry. She turned to Kathryn and said, "I hate to cause you any trouble, but I have to get back to my apartment. My boyfriend will start freaking out. It's almost one in the morning. I can get out and call an Uber or Lyft."

"Not in this neighborhood. Call him and tell him you're still running a little late. You ran into some friends you and Nina hadn't seen in years, and you're going to spend a little time with them."

"Wow. You really think on your feet, don't you?"

"Occupational hazard."

"Speaking of which, what do you normally do when you're not tracking a tractor trailer?" Frankie asked.

"Driving one," Kathryn said with a snicker.

"For real?" Frankie said with surprise. "I mean, well, I, I don't think I ever met a female truck driver."

"Less than six percent of truck drivers are women."

"How did you get into that business?" Frankie asked innocently.

"My late husband. He enjoyed traveling but then got multiple sclerosis and Parkinson's disease. I learned how to drive so we could continue together. I kept it up after he passed."

"Oh, I am so sorry. That is incredibly sad."

"Yes, it was, but I have a great network of friends, and I

think I've finally come to the last stage of grief: acceptance. It has taken me a long time. A really long time. In fact, I think I'm just pulling myself out of it now." Kathryn was surprised at how much she divulged about her emotions. But it felt good. She could share without the sadness. She smiled at Frankie, remembering what it was like to have someone who cared. "Now call your guy and let him know you'll be home within the hour. I am going to drive you back to Maggie and Nina."

"What about those guys in the truck?"

"As long as I get the trailer back, I can't worry about them right now. We'll catch up with them eventually. We know at least one of the places they frequent."

Several minutes later, Kathryn got a ping on her phone. It was from Charles. He and Fergus were able to find out who the property owner was. According to what they discovered, the warehouse was in the name of an LLC that also owned a pizzeria in Brooklyn. "Looks like we got another location."

Frankie was about to ask, but decided the less she knew, the better, and she got the impression that Kathryn wasn't going to be forthcoming with additional information.

"Now call your dude," Kathryn said with a smile, then sent a text to Maggie telling her they were on their way back.

Frankie hit Giovanni's speed dial number, explained the make-believe situation, and assured him she would be home soon.

Twenty minutes later, Kathryn arrived at the terminal, where the trailer still sat in front of the gate.

"What happened?" Maggie asked.

"Nothing. Well, not exactly nothing. Charles got the name of the property owner and a second location."

"You're right. That's not nothing. Do you think the trailer thing was a mistake?" Maggie asked.

"It was a mistake, alright, but I think they thought they

were hijacking something they could fence and not dozens of Legos, socks, stuffed animals, and dolls."

"That warehouse looked a bit shady," Frankie added.

"Yes, and it's a good thing you didn't get caught spying on them!" Maggie admonished the two other women.

"Well, I was able to get a photo of the guy with the cap." Frankie opened the camera app on her phone. "So at least I can give the police something to go on."

Kathryn and Maggie began to laugh. "As if."

Frankie looked downtrodden. "I suppose you're right. They don't have time for this sort of thing."

Kathryn and Maggie looked over at each other. "No, but we do!" Kathryn hooted. They gave each other a high five. "Text me the photo," Kathryn directed to Frankie and gave her the number.

Nina and Frankie weren't quite sure what to make of their new friends, but they somehow trusted that they would indeed take care of everything. They waved goodbye as Nina started her car. They certainly had had an adventure tonight.

As Nina's car drove out of sight, Kathryn pressed the button on the gate. A few minutes passed, and she pressed it again. A sleepy disembodied voice came over the speaker. "Yeah?"

"Kathryn Lucas here. The one whose goods went missing."

"Yeah."

"Well, they've been returned."

"Whaddya mean?"

"The trailer is sitting outside, right in front of the gate."

"Okay. I'll let you in."

"I don't have the cab. I'll be back in the morning, and this baby better still be here. Got it?"

Suddenly the person on the other side of the voice box perked up. "Got it. What time do you think you'll be here?"

"Nine," Kathryn announced back.

"But what if someone else has to gain access to the lot?" the feeble voice asked.

"Deal with it. See you in the morning." Kathryn and Maggie returned to Kathryn's vehicle and drove back to Jerry's apartment.

Once they arrived, Kathryn called Myra and Annie, bringing them up to speed. She also explained the bad Santa stunts, which they were extremely interested in pursuing.

"We'll chat more tomorrow evening," Myra said. "And see if your two new besties are available."

"You want to bring them in on this?" Kathryn asked.

"I think they already are," Myra said calmly as she stroked her pearls.

Chapter 14

New York City

The following morning, Giovanni was asking Frankie a multitude of questions about her evening with her friends. "How was the concert? Where did you go? Are your friends living here now?"

Frankie's stomach was beginning to churn. She couldn't keep lying to Giovanni. She had to tell him the truth. She sat across the table and took his hands into hers. "This is not easy for me, Gio. I do not want our relationship to be riddled with lies, and untruths."

"Of course, *cara.*" The expression on Giovanni's face was bleak. He was expecting the worst, even though he had no reason to, but he had to admit Frankie's behavior the previous evening was odd. "Tell me. What is on your mind?"

"I lied to you about last night." She paused. "Before you think I did anything that would hurt you, please don't go there. I was out with Nina, but we weren't at a concert."

"Okay. So, what is the big lie?"

"I lied about what we were doing," Frankie said, and continued. "Remember the woman, Carol, who got mugged outside my building?"

"Yes. The bad Santa."

"Yes. Anyway, I saw it happened to two other Salvation Army people."

"It is not such a nice thing." Giovanni's face relaxed slightly, but he knew there was more to Frankie's story than informing him of the news.

"You know how much I enjoy solving mysteries, right?" she asked, and Giovanni nodded.

"I had one of my funny feelings, so I opened a map and pinpointed the muggings."

Giovanni's expression began to change again. This time he closed one eye and tilted his head. "What did you do, Frankie?" he asked calmly, but knew the answer was going to be *pazzo.* Crazy.

"I triangulated where the incidents happened and drew a line from each one and found an address where all the lines intersected."

Giovanni folded his arms and leaned his elbows on the table. "Tell me you and Nina did not go to that place?"

"I can't do that; otherwise, I'd be lying again." Frankie waited for an explosive reaction.

"Where was this address?" he asked, and inhaled a huge volume of air. Then he let it out as he waited for her response.

"A warehouse area in Brooklyn."

"You went to Brooklyn with Nina to find a warehouse?"

"Yes, but we didn't do anything. I mean, not anything that had to do with the men in the truck."

Frankie knew she could not un-say what she just said, knowing Giovanni was certainly going to blow a fuse.

"Two men. A truck. A warehouse in Brooklyn." he said,

slowly piecing it together. "Frankie, you put yourself in an extremely dangerous position. You are not stupid, so I don't understand why you would do such a thing." His voice was still calm, but stupefied.

"I know. But I was so shaken by what happened to Carol, I wanted to do something. I know the police are too busy. Then when I did the research, I got one of those vibes." She reached over and gently touched his cheek. "All I wanted to do was see if my hunch was correct. I wasn't going to do anything. Just scope it out. Take a photo if possible and send the information to the police."

Giovanni had a distinct Italian accent, but his English was impeccable. It was only when his emotions were heightened, or he got excited, that his accent became much more obvious. "You make-a the cookbooks. Not a Sherlock-a Holmes." He took her hands again. "Frankie, you lead-a with-a your heart, but sometimes, I wish you lead-a more with your head."

Frankie bit the inside of her lip. There was much more to the story, but she didn't think Giovanni could handle the wild-goose chase part of the escapade. She also wasn't sure she should mention her new friends. Maybe she would never see them again, so maybe she should keep that information on the down-low for now.

"I am happy you are okay." He kissed the back of her hands. "And you tell me the truth."

Her stomach churned again. Better go for it and tell him everything. "We met two other women. A reporter and a long-haul truck driver."

"Where?"

"While we were on the stakeout," she said, and held her breath.

Giovanni blew a huff of air through his lips. "We can discuss later. I have to pick up Mama and Aunt Lucia. We have dinner with them tonight, remember?"

"Of course. And thank you for bringing the things for the memory book," Frankie said when she spotted them on the table.

"For you? Of course." He got up from his chair and placed his arms around her. "I'll see you later. You stay out of trouble. Please?" He kissed her on the forehead.

"I'll do my best," Frankie said, with a huge amount of relief. The rest of the story would be brief. Or so she thought.

Pinewood

Charles and Fergus spent a good part of the night tracking down information regarding the warehouse and pizzeria. Like most illegitimate businesses, the real ownership was buried behind one shell company after another. But that wasn't usually a problem. It was simply time-consuming. They finally found the name of the proprietor. It was Buchwald Barflow, who once worked for an organized-crime family in Belarus. As they checked further, they discovered he was implicated in money laundering, human trafficking, and illegal off-track betting on the side.

Charles began to read the rest of the dossier. "The pizzeria was once owned by Louis Amato, who also had mob ties, but his was central to New York, and it was limited to illegal betting. Lots of punters back then." Charles was referring to gamblers. "When sports betting became legal, he retired and sold the business to Barflow."

"So Barflow has maintained the bookie business but is also operating from the warehouse, you think?" Fergus asked.

"Probably. He's a dodgy bounder from what I can tell," Charles continued. "He's not big or bad enough for the DEA. Small-time in comparison."

"Still, what he is doing is horrid at any level."

"I totally agree. I think he deserves an evaluation from

Myra and Annie. If the FBI, NYPD, or Interpol don't have the resources to go after him and his little gang, perhaps there is something we can do to facilitate the dismantling of his business enterprises and assist in his deportation."

"Splendid idea. They should be at the townhouse by now." Charles phoned Myra in New York and brought her up to speed with Mr. Barflow. "I suspect they nicked the wrong trailer, which is why they returned it. There couldn't be any other reason."

"I am sure you are correct. We also have this Santa thing. I'm not sure how we are going to approach it. I asked Maggie to invite Nina and Frankie over later this evening, after we have dinner."

"Crack on, love. We'll keep on the Barflow situation. Meanwhile, we're running facial recognition from the photo Kathryn sent. The tosspot in the Santa hat. Everything else on schedule?"

"Kathryn met with the other drivers, and they are en route to the Hilton. It seems like we are back on track," Myra said.

"Bloody good. Chat later."

"Bye, Charles." Myra ended the call. She turned to Annie and said, "They've identified the owner of the warehouse. As Charles said, 'very dodgy.' Fergus is trying facial recognition on the Salvation Army kettle-pilfering Santa."

"Excellent. So, what do we do between now and dinner?" Annie asked.

"Shop? Check out the decorations?"

"Sounds like a good plan," Annie agreed.

Brooklyn

Vinny was about to do the unthinkable, but his physical well-being was in jeopardy. He went downstairs to his mother's apartment after she left to go to the beauty parlor. He entered the room where his mother kept a desk and a filing cabinet with all the family paperwork. Lucky for him, she was well-organized, and he was easily able to locate the deed and property bill for the house. He wasn't going to mortgage the house to the hilt. Just a small equity line of credit. Enough to cover his debt to Bucky. He'd find a legitimate job and pay it off. It was the holidays, and lots of businesses needed extra help. He knew his position as one of Bucky's lieutenants and enforcers was over. Besides, he hated the job. Like Jimmy said, they had no manners. He had enough skills for construction work, but for now he had to hustle to the bank.

The loan officer had known the Massella family for years and expedited an approval for 60,000 dollars. The house was worth well over 650,000. The neighborhood was being gentrified, and the value would only go up. The money was available within an hour, but Vinny could only withdraw 20,000 per day. That should keep Bucky from bashing his brains out for one more day.

He took the cash in hundred-dollar bills and placed them in a leather pouch. Jimmy was waiting outside in his uncle's truck to drive him to the warehouse where Bucky had been spending more of his time lately.

Bucky was surprised to see Vinny so soon, especially with a good chunk of money. "Maybe you not such bad worker. Maybe I keep you on the payroll." Of course, Bucky's payroll was on a cash basis, and there were no contributions to the IRS. No health care or retirement plans, either.

Vinny wasn't about to contradict his lender and current employer. He was going to wait until he paid off his debt, which should be within the next forty-eight hours.

Fergus was able to get a hit on facial recognition. "The name is James 'Jimmy' O'Mara. Small-time stuff. Breaking and entering, shoplifting."

"What do you suppose he's doing with Barflow?"

"Once I discovered his name, I reached out to Snowden, who gave me a little more background. He's mates with a Vincent Massella, who was busted for assault. The person dropped the charges."

"Of course they did," Charles said, and grunted. "We can easily imagine the assault was more of an incentive."

"Right. Vinny worked for Louis Amato, and Bucky kept him on."

"So, this Jimmy person and Vinny run together?"

"Seems so."

"Then the other person with Jimmy the other night was probably Vincent."

"Let's run the financials on this Vincent chap," Fergus said, and the two men went back to their investigating.

Frankie was surprised and delighted when she got Kathryn's call. "How did the toy transfer go?" Frankie asked.

"All good. That's one issue we can put behind us."

Frankie's interest piqued. "And what is the other one?"

"The bad Santa."

Frankie shuddered. On the one hand, she wanted the people to pay for stealing the money, but on the other hand, she did not want to get in over her head, especially with Giovanni. "What do you have in mind?" she asked with great trepidation.

"Are you available to meet for lunch tomorrow?"

"I have a few things to do in my office. Can we meet around Rock Center?"

"So funny you should say that. Annie suggested Limani, which is right there."

"Perfect. I haven't been in a while."

"Do you know if Nina is available?"

"Possibly. I'll give you her contact info."

"Excellent," Kathryn replied, and wrote down the information.

"Looking forward to seeing you in the daylight," Frankie said, and signed off.

Vinny and Jimmy hauled out of the warehouse parking lot, just in case Bucky had changed his mind about giving Vinny one more day.

"You still got that Santa suit?" Vinny asked.

"Yeah. Why?"

"Can you get your hands on another one?"

"Why?"

"Can you or can't you?"

"But why?" Jimmy said with a huff.

"I'll explain tomorrow. Find one that'll fit me. Pick me up tomorrow at three."

Giovanni's restaurant was brimming with laughter and music. This was the first big family meal they were having together in almost a year. Marco and Anita took the children to Italy during the summer, and Giovanni had a short visit when he was in Campania for business, but now they were all together. It was a season to celebrate.

Over a dozen live fir trees with tiny white lights served as area dividers, creating cozy seating areas, and accommodating large private parties. Large matching wreaths with lights hung along the walls, and fifty small crystal angels were suspended throughout from the ceiling. Soft classical holiday music floated through the air. It was magical. It was inspiring.

Frankie played a major role in the decorating. Lucia hadn't been to the restaurant in several years, and it was the first time ever for the Parisi brothers. Frankie's goal was to make a banger of an impression. She knew she had hit it out of the park when both Lucia and Rosevita's mouths dropped open as they entered the holiday fairyland. Elio and Anthony were also speechless.

"*Magnifico,*" Elio remarked.

Giovanni put his arm around Frankie. "This is all Frankie's idea."

"*Bellissima,*" Lucia said in awe.

The table was set with fir branches that ran down the center of the table, interspersed with candles covered in bark, pine cones, and small cache pots with live rosemary plants. More *oob*s and *aab*s echoed around the room.

Frankie's part of the evening was over, except for handing out the envelopes with the tickets. "Before we start, I wanted to give you my holiday gift."

"But we don't have your gift; it's not Christmas yet," Rosevita protested.

"It's okay, because if I wait until Christmas, then it won't be a surprise. Well, it will be a surprise, but not a good one," she said, and chuckled. "Whatever your plans are for tomorrow, you will have to change them."

Rosevita looked at her sister and shrugged.

"Please. Open them."

Everyone eagerly opened the mysterious envelopes. Inside were tickets to the *Radio City Christmas Spectacular!*

Cheers of delight from the adults, and squeals of glee from the children, rang in the air. Frankie was once again relieved. Her mission for the evening was complete. Now all she had to do was enjoy the company of loved ones and indulge in some fabulous food.

It was almost ten by the time dinner was over. Everyone was stifling yawns and congratulating Giovanni and Marco for a wonderful meal. Marco hired a van to bring the family back to Tenafly, and Giovanni and Frankie walked to her apartment a few blocks away.

The air was crisp as they casually strolled through Madison Square Park, where a large Christmas tree with twinkling lights stood in the middle of the reflecting pond.

"It's a beautiful night." Frankie sighed and rested her head against Giovanni's shoulder.

"*Bellissima,*" he said in response, "you make it beautiful."

And Frankie's legs turned to Jell-O once again.

Chapter 15

Mayhem and Magic

New York City

The following day was packed with activities. Giovanni's family was getting ready for their afternoon at Radio City Music Hall. Marco's children, Sophia and Lorenzo, were racing all over the house with excitement.

Across the river, in the Flatiron District, Frankie was trying to decide what to wear to lunch with a countess and a candy manufacturer magnate.

Giovanni grinned as Frankie kept changing outfits. "How does this look?" she said, modeling a navy-blue pantsuit.

"Maybe a little too much like the office." He continued to read the newspaper and sip on his espresso. Two minutes later, Frankie reappeared in a black leather pencil skirt with a cropped white jacket.

"Very nice," he said, nodding.

"But?"

"There's no *but*."

"Yes, there is. I heard it."

"But I didn't say it."

"I still heard it." Francesca stood with her hands on her hips.

"I think you look beautiful in the white cashmere turtle-neck. Wear it with leather pants and the over-the-knee boots," he suggested.

"*Perfetto!*" Frankie said and snapped her fingers. "You are such the fashion maestro."

"*Si.* It's an Italian thing." He smiled and looked up from the newspaper. "No matter what you wear, Frankie, you will impress them. All you have to do is smile," he said, and winked.

Frankie changed into the outfit Giovanni described, pulled her hair back in a long ponytail with a white satin and silk plissé scrunchie, then donned the emerald earrings he had given her the Christmas before. "Ta-da!" She said, and reappeared in front of him.

"*Bellissima!* You look stunning, casual, and festive! *Brava!*"

"Thanks to you." She gave him air kisses on each cheek. "Makeup, darling."

Giovanni understood. Frankie normally wore a minimal amount of makeup to work, but she knew how to get "dolled up" when the occasion called for it.

"You will greatly impress everyone. Maybe I should go as your bodyguard," he joked as he pulled her closer. She playfully resisted.

"Come on. You know the rules. No shenanigans after I'm fully dressed!"

"Shame on me for not paying attention to the time." He patted her on the fanny. "Now you go and make some new friends."

"Thank you, *mi amore!*" Frankie bent over to give Bandit a pat on the head, while Sweet P rubbed against Frankie's ankles. "You kitties behave," she said, and blew a kiss as she headed out the door.

* * *

Charles and Fergus arrived in New York City early that morning. They met up with Annie, Myra, Maggie, and Kathryn at Annie's townhouse for breakfast and a briefing. Unbeknownst to Frankie, Charles and Fergus were able to get a good lead on Jimmy the bad Santa, and his pal, Vinny.

"Jimmy drives a delivery truck for his Uncle Frank's liquor store. Avery Snowden had his operative Sasha place a GPS device on the vehicle early this morning."

"What about Vinny?" Myra asked.

"Jimmy usually picks Vinny up at his mother's house around lunchtime, and then they go to the pizzeria to run errands for Barflow using Uncle Frank's liquor store truck," Fergus explained.

"Very inconspicuous," Charles added.

"Do you have a plan in mind?" Myra asked as she stroked her pearls.

"Not yet. We want to get a handle on their comings and goings. Once we corner them, we can transport them to Pinewood."

"And torture them?" Annie chuckled.

"At the very least, we want to teach them a lesson," Myra said. "What about this Buchwald character?"

"Oh, he's the bee's knees when it comes to corruption. And he is audacious. He was cheeky enough to poach from one of the bosses of their version of 'the mob,' and now there is a bounty on his head should he ever set foot in Belarus again."

"Looks like it might be time to give Pearl a call," Annie said, eyeing Kathryn.

"We're copacetic now. All good," Kathryn said, and grinned.

"It should be relatively easy to locate Barflow. Getting past his thugs might be a bit of a challenge."

"Not if I make an offer he can't refuse." Annie raised her eyebrows.

"What do you have in mind?" Fergus said, eyeing her curiously.

"I need some quick cash and want to unload some of my diamonds."

"Won't he ask why?" Charles queried.

"I don't think he really cares, as long as he can get his take."

"Or steal the goods for himself?" Maggie asked.

"But they won't be real. Remember my friend Lincoln Gladwell?"

"Yes. The gemologist. What about him?" Myra asked.

"He created replicas of some of my jewelry," Annie said, and grinned. "After the masterful job he did when we were in London chasing down those terrible longevity doctors, I thought I should have the tiara and a few of my baubles duplicated so I could wear them in public without being concerned about losing them."

"Brilliant!" Fergus said, and chuckled. "I often wondered why you were so casual with that crown of yours."

"I have two rings and a bracelet that I'll ask that Barf fellow to fence. I keep them here for when we have to go to a gala. Retail value of the originals is over a hundred-fifty thousand. I'll offer him thirty percent. That's five percent higher than street value."

"When did you become an expert in jewelry fencing?" Maggie asked with surprise.

"There's still much to learn about your boss," Annie said, and wiggled her eyebrows.

"Sure is. Now pass that basket of croissants, please," Maggie replied with an outstretched hand.

"Sounds like some of the pieces are falling into place," Myra remarked.

"Meanwhile, we have to figure out how to round up the other two knuckleheads," Kathryn added.

"That shouldn't be too difficult. We can follow them tomorrow afternoon. I'll ask Sasha to put a slow leak in one of the tires. When they pull over, we'll be right behind them in a van. We'll nab them, bring them to the airport, and transport them to Pinewood," Fergus said.

"Where they'll spend a horrible Christmas in the cellar," Myra said with a devilish grin.

"But then what?" Maggie asked.

"We'll scare the bejeezus out of them, drive them to the mountains in Virginia, and make them figure out a way to get back to Brooklyn. They're two-bit criminals. Once Barflow is out of the way, I suspect they will have to find gainful employment. I doubt if Uncle Frank will keep Jimmy on the payroll after his truck goes missing."

Myra was frowning.

"What is it, love?" Charles asked with a concerned expression.

"Do you think it's punishment enough for stealing money from the Salvation Army?" she asked.

Annie's face lit up. "Here's an idea. After we keep them in the basement for a few days, we bring them back here. I'll call my friend Captain Dag Dorph of the FDNY and cajole him into doing me a favor."

"And what might that be?" Myra asked.

"Let me talk to the captain first and see if what I have in mind is a possibility. Otherwise, we'll set these city boys on the side of a mountain."

"How do you plan on contacting Barflow?" Kathryn asked.

"I know people," Annie said, winking.

"Whatever it takes!" came the battle cry from the four women seated at the table.

"Tomorrow we are on the move. Today we are having a lovely lunch at Limani with Kathryn and Maggie's new pals."

Charles placed a box on the table. "Since we're going to be in the middle of holiday madness in the Big Apple, I thought each of us should have an Apple watch. But it's not exactly an Apple watch." He handed one to each of the women, and then one to Fergus.

"It's a two-way radio. Fergus and I thought it would be a good idea for us to be readily able to communicate without using our phones."

"Oh, cool," Maggie said as she strapped the smart-looking timepiece on her wrist.

"It will emit a slight vibration when someone wants to communicate. All you have to do is hold it near your ear. Pretend you're scratching your face. Or you can use the earpiece." He handed everyone an object the size of a pushpin. "No one will know you're wearing it."

"It's the most current technology available," Fergus said proudly.

"I wouldn't expect anything less," Annie said, and chuckled.

"The Secret Service doesn't even have these yet," Charles remarked.

"This is very cool," Maggie said. "Give us a tutorial, please."

"Annie, you go downstairs to the first floor. Myra, you go upstairs to one of the bedrooms. Kathryn, you stay here, and Maggie, you to inside the kitchen."

The women went to their assigned places. A few minutes later, everyone's wrist got a tingle. "Charles here."

"Coming in loud and clear," Annie said from the lower level.

"Ditto," Myra concurred.

"Me too," came from Maggie.

"Roger that," was from Kathryn.

"Right! Now everyone back to the table."

A minute later, they reconvened. Charles was the first to speak. "I am much more comfortable knowing we can reach each other easily. The city is bustling with people, and simply getting through a crowd can be challenging, let alone making a phone call."

"You and Fergus may have outdone yourselves this time," Annie said.

"We can celebrate our mission when we've completed all the tasks," Charles said. "And of course, Fergus and I shall prepare a meal for the victors."

Everyone's hands went up in high fives, followed by fist bumps.

When Frankie walked into her office, Matt let out a low whistle. "Oh. Sorry. H.R. will be all over that," he said, and hung his head.

"I'll let it slide this time, buster," Frankie said, laughing. Matt played for "the other team." His acknowledgment of Frankie's appearance was a compliment as far as she was concerned.

"All dressed up, dearie. What's the occasion?"

"Lunch. Limani." Frankie stuck her chin up in the air. "With Countess Annie De Silva and Myra Rutledge of the eponymous candy fortune."

Matt spun around in his chair. "Well, aren't you fancy? How come I didn't know about it?" He placed his hands on his hips. "I am the keeper of your calendar. How am I supposed to keep it if you don't inform me?"

Frankie knew he was kidding and replied with the same feigned annoyance. "There are the rare occasions where it's none of your beeswax."

Matt spun around again. "Okay. Fine. But do tell!"

"Long story. Very, very long. Too long to share right now, but I met two colleagues of theirs last night, and they invited me and Nina to lunch."

"You and Nina?" he said, and eyed her suspiciously. "Where were you, exactly? I want details."

"Around town. That doesn't matter," Frankie said, knowing it would take too long and sound very crazy if she told him *exactly* where she was the night before. "What matters is I am meeting the owner of Washington, D.C.'s most prominent news media company, who also happens to be a countess; the magnanimous Myra Rutledge, who donates bulletproof vests to K-Nines all over the country; Maggie Spritzer, star reporter; and Kathryn Lucas, former engineer, current cross-country truck driver."

"Plus Nina, former star of *Family Blessings*. Well, that is quite an interesting group."

"It is, isn't it?" Frankie said thoughtfully. She had gotten so caught up in the previous night's escapades and the invitation to lunch, she barely had time to put it all together in her head. "I'm very excited!" Frankie wondered how much adrenaline one could release at once without having a heart attack. She placed her thumb on her wrist and checked her pulse.

"You alright?" Matt sat up quickly.

"Yes. Just getting a bit of a rush."

Matt eyed her carefully. "Okay. No double cappuccino for you today."

"Good idea," Frankie said, and hung her coat on the back of her office door. "What's on the agenda for the morning?"

"Just need you to check a few things before they go to the printer. The BLADS are in for next season," he said, and handed her a large folder. "Should be a relatively quiet day except for your fabulous lunch."

"Yes, indeed."

"How are Giovanni's family members doing?"

"Great. They're going to Radio City this afternoon. And the gang chipped in for a weekend in Atlantic City for New Year's Eve. Dinner, a show, fireworks."

"What about Christmas?"

"Marco and Anita are hosting Christmas Eve and Christmas at their house. This way the kids can get to bed early, and they don't have to shuffle everyone around. I am sure

Rosevita and Lucia will wrangle their way into the kitchen. But Giovanni is preparing a few dishes at the restaurant to try to keep the chaos to a minimum," Frankie said, and chuckled.

"I never appreciated the many benefits of cooking."

"What do you mean?" Frankie asked.

"It's therapeutic. It's creative. It offers interaction between people with a common goal of nourishing each other."

"Wow, Matt. When did you become the cuisine philosopher?"

"When I started working for you!" he said, and grinned. "You created an imprint for cooking with a cause. I believe that's the *name* of the imprint."

Frankie snickered. "Good point! Okay, let me get to these before lunch. I might be having too much fun and not return."

"Right," Matt said sarcastically. "When has that ever happened?"

"Never," she said, paused, then raised her eyebrows. "Up until now."

Reservations were set for twelve-thirty. It was mild enough outside that Frankie didn't need to wear a jacket to walk from one building to another. Nina was waiting for her on the sidewalk.

"Hello, dahling," Nina said in a deep, exotic voice.

"Kiss, kiss," Frankie replied, giving her friend air kisses.

"How excited are you?" Nina asked.

"I had to check my pulse earlier this morning," Frankie admitted, chuckling.

"That was quite a scene, eh?" Nina said in amazement.

"You ain't kidding. And thanks for humoring me."

"It could have turned out a lot worse than being invited to lunch at Limani."

"So true. I wonder why," Frankie said pensively.

"You mean why on earth would a countess and a confectionary tycoon want to have lunch with us?"

"Exactly," Frankie replied. "I think it's great, but odd. In a good way."

"Maggie and Kathryn seem to be pretty normal, if you can call being on a stakeout at a semi-abandoned warehouse normal."

"They were tracking down the toys," Frankie said, reminding her friend.

"True. But how did they know where to find the truck?" Nina pondered.

"You're the one with the creative and sometimes criminal mind," Frankie joked.

"I guess we are about to find out." Nina opened the big brass doors and approached the maître d'. "Good afternoon. We have a reservation with Countess De Silva," Nina said, trying to hide her tinge of nervousness.

"Ah yes. The rest of the guests have already arrived. Follow me, please." The gentleman led the way to a table toward the rear of the Mediterranean restaurant.

"This place is beautiful," Nina whispered as she took in the ambiance of the décor. She felt transported to Greece.

"I can't believe I haven't been here in years, and I work across the street," Frankie whispered in return.

Four smiling faces greeted them. "Hello again!" Maggie's said with a huge grin. "Long time no see," she giggled.

Annie held out her hand. "I'm Annie. So nice to meet you."

Myra followed with her introduction. "Myra. Glad you were able to join us on such short notice."

"I wouldn't have missed this for anything." Nina shook hands with the two women.

"Except maybe an Emmy," Maggie said, teasing one of her TV idols.

"Francesca—Frankie—Cappella," Frankie said, and followed with handshakes.

The maître d' held the chairs for them to be seated.

"Thank you very much for inviting us. This is really a treat. I usually have a salad at my desk from the commissary."

"This will be a vast improvement, I can assure you," Annie said, and gave her a warm smile.

A server approached the table with a bottle of Dom Pérignon. "Madame?" he asked Frankie.

She was a bit startled at the offer, but then again, she had no idea what to expect. Champagne at lunch? Why not? This was a special occasion.

"Yes, thank you," Frankie replied.

He turned to Nina. "Madame?"

"Please. Thank you," she answered.

Once everyone's glasses were filled, Annie lifted hers. "Here's to making new friends! Cheers!"

Frankie responded with "Cin! Cin!"

Everyone else voiced their own toast.

Annie began the conversation. "Nina, I know you are an actress, writer, and podcaster. What are you working on now?"

Nina was surprised Annie knew as much as she did about her. "I'm collaborating with Jordan Pleasance. We're attempting to pitch a series."

"Can you tell us what it's about?" Myra asked, and took a sip from her glass.

Nina explained it was a mother-daughter mystery, focusing on small towns in the U.K.

"That sounds like something I would enjoy," Myra said.

"Ditto," Annie added. "There isn't much on network television these days."

"Exactly. And when you are a woman of a certain age, such as me, it's tough to find work in this industry unless you create something for yourself."

Maggie chimed in, "I saw Billy Bob Thornton doing an interview. Apparently, he got that advice from Billy Wilder while he was working for a catering company at a posh Hollywood party. I'm paraphrasing, but Wilder approached Thornton and said, 'You want to be an actor. You're not good-looking enough. Write your own material.' Or something to that effect."

"Seriously?" Nina asked.

"Yes, and the funny thing about it was Thornton had no idea who he was talking to. When he went back to get another tray of pigs in a blanket, his friend asked him what Wilder had said to him. Imagine that!" Maggie said.

"Now *that* sounds like a plot for a movie," Nina responded.

"And so, the movie *Sling Blade* was born," Maggie said as she finished her story.

"And what about you, Frankie?" Myra asked.

"I'm an editor at Grand Marshall."

"She is being modest," Nina chimed in. "She created an imprint called Cooking for a Cause."

"I heard about that," Myra said. "Celebrity chefs, and part of the proceeds go to their favorite charity, correct?"

Frankie tried not to blush, but she was impressed that her work was known to someone as prestigious as Myra Rutledge. "Correct."

"The reason I'm aware, is because my husband has become a foodie and is always trying new recipes on us."

Kathryn finally spoke. "I try to be in town when he and Fergus are rummaging through the kitchen."

"Fergus is my plus-one," Annie said, and grinned.

The server approached the table and asked if they wanted to hear the specials. Indeed, they did. Annie ordered the Mediterranean mezza, an assortment of dips and pita bread. "Anyone interested in octopus?" she asked.

"Count me in," Frankie replied.

"Ew. No," Maggie and Kathryn said in unison.

"I would love some," Nina added.

The two-hour lunch was filled with lively conversation, including how the four women happened to meet on a dark deserted street in Brooklyn.

"I would really like to get my hands on those buggers who stole the money," Frankie said, then sighed. "I met the woman who was mugged by Rockefeller Center. Her name is Carol. She's been ringing that bell for years." Frankie paused and decided to finish her story. "I got there a few minutes after it happened. Then I coaxed her to follow me to St. Patrick's Cathedral. I figured a little prayer and some solace might help her jangled nerves."

"That was very kind of you," Myra said. "It's shocking that something like that would happen with so much security," Myra said.

"True, but there were a bunch of SantaCon merrymakers, and it happened very fast. There were too many of them to finger any particular one of them," Frankie replied.

Nina cleared her throat. "My dear friend here heard about a few more kettle grabs and made a map of the incidents. She pulled out her handy drawing compass and triangulated the distances and produced a location. She had a hunch. And when Frankie gets a hunch, she is like a dog with a sock in its mouth. I knew she wasn't going to let it go, and I allowed her to talk me into this wild idea of checking the address."

Myra addressed Frankie. "Well, your sleuthing and quick thinking with your camera app may prove to be quite useful," she said with respect, and glanced at Annie, wondering how much information they should share with the two newbies.

Frankie had a confused expression on her face. "How so?"

"We have a group who, shall we say, work behind the scenes," Annie said.

Frankie tilted her head, waiting for more information.

"Myra and I, along with Maggie and Kathryn and a few other remarkable women, have righted some wrongs along the way."

As obtuse as it sounded, neither Nina nor Frankie wanted to press the issue. They could tell these women were serious. Serious, but not scary.

Annie's wrist got a tingle from her watch. "Would you excuse me?" She got up and walked to the ladies' bathroom just in case Fergus or Charles was sharing sensitive information. She peeked under the stalls to make sure there was no one else in the room, then whispered into the face of the watch. "What's up?"

Fergus's voice was in her ear. "According to the tracking device, the two goons have been driving across Brooklyn. It appears they are on their way to Manhattan."

"What should we do?" Annie asked.

"Sit tight. We're bringing the limo around to where you are. If they are heading to where I suspect they are, things may get a little dicey."

"Ok. We're about to have dessert."

"Enjoy. I'll check back in a few once we can figure out which direction they're headed."

"Great. Can you buzz the info over to Myra? I don't want to say anything in front of our guests."

"Right. We'll get these bounders!" Fergus said with authority.

"Super," Annie said into her wrist. She washed her hands and went back to the table.

"Everything alright?" Myra asked casually.

"Yes. At this age, sometimes nature calls too often," she said, and chuckled.

Everyone at the table giggled. Bladder issues often arose at the worst possible moment. "Wherever I go, I always look for the exit signs first, and then the loo," Annie said, and continued to chuckle.

Meanwhile, Myra heard a voice in her earpiece whispering information to her. She tapped Annie's foot to let her know she knew.

When the meal was finished, Annie and Myra stood first. Nina and Frankie noticed the check had not arrived. *Surely they weren't going to dine and dash*, Frankie thought, chuckling to herself. Then she spotted Annie nod toward the server, who nodded in return. *Must have a house account*, Frankie surmised. Several of Giovanni's clientele were sent monthly bills instead of paying for each meal at a time. It was convenient for the power-lunch people. They didn't have to bother filling out an expense form. The bill went directly to their company's accounting offices.

The six women decided to take a stroll around the perimeter of the ice-skating rink. In spite of the throng of people, everyone was in a festive and cheerful mood. It was delightful sharing this upbeat group energy, until Frankie spotted two men dressed in Santa suits approaching the orange kettle managed by Carol.

"Oh no! Not again!" Frankie cried out. She was stunned when one of the men turned his face in her direction. "It's him!" she yelled to her lunchmates.

Frankie instantly began to scramble through the crowd, saying, "Excuse me . . . pardon me," over and over again.

Following close behind was Kathryn. She was yelling toward Frankie, "What are you doing?"

Frankie didn't take the time to stop and turn. Instead, she made wild *follow me* gestures. The other women followed, everyone excusing themselves as they made their way toward the red-flocked phonies.

One of the two Santas shoved a bag he was holding toward Carol and took off in the direction of 51st Street. The second Santa was right behind him. They made a quick turn toward Sixth Avenue, with the six women hot on their heels.

Tourists, office workers, and delivery people watched the chase and jumped out of their way.

The skinny Santa pulled open the stage door of Radio City, and the two men quickly slid inside. Frankie, Kathryn, Nina, Annie, Myra, and Maggie followed. It was pandemonium backstage, with the stage elevators being dismantled and reset by the crew. Singers and dancers were standing by for their cues, including Randy, who got shoved by the bigger Santa.

"Hey, watch it!" he yelled before spotting Frankie. "What on earth . . . ?" He didn't have time to finish his sentence when Frankie grabbed a Santa cap from a box with several dozen of them. The other women did the same and dashed behind Frankie as she jumped on one of the moving stages. With quick reflexes and agility, the other women hopped onboard.

Vinny and Jimmy kept barreling forward, but the ladies were not far behind. Suddenly, the curtains opened, and the audience got a special addition to the show: a Santa chase across the massive stage. Some people laughed, others gasped, and some of the dancers shrieked. It was something never seen before at the Holiday Spectacular.

Vinny and Jimmy jumped off the platform and knocked their way through the crew, with six wild women keeping pace. They found their way to the exit and were about to dash toward the subway when a man stood in front of them, blocking their escape. Vinny and Jimmy turned to run in the opposite direction, but there was another human obstacle standing in their way. They couldn't turn back. The women were within a hairbreadth away.

Charles opened the door of the stretch limo. "Get in," he demanded of the two men, who were beginning to panic.

Vinny thought Bucky was finally going to exact his revenge for having to wait so long for his money. He knew they had no choice and followed the instructions of the man with a British accent.

"We'll take it from here," Fergus said to the ladies as they arrived on the scene.

"Marvelous, darling," Myra said, and blew them kiss. Annie did the same.

The six women huddled together and began to laugh hysterically. Their cheeks were bright red, and they were out of breath.

Everyone began talking at once.

"What in the heck just happened?" Maggie asked incredulously.

"A game of tag?" Myra said, half-winded.

"That was fun!" Kathryn roared.

"Sure wasn't what I expected," Nina added.

"Now that's what I call an excellent ending to a fabulous lunch," Frankie said, and began to hug everyone.

The group began to walk back to the promenade. They wanted to get out of there before the police arrived. They really did not want to answer any questions, but if they had to, Myra suggested, "We thought it was a purse snatcher."

Annie added, "They'll tell you it's never a good idea to chase someone in case they have a weapon."

"And we'll all agree with them and promise never to do it again," Maggie said. She raised her hand in a fist bump, to which everyone joined in.

As they were rounding the corner of the great music hall, a voice yelled out to them. "Hey, missy. What in the heck was that all about?" The recognizable voice was Randy's.

"I'll explain later." Frankie placed her index finger on her lips. "Big secret."

Randy stood on the sidewalk with a befuddled expression on his face. Then he remembered whom he was dealing with. You just never knew what was going to happen if Frankie Cappella was around.

The six women approached Carol, who was holding onto the pouch when the pursuit began.

"You okay?" Frankie asked the confused woman.

She was visibly shaken. "The man shoved this at me."

"Did you open it?" Nina asked.

"No. I was too afraid," Carol answered.

Frankie took the bag from her and untied the cord. "Well, looky here." She held it open. Inside was a wad of cash wrapped in a note. Frankie unwrapped the note and handed the cash to Annie, who began to count it.

"Ha!" Frankie yelped. "Check it out!" She turned the paper around so everyone could read what it said: *Sorry.*

"There's five hundred dollars here," Annie said, and handed the money to Carol.

"But that doesn't belong to me," Carol protested.

"It does now," Myra insisted.

Frankie furrowed her brow, then said thoughtfully, "So they were returning the money."

"That's way more than he took," Carol tried to explain. "It was maybe two hundred, tops."

"Payment made plus interest is what I say," Kathryn added to the conversation.

"Merry Christmas, Carol," Frankie said, and gave the woman a big hug.

Annie reached into her purse and pulled out another five hundred dollars. Myra matched it, and they placed it in the bundle of money. "Now you can feed a lot of families this week," Myra declared.

Carol's eyes began to tear. She pointed to Frankie. "I don't know who sent her to me, but I am surely grateful."

"There are always angels among us," Frankie said. "We just have to pay attention."

As the group began to disperse, Annie extended an invitation to the block party for New Year's Eve. "My friend Camille lives on Sniffen Court, and she arranged for a block party. My townhouse is just around the corner. We'd love for you to join us."

Frankie was the first to respond. "That sounds lovely, but we have plans to meet two of our other friends and their dates." She hesitated to say *significant others*, because she had no idea who was going to be significant to Rachael over the next ten days. "It's become a tradition."

"Well, then, you can continue that tradition by bringing them along. Party starts at ten. Then we go to the roof of my townhouse to get a glimpse of the glow from the fireworks in Central Park."

"Sounds spectacular! Thank you very much," Nina said.

"Excellent. I shall text you the address. Oh, and we have outdoor heaters for the courtyard, so you don't need to bundle up too much."

Frankie gently grabbed her hand. "Wonderful. It shall be an evening to remember."

"Just like today!" Annie said, and chortled.

They hugged and wished each other a Merry Christmas. As they were leaving, Frankie turned and asked, "What is going to happen to the two men?"

"We shall let you know," Annie said, and winked. She sensed some nervousness in Frankie. "Oh, don't worry. We're not going to kill them or anything. Just torment them a bit."

"Whew," Frankie said, grinning. "Glad to hear it's only torment and not torture."

Annie, Myra, Maggie, and Kathryn looked at one another and burst out laughing. "Maybe just a smidge."

Frankie and Nina locked arms and walked over to St. Patrick's. "I think we both can use a little candlelight and some prayers."

"How did I ever let you talk me into this?" Nina asked half-jokingly.

"Because you're my bestie." Frankie gave her a kiss on the cheek.

Frankie kept her threat of not going back to the office after lunch. Instead, she went home to change and spend a little quiet time with her kitties. It had been a surreal day, and she needed some space to clear her head. Dinner with Giovanni's family later that evening would require a mental tune-up from the day's activities. She slipped into a pair of fleece pajamas and threw herself on the bed. Bandit joined her lickety-split. His latest "thing" was to pull the scrunchie out of Frankie's hair and make a nest with it. Once he was satisfied, he curled up on her hair and rested his head against hers. Frankie thought it was the sweetest thing, and kept trying to figure out how she could catch a photo of him doing it. Maybe next time, she'd bring her phone to bed with her—that is, if she ever took a nap again. She considered it a luxury. She set her alarm for a two-hour doze, which gave her time to freshen up before Giovanni got home and they had to leave for the restaurant.

Giovanni got home earlier than expected. He, too, wanted time to freshen up and put a little space between work and the next family dinner. The holidays were a wonderful time of year, but also very demanding. Giovanni thought it might be because Thanksgiving and Christmas were only four weeks apart. A lot to pack in over a truly short window. But everyone in his orbit did their best to *keep calm and carry on.*

Frankie didn't hear Giovanni enter the apartment and was startled when he approached the bed. She had been out cold. Like a light. Gonzo. La-la land. She bolted up. "Oh, geez!" she gasped. "I wasn't expecting you this early." She glanced at the clock next to the bed.

"I wasn't expecting you to be here, either." Giovanni sat on the edge of the bed and stroked whatever hair Bandit wasn't sleeping on. "Everything alright? How was your lunch?"

Frankie blinked several times. "Everything is fine." It was the truth, but Giovanni could tell something else had happened.

"Che cos'è?" he asked—*what is it?* in Italian.

"Lunch was wonderful. Lovely people. Fun and funny. Food was scrumptious."

"So, what's the face you make?"

"Well," she said, and paused, trying to construct the right words to explain the antics of the afternoon.

Giovanni got close to her face. "Frankie?"

She wriggled her way out from under Bandit and sat upright. "Let's turn on the news."

"Why?"

"I'd like to see what happened today," Frankie said, still searching for the right words, and in which particular order.

Giovanni gave her his quizzical look of one eye closed and his head tilted to one side. He got up from the bed and held his hand out to Frankie. She stood, grabbed the remote, and clicked on the local news station. She was anxious to see if anyone caught the spectacle on the stage at Radio City, and she didn't mean the one that had been rehearsed by the performers.

Giovanni went into the bathroom and put on a robe. When he returned, the program showed a chaotic scene traveling across the famous stage. He got closer to the television, staring at the scene intently. He slowly turned his head toward Frankie. She grabbed a toss pillow and stuck it in front of her face. "Frankie? Those look like your sweater and your boots."

Frankie pulled the pillow below her chin. "I can explain."

Giovanni couldn't help but grin. "I hope so."

"Let's say some justice was done today, and I didn't go to jail."

"Okay. That's a good start. Continue, please." Giovanni pulled the pillow away from her and took her hand. He couldn't

help but think all of this had something to do with the bad
Santa.

Frankie began her story with, "Remember the woman,
Carol, from the Salvation Army?"

"Yes, and the dangerous trip you and Nina took."

"Right. Well. . . ." And she revealed the rest of the adventure in great detail, all the way down to the two British men
who forced the bad Santas into a stretch limo.

Giovanni's eyes went wide. "Kidnapping?"

"No, I don't think that's the whole story." Again, Frankie
tried to find the right words, but she honestly didn't know.
"But they assured me the men would be taken into custody,"
Frankie said, even though she wasn't clear as to what that entailed. And she wasn't about to ask Annie, Myra, Kathryn, or
Maggie, either. "Besides, who would kidnap people with a
stretch limo?"

"I think maybe we should stop now."

"Good idea. Oh, and we've been invited to a New Year's
Eve party on Sniffen Court."

"Ah, that side street with the townhouses? It was a stable
at one time." Giovanni had always been interested in the history of New York.

"That's the one. Apparently, Annie has a townhouse on
East Thirty-fifth Street. Her friend Camille arranged for the
Sniffen Courtyard to be transformed into a party plaza."

"What about dinner with everyone?"

"The party starts at ten. Everyone has been invited, so we
can have dinner as planned and head cross-town afterwards.
If it's nice weather, we can walk. Shouldn't take more than
twenty minutes; plus, we'll be walking in the opposite direction of Times Square."

Giovanni was smiling. "That sounds like a very fine way
to spend New Year's Eve, especially since nobody is cooking
this year."

"Exactly. Even your mother doesn't have to do anything except throw some money on the roulette table."

"Oh, she is going to love that!" Giovanni said happily. "It was so nice for everyone to help pay for it."

"Are you kidding? It was the least we could do!"

"Let's hope this New Year's will be a little calmer than last year. Just a dinner and a party, and not on the roof of a police department jail," Giovanni said, chuckling.

"We have two hours before we have to be at Keens. Let me jump in the shower first so I can primp while you take yours."

"Perfetto." Giovanni kissed her forehead, an affectionate gesture Frankie appreciated.

As she was setting the water temperature, she called out, "Did you speak to your mother yet? How did she enjoy the show?" It wasn't until that moment Frankie froze, realizing Giovanni's family must have seen the crazy antics in which she was involved.

"No, we haven't spoken. She sent a text saying they were going to Macy's to see Santa; then Marco arranged for the sitter to pick up the kids and take them home. The rest will meet us at the restaurant."

"Uh, boy," Frankie said quietly to herself. Then she spoke louder so he could hear her: "Well, I am sure they are going to tell us everything about their day."

That's when it occurred to Giovanni that his family was most likely in the audience when the wild chase behind the dancing Rockettes took place. He stuck his head inside the bathroom door. "We will not say anything. You will not admit anything. *Capisce?*"

"Capisce!"

Several minutes later, a newscaster made another announcement:

> *Two days after three Salvation Army buckets were robbed, three packages containing five hundred dollars appeared at the sites with a note that simply said, "Sorry." No one knows who made these contributions, but witnesses said they thought they saw two men dressed as Santa drop something into the kettles. In another bizarre story involving Santa, there was a disruption in the famous Radio City Christmas Spectacular this afternoon, when two men dressed in Santa garb were being pursued by six women also wearing Santa caps. None of the participants in this rave have been identified, but one of the women was wearing white rhinestone cowgirl boots. The police say they are investigating both situations, but do not believe they are related.*

Vinny and Jimmy had no idea where they were or what was going to happen to them. Somehow, they had been drugged. When they came out of the effect of the narcotic, they were in a fetal position, their mouths were taped shut, and their hands and ankles were bound with zip ties. They assumed they were in a trunk of some sort. Jimmy tried to speak, but the only thing that came out was a muffled *whuffwemerf*, which, of course made no sense to Vinny. The vehicle seemed to be parked, and they could hear what sounded like jets in the background. The only shred of optimism was that they weren't dead. At least not yet. Vinny decided it wasn't worth the effort to try to disentangle themselves. The only thing they could do was wait until they met their fate.

Then he heard voices: the British guy, and two, maybe three women.

A key fob clicked, and the trunk opened. The two men were staring down at them.

"Looks like they're no worse for the wear," Fergus said.

"Okay, gentlemen, you shall accompany us." He and Charles helped them unfold themselves from the trunk and assisted the weary men up the short flight of steps to the aircraft. Vinny and Jimmy were still in a twilight stage as Charles buckled them into two seats in the rear of the plane. The minor exertion must have tired them, because in a minute, they were fast asleep again.

"Looks like we got most of this sorted," Charles said to Myra as she ascended the stairs.

"I knew you would." She kissed him on the cheek.

"What are your plans for these two clowns?" Maggie asked.

"I think they shall be our guests in the basement, just long enough to learn their lesson. After all, they didn't inflict any bodily harm, and from what we can surmise, they actually returned the money and then some," Myra said.

"So, they're not bad people. Just have bad judgment, would you say?" Maggie asked in her reporter voice.

"That's a good summation," Annie said. "You can put that in the article you're going to write about *Bad Santa Makes Good*. We'll just leave their names out of it."

"How long are they going to be our guests?" Charles asked.

"We can't do anything before Christmas, and we have the gala in two days."

"I suggest the two of you stay here in New York, and we'll get them settled at Pinewood. We should be back in a pinch," Charles said.

"Who is going to mind these lads while we're gone?" Fergus asked.

"I already spoke to Pearl, and one of her people agreed to babysit. Next, we have to plan our move on extraditing Mr. Barflow. Meanwhile, you can give each of these men a cell of their own," Annie said.

"I'll even put a Christmas tree at the end of the tunnel. Just to remind them of what they're missing," Fergus said with a gleam in his eye.

"Speaking of missing. What do we communicate to Vinny's mother?" Fergus asked. "And Jimmy's family?"

"We'll send Mrs. Massella a text from his phone, informing her he was comped for three nights in Atlantic City and that Jimmy is driving. They'll be back in a few days, and to please let everyone else know," Myra replied.

"She is not going to be happy about that," Charles said, and chuckled.

"That will be one more penalty for his misdeeds," Fergus said to everyone's delight, with hoots and cackles.

An announcement came over the PA system. "Ladies and gentlemen. This is the captain speaking. We have been cleared for takeoff. Please fasten your seat belts."

Everyone looked at one another and roared, and then Myra and Annie stepped off the plane and headed back to the townhouse.

Chapter 16

Later that Evening

Frankie made sure she wasn't wearing anything that could identify her as one of the rowdy women at Radio City. She put on a double-breasted beige pinstripe pantsuit with black threads, and a matching black camisole underneath. She added a pair of gold, chunky earrings to match the buttons, and pulled her hair in a chignon. She thought her signature ponytail might give someone a clue if they had been paying attention to the skirmish behind the dancers.

Giovanni was already dressed in a pair of black slacks, white shirt, and a black and blue tweed jacket. He was sitting in front of the television with the remote, watching the news on another channel.

"What are you doing?" Frankie asked.

"Watching the woman I love dance on the stage of Radio City," he said jokingly.

"Ha. Not exactly dancing." Frankie laughed as she took the remote from his hand.

"But *cara*, you can tell people you graced the stage at the famous venue," he said, grinning.

"Graced the stage is a wild exaggeration," Frankie said, and chuckled. "Let's hope no one recognizes any of us."

"Ah, but Randy knows it was you and Nina."

"Then we're going to have to kill him," Frankie said, raising her eyebrows. "Kidding."

"I hope so. I don't want you to turn to a life of crime."

"I think we did that last year."

"Ah, but it was your friend Rachael who got arrested."

"Yeah, but we were co-conspirators by letting her loose in Campagna."

"You are not her babysitter," Giovanni said, looking up at her.

"Have you met Rachael?" Frankie said with a grin.

Giovanni laughed, then remarked how lovely Frankie looked. "*Bellissima!*"

"*Grazie. Sei bello!*" Frankie said in return.

"Ah, your Italian is getting better every day." Giovanni got up and took her hand. "*Andiamo!*"

"Let's go!" Frankie replied in English.

It took less than twenty minutes for them to walk from Frankie's apartment to Keens Steakhouse. The air was crisp, and holiday lights twinkled from windows, trees, doorways, and around lampposts. There were banners of lights from one side of the street to the other.

"It's another beautiful night in the city," Frankie cooed as they walked arm in arm past Madison Square Park. "I'm glad we decided to stay local this year. The past three were exhausting," she said with a bit of an ironic chuckle.

"I'm glad we are here, as well. And I am happy Mama and Aunt Lucia are here, too."

"With their boyfriends," Frankie replied with a devilish grin.

"*Si.* I don't remember the last time I saw Mama this happy.

She is with her whole family, and with a genuinely nice man in her life."

He continued, "Also, Aunt Lucia? *Madonna mia*! What you and Nina did was like a miracle. First, you make her look beautiful. Ten years younger. Then you encouraged her to have fun at a party. She never went to parties."

"No wonder she was so unhappy. We need people."

"It's a funny—well, not so funny—thing, but widows are expected to suffer for the rest of their lives." He hesitated, then snickered, "As if they weren't suffering enough when their husbands were alive!"

Frankie hooted, "Giovanni! I can't believe you said that about your father!"

"You know what I mean. Sometimes men can be very demanding. Difficile."

"How did you manage to escape the DNA?" Frankie said, and tugged on his arm.

"You see, I met a woman who was incredibly special. I knew if I did not behave myself, she would fly away."

"Oh?" Frankie asked wryly. "Anyone I know?"

"*Probabilmente*. But maybe not."

She lifted her leg behind her and gently kicked him in the butt.

"And she has very long legs."

They were the first to arrive at the restaurant. The maître d' brought them to a round table on the rear platform, two steps up from the main floor, and behind the baby grand piano. They could view the historic dining room from that vantage point.

Keens opened in 1885 and was part of the historic Hearld Square Theatre District. At the time, it was a gentleman's only club. It wasn't until Lillie Langtry, paramour of King Edward of England, sued the club in 1905 and won access to the once male-only establishment, that women were allowed inside.

Giovanni continued to share additional history of the restaurant. A churchwarden "pipe membership" dated back to the early 20th century, where patrons would leave their pipes with a warden until they returned. The tradition started during the Elizabethan era. Due to the fragility of the pipe's stem, travelers kept their clay at a favorite inn when they traveled. Keens's roster of their Pipe Club membership included such luminaries as Albert Einstein, Teddy Roosevelt, Babe Ruth, Will Rogers, and Buffalo Bill, to name a few. Giovanni nodded in the direction of the pipes on display.

"You are a fountain of information, Signor Lombardi," Frankie said in awe.

"I like New York history. I like restaurants. But pipes? Not so much," he replied.

Frankie spotted the Lombardi family entering the dining room. Everyone was wearing smiles from ear to ear. The two stood and welcomed the rest of the dinner guests with two-cheek kisses and lots of greetings and gabbing.

Once everyone was settled, the wine Giovanni had ordered earlier had aerated, and the waiter poured everyone a glass. Again, cheers in English and Italian went around the table.

Giovanni started the conversation. "How was Macy's?" He decided to wait until everyone had a little of the vino in their veins before he asked about the show.

Lucia was enthralled with the decorations. "So many trees, and lights, and wreaths! I didn't know where-a to look first! It's a wonderland."

Frankie was grinning from ear to ear. At least the interlude at the theatre hadn't ruined their day.

"*Magnifica!*" Rosevita echoed her sister-in-law's assessment.

"*Brava!*" one of the Parisi brothers offered.

Giovanni couldn't contain his curiosity any longer. "How was the show?"

Frankie thought she might spit out the hundred-dollar-a-bottle chianti. She grabbed Giovanni's thigh in a death grip. He tried to mask a wince.

Elio began, "It was for sure spectacular! And funny, too!"

"Oh, they had a comedian?" Frankie asked innocently.

"No! No!" Anthony chimed in with a big smile. "There was a race."

"A race?" Giovanni feigned ignorance.

"*Si*! Two men dressed like Santa ran behind the dancers!" Lucia said.

"And six women chased them! One had-a white-a rhinestone-a cowboy boots!" Rosevita said, and giggled. "It was-a so funny!"

Elio looked over at Frankie, whose face was slowly turning red. "One-a look-a like-a you, Frankie!" he said gleefully. "And another one look-a like your friend, Nina. With the curly hair!" he continued to laugh.

Frankie tightened her grip on Giovanni's leg. "Really? Now *that* is funny!"

Pinewood

Vinny and Jimmy were in mental limbo-land. Neither could figure out what was happening or where it was happening. All they knew was they had hightailed it through the Radio City Rockettes' high kicks and were "escorted" into a limo. The rest was a haze, including the current moment. At least the duct tape was off their mouths as well as the zip ties off their extremities. Vinny looked around the six-by-six concrete cell. He heard whimpering echoing off the slab walls.

"Jimmy? Z'at you?" Vinny asked with a croaky voice.

First a sniffle, then a response. "Yeah. That you, Vin?"

"No, it's Marie Antionette," Vinny said, and huffed. "Who do you think it is?"

"Where are we?" Jimmy asked meekly.

"How should I know. We traveled together."

Vinny could hear Jimmy rustling and approached the steel rods. "You okay?"

Jimmy stuck his fingers through the bars. "Can you see me?"

"Just your fingers," Vinny said. "At least they're still attached."

"Yeah, but for how long do you suppose?"

"I have no idea. Like I said, we were traveling companions, and I don't know who booked this trip."

"What did you make of those Brits?" Jimmy asked.

"They had nice clothes."

"The bald one reminded me of Captain Picard. You know the guy from *Star Trek*?"

"You mean Patrick Stewart?" Vinny asked.

"Yeah. That's the one. And the other guy looked a little like the dude from the movie about the King who had a speaking problem."

"The King's Speech?" Vinny replied, and shook his head. He loved his friend, but sometimes he wondered how Jimmy had lived this long without getting hit by a bus.

"Yeah. Yeah. That's the one. This guy isn't as good looking, though."

"You better keep your voice down. We don't know who is watching or listening."

No truer words were spoken, as Fergus and Charles listened to their conversation. Charles burst out laughing. "Not as good looking! That's brilliant!"

"Well, Captain Picard, beam me up," Fergus said in return.

"At least we're being compared to movie stars," Charles said with a chuckle. "I suppose we should bring them something to eat and drink."

"Right. I'll grab the tree." Fergus went outside and then to a shed where Myra kept a bounty of holiday decorations. Every room in the house had to have at least one Christmas tree. He fetched the smallest one and brought it through the kitchen and down the stone steps. Charles followed with a tray of sandwiches and thermoses of water.

Vinny and Jimmy began to shake when they heard footsteps heading in their direction. They both thought it was going to be curtains for them.

"Good evening, gentlemen," Charles said in his deep baritone voice.

"Huh . . . huh . . . hello?" Vinny and Jimmy answered simultaneously.

"You are going to be our guests for the next few days," Charles said, as he slid one of the plates under the small opening at the bottom of the gate.

"Where are we?" Jimmy asked.

"Our version of The Grey-Bar Hotel," Fergus answered.

"Who are you guys?" Vinny asked, as politely as he could muster.

"Friends of Lady Justice," Charles answered.

"Who?" Jimmy asked.

"Lady Justice, Jimmy. You know, the statue of the woman with the blindfold and the scales."

"Oh, is that her name?"

Again, Vinny wondered why his friend didn't have tire tracks along his back.

Charles proceeded to explain the rules. "You shall be fed three times per day. You will have the opportunity to use the loo three times per day. You will have access to a shower every other day. And of course, you shall be escorted to the facilities one at a time. I strongly suggest neither of you try to make a break for it. I can assure you, you will not make it to the stairs."

"What if I have to pee before we can go?" Jimmy asked, because he was in that very situation.

"We'll provide a receptacle, which you will clean yourselves." Fergus said.

Vinny took in an exceptionally long breath and exhaled.
"What about my mother? She is going to worry."

"We've got that sorted. She thinks you and your pal were
comped for a hotel in Atlantic City."

"But what about Christmas?" Vinny asked. He was fairly
sure it was still a couple days away.

"Christmas?" Charles asked. He turned to Fergus, but did
not address him by name. "Do you know about Christmas?"

"I do, indeed." Fergus set the three-foot-high, pre-lit tree a
few feet from the cells. "We're not barbarians, after all."

"Can someone take me to the bathroom?" Jimmy was
whining at this point.

Charles looked at Fergus. "Right. We're not barbarians."
He pulled out a huge ring containing over a dozen keys of
various colors, shapes, and sizes. "I will remind you, do not
attempt to do anything foolish."

Charles unlocked his cell and motioned for Jimmy to walk
forward. "Turn right. First door on the right."

Jimmy followed the directions and came upon a rudimentary toilet area with a bowl, a sink, and a shower pan. He
also noticed there was no door between the plumbing and
the hallway. Not that he was modest. It clearly affirmed that
this was a serious situation.

"Don't forget to wash your hands," Charles called out,
and chuckled to himself. He was actually enjoying this fly-in-
the spiderweb situation. Myra would be proud. The purpose
wasn't to torture them, but to teach them a lesson, and serve
as a reminder to never do it again. It was relatively light weight
for the Sisterhood. But it was the holidays, and the penalty
was commensurate with the crime.

New York

Annie and Myra were back at Annie's townhouse. They turned on the television to watch the evening news when they heard the announcer say:

> *According to police, there are no suspects at this time in the raucous disorderly event that took place this afternoon at Radio City Music Hall. A few audience members were able to capture this episode on their phone's video app, and one dancer mentioned a woman wearing white rhinestone cowgirl boots; however, no one had been identified.*

Annie looked down at her prized footwear. "I hope I don't have to ditch these babies."

"Just keep them on the down-low until this blows over," Myra said. "We still have a couple of things to accomplish."

"You're right. Speaking of which, I shall call my contact, who will reach out to Bushwhacker."

"You mean Buchwald Barflow?"

"Close enough!" Annie hooted. She pulled her phone from her purse and pressed one of her speed dial buttons. "Hey, Desie. Annie here. How are you doing?"

"Annie! I'm great. And you?" the woman replied.

"All good here. Listen, I need you to get me hooked up with Buchwald Barflow."

"Really? That creep?" Desie asked.

"Yeah."

"He's a menace. He and his gang are ruining the neighborhood," Desie said with despair.

"So, I've heard," Annie agreed.

"Can you get rid of him? Please?" Desie asked, half-joking.

"That's the plan."

"Oh goodie! How can I help?" Desie asked. She and Annie

went way back to one of the first Sisters missions. Desie owned a bottega, and her finger was on the pulse of the borough for many years. Unfortunately, she had no clout, but people went to her if they needed information. She was considered the "directory assistant" in town.

"I want to fence some of my diamonds."

"Really?" Desie was shocked at the thought of this rich and powerful woman having to hock her jewels.

"Not really. Just paste. But good paste. Paste that only a serious expert could recognize. A jeweler's piece isn't going to do it. At least not by Buchwald standards."

"Sounds intriguing," Desie responded.

"I want to set up a meeting with him so I can show him one of the diamonds. Whet his appetite."

"Okay. What do you want me to do?"

"Get word to him that the countess wants to meet. Tell him I have over a hundred-fifty-thousand dollars' worth of diamonds that I want to get rid of, and I'm going to offer him a thirty percent commission, five percent higher than the street. It has to be discreet. Not the pizzeria. Maybe a coffee shop. Once he takes the bait, I'll arrange for a drop."

"You got it!" Desie said with enthusiasm. "I'll get back to you ASAP."

The wheels were in motion. Annie was sure Buchwald would agree. How could he turn down an opportunity to make thirty grand in a day? Annie planned to tell him to meet her in the hangar where she kept her plane. Alone. "I don't want anyone to know anything about this," she would explain. The only thing he was allowed to bring with him was the cash. Once he arrived and everyone was certain he's alone, Annie would offer him a cocktail to toast their deal. Within seconds, he'd be lying on the tarmac and shipped back to Belarus, never to return to the States, or possibly anywhere, for that matter.

Annie turned to Myra. "Now we wait."

"Excellent. Let's check in with Charles and Fergus and see how our houseguests are doing."

Frankie hadn't had a chance to talk with Nina since their afternoon adventure, but the text messages had been flying back and forth since the earlier edition of the local news. Frankie promised she would call Nina as soon as she got back to her apartment after their dinner at Keens.

The eleven o'clock news was on at Annie's townhouse, Frankie's apartment, and Nina's parents' place, where Nina was living. It hadn't hit the national media yet, but by morning it would certainly be one of the leading stories on the talk shows. Frankie and Nina were on the phone watching it virtually together. Annie and Myra were glued to the big screen TV in Annie's townhouse. The commentator began with grainy video footage in the background:

This afternoon, a group of wild Santas dashed across the stage and disrupted the famous Radio City Rockettes routine. Six women wearing Santa caps were in hot pursuit of two men dressed as Santa. The incident lasted only a few minutes but was captured in part by some members of the audience. Randy Wheeler, one of the performers, was interviewed.

"They ran in and grabbed a bunch of hats that were sitting in a box backstage. They practically knocked me over."

Apparently, the unknown intruders have not been identified, although one witness said she saw a pair of white rhinestone cowboy boots flash by. Police are asking if anyone has any information, they should contact the police hotline number seven-seven-seven.

Frankie's phone began to blow up. First it was Randy, claiming he was not an accomplice, and he did not give them up to the police. Then Rachael, who had gotten the news from Randy in the aftermath. Myra and Annie were also fielding calls from Maggie and Kathryn, who'd caught it on their news feed. Finally, Annie put everyone on a conference call, including Frankie and Nina.

"Do you think they'll figure out who it was?" Maggie asked.

"Who is going to tell?" Annie asked.

"Randy had his two minutes of fame and didn't rat us out," Nina said.

"I think we're good, but I also think Annie is going to have to retire those boots. At least for a while," Myra reiterated her earlier comment.

Annie looked at her favorite bedazzled boots. "Sorry guys. Time to pack you up until the season is over."

There was a few more minutes of chatter and Maggie asked, "Annie, do you want me to run a story about today's holiday shenanigans?"

Myra jumped in, "Call it 'Santa's Holiday Spectacular!' "

"Great turn of a phrase," Annie added. "And be sure you throw the light away from us."

"But I report facts," Maggie said proudly.

"Then keep them vague and simple," Myra suggested.

"Roger that," Maggie said gleefully. "No suspects have been named."

"You got it!" Annie bellowed. Everyone laughed and applauded. "Okay, pals. Time we all got some rest. Sweet dreams, everyone!"

Once the call was over, Myra checked in with Charles. "How are our guests?"

"Hunky-dory. We fed them and gave them an opportunity to relieve themselves. I almost feel sorry for them. Almost. I think one day in our version of the pokey was enough. By the time we get them back, they'll be altar boys."

Myra whooped and said, "I seriously doubt that, but I do believe they will leave their life of petty thievery behind."

"We'll tell them we'll be watching." Charles chuckled. "Have you and Annie figured out part two of this caper?"

"Annie has a brilliant idea, but she has to check with someone first."

"Do tell," Charles coaxed her.

"No can do, darling." She looked over at Annie. who mouthed the word *tomorrow*. "But I can bring you up to speed in the morning. How does that sound?"

"Splendid. Meanwhile, I'll go tuck the boys in."

Myra laughed out loud. "Do give them a fresh pair of pajamas. We don't want them to think we're terrible hosts."

"Will do. Fergus has some clean jumpsuits for them," Charles said. "And one of Pearl's people will be here in the morning to take over our shift."

"Perfect. Sleep well, dear."

"You too, love. I am sure you can use some rest after today."

"Yes, but I have to admit, it was rather fun!"

Giovanni watched the expressions on Frankie's face. She was giddy. It made him smile. He absolutely loved this unpredictable woman. When she got off the phone, he swooped her up in his arms and planted a passionate kiss on her lips.

Chapter 17

New York City

The night of the gala at the Hilton had finally arrived. The large ballroom was festooned with holiday decorations, and mountains of toys were piled next to the twelve-foot tree. A big band was playing holiday favorites including "Santa Claus Is Comin' to Town." Myra and Annie burst out laughing. "Let's hope not," Annie said cheerfully.

"Only the *real* Santa," Myra suggested.

The two couples looked like movie stars, with Fergus and Charles decked out in Emporio Armani tuxedos. Annie was wearing a bronze, portrait-collar, faux wrap dress with three-quarter sleeves and a sweeping high-low hem. Myra donned a floral-embroidered, beaded trumpet gown in a smoky gray.

They were seated at the same table as Camille and her husband and son. Camille was dumbstruck when she saw the abundance of toys and socks. "How did you manage all this?"

Annie and Myra looked at each other and shrugged. "All in a day's work," Myra replied coyly.

When the group of children arrived, the expressions on their faces brought Myra and Annie to tears. It was truly a joyous occasion, considering the events the days before. Once again, the Sisters pulled off an amazing coup. There were just a few loose ends that needed tending to, but that would come soon enough.

The Following Day

Giovanni decided to let Frankie sleep in that morning. He fed the cats and did the chores, showered, and got ready for work. As he was about to leave, his phone rang. It was his mother.

"Mama! Everything alright?" he asked with a tinge of concern.

"*Si*, but no."

"What's the problem?"

"Anita," Rosevita said with a slight edge to her voice.

"Is she alright?" Giovanni pressed on.

"Yes, but there is a small problem." Rosevita remained calm, spoke slowly, and in her best English. That was a rule the family had. *In America, speak like Americans,* unless you didn't want the grandchildren to know what you were talking about. "Anita's women's group was to make cakes for the church bake sale, but everyone has the flu. Anita cannot do it by herself."

"What can I do to help? I have to be at the restaurant by ten."

"Can you ask Frankie to call her friends to help?"

"Of course I can ask, but let me call you back in a few minutes."

He gently tapped Frankie's shoulder. She bounced with a start.

"Everything alright? What time is it? Geez, I was out like a light," all came tumbling out of her mouth.

"Everything is okay, but Mama and Anita need help to bake something for the church. The other women got sick, and they need cakes for tomorrow."

Frankie sat up straight. "Okay. Hand me my phone, and I'll call Nina and Rachael. What time and where should we meet?"

Giovanni called his mother. "Mama? What do you need and when?" He nodded as she explained; then he responded, "Okay. I will call the restaurant supply company and order the panettone pans and the paper. Frankie can pick them up on her way to Anita's house. In an hour?" Giovanni looked at Frankie with wide eyes. She nodded. "Okay, Mama. Frankie is on it. *Ciao!*"

"What's going on?"

Giovanni explained the situation, and Frankie immediately phoned Nina and Rachael. "Hey, kids, we have an SOS from Rosevita and Anita. They need help with some baking ASAP. From what I gleaned from Giovanni's conversation with her, we will be baking panettones, but we've got to get to Anita's in an hour. You in?"

Nina and Rachael were always available when Frankie needed them. It was true of all of them. "Great! I'll text you the address and meet you there." She quickly pulled up Anita and Marco's contact info and sent it off to Rachael and Nina.

Frankie scrambled out of bed and into the shower. Giovanni had a double cappuccino and a croissant waiting for her when she stepped out of the bathroom. "You are the best!" She kissed him on the cheek.

"No. *You* are the best!"

"Okay. I won't argue with you." Frankie smiled and took a swig of her coffee.

Giovanni wrote down the address of the restaurant supply company. "I already spoke to them while you were in the shower. Everything will be ready when you get there."

"Excellent," Frankie said, and then stopped. "Is it my imagination, or do we have a food emergency every year?"

Giovanni laughed out loud. "You are very observant, *cara mia*!"

She snatched the paper out of his hand, gave him a kiss, and hurried to the lot where Giovanni kept his car. Fortunately, traffic was light in her neighborhood, and she navigated her way to the Lincoln Tunnel with ease. She hoped the rest of the day would run as smoothly.

When she arrived at the supply house, the order was sitting on the counter with her name on it. One of the employees helped carry the box to her car. So far, things were moving along. She arrived at Anita's twenty minutes later as Rachael and Nina were pulling in.

Lots of hugs, then questions, erupted as they helped Frankie unpack. Frankie shared what little information she had and assured them they would be brought up to speed as soon as they got into the house.

The kitchen counter was piled high with ingredients.

"Wow! How many of these things are we making?" Nina asked.

"We need fifteen," Anita said. "I cannot thank you enough for helping."

"Don't thank us yet," Rachael quipped. "This is my first Panettone Rodeo."

It occurred to Frankie that there wasn't time to soak the raisins. They required a couple of days. "What about the raisins?"

Rosevita had a sly smile on her face, then pointed to three jars sitting next to the sink. "I bring. Raisins and cherries."

"How did you get it through customs?" Frankie asked with her mouth agape. She wasn't sure what was more surprising: the raisins, or the idea Rosevita was a smuggler.

"I wrap them in toy boxes," Rosevita said, and grinned.

"Oh, you are one sharp cookie!" Nina said with admiration.

"No cookies. Panettone!" Rosevita responded.

Rachael was next with a question. "How are we going to bake fifteen in two ovens?"

"The dough has to rise two times. The second time is for one hour. That's when you each take three to your houses and bake there. When they are finished, you bring them back here. Four ovens, three panettone each. No problem," Rosevita explained. "We bake the other three here."

Frankie had to admit it was a good plan. Rachael and Nina lived about twenty minutes away, and Frankie's parents' house was twenty-five. "Oh, I better call my mom and tell her I am commandeering her oven!" she said excitedly.

Fortunately, Anita and Marco had a large U-shaped chef's kitchen with lots of counter space, a center island, and two ovens.

Rosevita and Lucia had already created a working area for everyone, with all the ingredients pre-measured and prepped. Everyone was handed an apron and stood in front of their station. Rosevita and Lucia began to give them a cooking class for the traditional panettone. For years, Rosevita had kept her secret recipe a secret, until she finally succumbed to Giovanni and Marco's nagging and passed it along the year before.

Having everything pre-measured made quick work of the long process. The holiday music of Michael Bublé, Harry Connick, Jr., Frank Sinatra, and Nat King Cole kept the line moving, with Rachael teaching Rosevita and Lucia a few side wiggles.

Once each batch of dough had been kneaded for the umpteenth time, they covered it to let it rise for two hours. In the meantime, the women cleaned up the kitchen, getting it ready for the next step—when the cherries and raisins are kneaded into the dough, and the dough is set in the pans.

SANTA'S HOLIDAY SPECTACULAR   243

While the dough was rising, the women went to the local pub to grab some lunch and relax until the second phase of this enormous project was at hand. During lunch, Rachael was compelled to ask: "Why so many panettones? Wouldn't a normal coffee cake be easier?"

Rosevita's head snapped to attention. "What, and not give Anita a chance to show off her heritage?"

Rachael wasn't sure if she'd insulted the woman. "No, that's not what I'm saying," she said defensively.

"I'm kidding." Rosevita placed her hand on Rachael's. "I figure if we have many hands to help, why not?"

Anita added, "Plus, we make the most money on panettone because of how laborious it is. Last year I made three, and they sold out the first ten minutes at twenty-five dollars each! The other women were going to make pies and cakes."

"Are fifteen going to be enough?" Nina asked.

"Marco called a friend in the bakery business who is donating cakes, cupcakes, and scones."

"But our panettone will be the best!" Lucia kissed her fingertips.

The women made a bit of a raucous scene as they clapped and cheered, but no one seemed to mind.

By the time they finished lunch and got back to the house, only half an hour remained in the rising of the dough. Anita clicked on the television to check the weather, and the same story about the disruption at Radio City was on again. Nina and Frankie shot each other a glance. Rachael stifled a giggle. For once she wasn't part of the skirmish, nor did she start it.

Rosevita and Lucia laughed again when they saw the footage. "I thought it was part of the show," Lucia admitted. "You know. Do something funny."

"I think they may have done things like that during the vaudeville era, a hundred years ago," Rachael added. She couldn't help but give Nina a light elbow in her side.

"I don't know why they keep running that piece," Frankie said plainly. "It's not as if it adds to the holiday celebration."

"True. But it is still very funny," Rosevita agreed with her sister-in-law. "Maybe not so funny on the television, but funny in person."

Nina and Frankie rolled their eyes, hoping something else would give the networks something else to talk about.

Rosevita doled out the drunken fruit, and the women added it to the dough. Once everything had been mixed together, each headed out to their respective ovens. When they finished baking and cooled down, the bread-like cake would be wrapped in holiday paper with a ribbon and a tag that announced:

LOMBARDI'S HOMEMADE PANETTONE
ORIGINAL "SECRET" RECIPE FROM ITALY

Hours later, the completed packages were lined up along the counter.

"*Bellissima!*" Lucia and Rosevita said in unison, then added in English, "Beautiful!"

"*Molto bene!*" Anita said with delight.

"*Brava!*" Rachael clapped her hands and did a little jig.

"We need to have a little toast!" Rosevita said.

"Toast?" Lucia balked. "We need a little champagne!"

Everyone burst out laughing. Rachael helped Anita with the champagne glasses, while Frankie popped a cork and poured.

"Mission accomplished, ladies!" Frankie cheered.

Greenwich Village

On the other side of the Hudson River, Annie sat with her back to the wall at a table in the rear of a coffee shop. From her vantage point, she could see patrons entering and exiting and who was loitering outside. A large, burly figure with tattoos and piercings swung open the door. Annie presumed it was Mr. Barflow. She looked up and nodded to him. His sour-looking face turned a bit cheerier as he approached the table.

"Mr. Barflow?" Annie said, more as a statement than a question.

"Countess De Silva?" he asked politely.

"Yes. Please. Sit." She motioned to the chair in front of her. She knew he wouldn't be comfortable with his back to the door. No good criminal is. "I'll be brief."

He leaned forward with his forearms on the table. "Let's have it."

"As I mentioned, I am in need of some quick cash." She reached into her purse and produced a velvet pouch. She glanced around the room to see if there were any prying eyes, then slid the pouch across the table. "This is a sample of what I am willing to part with. Here's a photo of the rest of it."

Barflow quickly scanned his surroundings and positioned himself so any view of their interaction was obscured. He reached into his pocket and produced a jeweler's eyepiece. Annie opened the pouch and placed the diamond ring on top of it. "Please take a good look."

Bucky did another quick look around, placed the eyepiece against his eye, and leaned closer to the diamond. "She's a beauty alright." He sat up quickly. "How soon do you want the money?"

"As soon as tomorrow. That is, if you can arrange it." Annie said it in a way that she knew would challenge him.

"You said one-fifty, and I get thirty percent?"

"That's the deal. But it has to be done tomorrow. Can you handle it?"

"Sure. No problem. Just tell me where and when." Bucky sat back and folded his arms.

"Tomorrow evening at six? My Gulfstream is at Teterboro." She slid a piece of paper with the hangar number over to him. "And you will come alone."

She placed the diamond back in the pouch and tucked it into her purse. "So do we have a deal, Mr. Barflow?"

He held out his hand. "We do, indeed. I don't need no escort."

Annie cringed at the idea of shaking this despicable creature's mitt, but it was all part of the game. She slowly got up from her chair. "See you tomorrow."

Annie confidently moved past the other patrons and handed the waitress a twenty-dollar bill. "Keep it."

Bucky couldn't help but notice a stretch limo was waiting for her outside. A man wearing a chauffeur's cap opened the door for her. Annie wasn't the flashy type, but under certain circumstances, she had to play her role to the fullest.

Annie got into the car, where Myra was waiting for her. "Tomorrow at six." Myra gave her a high five.

Chapter 18

Monday

Frankie could barely open her eyes when her alarm went off. It had been a whirlwind couple of days, and as she promised herself, she took the next two days off from work.

Frankie and her gang managed to make fifteen panettones for Anita's church bake sale, and they were a big success. People were willing to pay more to pry the secret out of Rosevita and Lucia, who stayed to help with the sale. The two women pretended they didn't understand English. Every time someone would ask, they would shrug and say *"Scusa, non parlo inglese."* It was all they could do to keep from laughing. By the end of the day, Anita's table raked in over eight hundred dollars, counting the sale of the pastries that had been donated. The entire bake sale collected over fifteen hundred dollars to pay for dinners for members of the congregation who couldn't afford a holiday dinner, or who were alone.

It didn't take too much coaxing for Frankie to convince

Mateo to bring his crew in to do the cooking, and she offered to volunteer to help serve.

Amy and Peter were due to arrive soon, and when Amy heard she missed the bake-off, she offered to help Frankie with the church dinner. Not to be left out, Rachael jumped at the idea, and Nina said it was a "no brainer" and they could count on her, as well.

The Christmas Day church dinner was scheduled for one o'clock, which did not interfere with the Lombardi plans. The Lombardis normally served their Christmas feast at three. It would be tight, but Frankie and her gal pals were used to doing things on the fly.

With two days left before the holiday, Frankie was busy putting the finishing touches on the memory book. She had to admit, it was quite fabulous. When she showed Giovanni the final product, it brought tears to his eyes.

"You are gonna make Mama cry." He paused. "But a good cry."

"I bought Lucia a pair of cashmere gloves and a scarf. I know it's not very personal, so I had one of the photos of your cousins cropped, retouched, and framed." She showed him the photo. "Do you think Lucia will like it?"

"It looks beautiful. I remember that day, too. I think we were maybe eight or nine, and Dominic dropped a bowl of meatballs on the patio. His shirt was covered in tomato sauce." Giovanni chuckled. "It looked like a crime scene. Good thing Mama took the picture before he made the mess."

"Originally I thought of doing one of her and your aunt and uncle's wedding, but with her and Anthony getting cozy, well, I wasn't sure he would want to see it every time he went to the house."

"You are so smart, Francesca Cappella. I think she will love this."

"And the thousand-dollar gift card to Saks!" Frankie added.

"She is going to have a lot of fun with it, I am sure," Giovanni replied. "And she will have time between Christmas and New Year's Eve to shop for the big night."

"Have you told them yet?" It had occurred to Frankie that no one actually asked them if they had made plans for the weekend.

"Not exactly. I made a little fib. I told them we were going to have a house party."

"Like the one we didn't have last year?" Frankie laughed out loud.

"Exactly," Giovanni said, smiling. "We can give them the reservations and tickets on Christmas Eve."

"Good idea. Everyone will be there, including Amy, Peter, Nina, Richard, my parents, your family, and Rachael."

"Do you know who she is dating this week?" he asked with a gleam in his eye.

"I think it's Robert, actually."

"Really? Rachael and a lawyer," he said thoughtfully. "What happened to the nurse from the retirement place?"

"She decided he was a little too young. Cute, but young. He liked to go out on the weekends, which would be fine, but he also liked to stay out until the bars closed. He told her it helped him let off steam from the pressure of work."

"I understand that. Me? I want to relax."

"Exactly. Rachael really puts a lot of time into dancing all week. One night of fun is okay, but not until three in the morning." Frankie stopped. "Does this mean we're getting old?" She frowned.

"No, *cara*. It means we are mature. Reasonable," he said kindly.

"That's not what you thought the other day when we were watching the news," Frankie said with a grin.

"True. But that is something you do not do every day," he said, and gave her a sideways glance. "Is it?"

"Not that I can recall," Frankie said, and wiggled her eyebrows.

The Game Is Afoot

As the sun was going down on the shortest day of the year, Myra, Charles, Fergus, and Annie arrived at the airport. Everything was in place, including the flight plan to Belarus, with only one passenger.

Charles was wearing a captain's uniform, and Fergus was in copilot garb. Myra was dressed in a flight attendant suit. Once Barflow was neutralized, the scheduled captain would take over with the proper crew, including someone from Pearl's organization, who would assure Bucky arrived at a designated location.

Annie stood at the top of the short stairs that led to the aircraft. She was regal and glamorous in a long, white, faux fur coat, with a matching headband. Even though it was evening, she'd donned a pair of Christian Dior sunglass for a bit of drama. She looked as "Hollywood" and as enigmatic as Elizabeth Taylor in the early 1960s. She casually leaned against the frame of the jet's door.

A black SUV pulled near the door of the hangar. A bald, bull-looking guy wearing a hoop earring in one ear and a ring in his nose climbed out. A security guard ran a wand over his body, making sure Barflow wasn't packing a gun, or any other type of weapon. After the guard finished with the metal detector, he also patted Bucky down, assuring there wasn't anything caustic or dangerous in his possession. Once he was satisfied, he nodded to Annie.

Annie raised her Dior shades, crooked her forefinger, and summoned him to join her. If Bucky could smile any wider, his lips would be around his ears.

"Good evening. You look lovely," he said, in a surprisingly gentle voice.

"Thank you." She turned and moved to the lounge area, while Fergus and Charles were listening to the exchange in the cockpit.

Bucky let out a low whistle. "This your rig?"

"Rig?" Annie said with a tinge of irritation.

"Sorry. I meant no offense." Bucky reverted to acquiescence at that point. He didn't want to blow this deal.

"Champagne?" Annie offered.

"Wow. You know how to do things right," he said effusively.

Annie did not respond to his comment, making sure she was in complete control. Even with all the planning, one could never be sure of the outcome until it came.

Without any prompting, Myra entered the cabin with a tray, a bottle of Dom Pérignon, and two champagne glasses, which were half-full. Each crystal flute was etched with a different pattern. The one with the *A* was for Annie.

"I believe one should always do the transaction before the celebration," she said calmly, allowing the Rohypnol, also known as "roofies," to dissolve in his glass.

"Sure thing." He pulled an envelope from his jacket. "It's all there."

"I have no doubt, but if you don't mind. . . ." She opened the envelope and proceeded to count the money on the top of a light box, to assure there were no counterfeit bills. "You took your cut, I see," she said easily.

"Yes, but I have it on me," he said apologetically.

"Not necessary." She nodded for Myra to top off their glasses as she opened the pouch with the fake jewels.

"Them is some beauties," he said, and stared at the bright, shiny gems.

Annie folded them back into their velvet wrapping and slid them across the table between them. "Now we can toast."

"Down the hatch." Bucky threw back the champagne as if it were a shot of cheap booze. Crude, but even better. The drug would go to work much faster. Myra gladly refilled his glass.

After a few minutes of small talk, Bucky's speech began to

slur, and his eyes got wider. His head began to wobble. "I don't feel. . . ." He never finished his sentence.

Myra quickly placed the evidence in her bag, while Charles and Fergus removed Bucky's commission from his pocket. Annie had the full one hundred and fifty dollars and her fake jewels.

As they were maneuvering Bucky's unconscious body, Charles put Bucky's seat back. "We're not barbarians, now, are we?" he said, and chuckled. He and Fergus were enjoying their latest slogan.

In a few short minutes, Pearl arrived with her own flight crew. She gave everyone a hug. "We'll take it from here."

"Thanks, Pearl. You are the best," Annie said, as they de-planed and got into the town car that was waiting.

"What is going to happen to his SUV?" Myra asked.

"The authorities will assume he fled the country and left it here," Charles replied.

As they began to drive past the hangar, Annie said, "I have an idea. Tell me what you think." She proceeded to describe her intention for the money. "We know Vinny took a sixty-thousand-dollar loan against his mother's house, unbeknownst to her. How do you feel if we use some of the money to repay it. I know it's Vinny's issue, but it shouldn't be his mother's problem. We just don't tell him." Annie paused as the others listened. "The rest of the money will go to rehabilitating the pizzeria and the rest of the block. I owe it to Desie to help get her neighborhood back."

"Sounds reasonable," Myra said. "But who will run the pizzeria?"

"Vinny. It will be his penance and get him on the straight and narrow. When we are ready to release him, we give him a list of rules he has to follow; otherwise, he goes back in the dungeon. We'll tell him we've got eyes on him, and one slip-up will cost him big time."

"I like the way you think, my friend," Myra said.

"Vinny will also begin to pay his mother rent, and repay the loan to an account we'll create, that looks like it's a commercial branch of the bank. We can work out those details after the holidays. Each month he'll make a deposit, and that money will be transferred to an animal shelter."

"Sounds brilliant," Charles said approvingly.

"This is why I keep her around," Fergus said with a big grin.

"But there's more," Annie continued. "He and Desie will work together to form a small business alliance in order to rebuild the neighborhood. There are government grants that are available."

"I can guide Desie on that front," Myra offered.

"Now that we have Vinny sorted, what about Jimmy?"

"Jimmy will continue to work for his uncle during the day and deliver pizza for Vinny at night. They'll both work on the apartments above the pizza shop, where Jimmy will take up residence."

"This is one of the best rehabilitation plans I've heard in a very long time," Myra said with enthusiasm. "Good on you, girlfriend."

"There is one more thing, however."

"What might that be?" Charles asked.

"It's a surprise." Annie winked.

"You can't leave us banging about," Charles said in protest.

"It will be worth the wait," Annie said slyly, and then nodded at Myra, who nodded in return. Once Annie got the green light, she shared her idea with Myra. It was going to be spectacular.

Chapter 19

Christmas Week
New York

Frankie walked briskly up Fifth Avenue. She was not scheduled to work, but she still had one more thing to do near Rockefeller Center. As she passed the holiday windows with the cool air brushing against her cheeks, she felt a sense of renewal. She couldn't quite put her finger on it. Perhaps it was all of the activity that put that extra bounce in her step.

She approached the famous Cartier building with its red awnings, red flags, and brilliant holiday lights. The building and the company had a long history. Cartier began in 1847 in Paris and was renowned as one of the finest in the jewelry design business. She couldn't think of anything finer for her beloved Giovanni. He deserved something exceptional. Frankie appreciated Giovanni's sense of style. He was elegant without being fussy. When he walked into a room, you noticed him. The best part was that he had no idea he had that kind of effect, and if he did, he never let on. He was humble and sincere.

The doorman greeted her and asked if she had an appointment. That was the one thing she found annoying. She told him she was picking up something she ordered, and the uniformed man allowed her to pass through. She supposed it was a deterrent to thievery. She approached the concierge, who escorted her to the counter, where the cuff links awaited her arrival. Each was a simple silver bar with two gold iconic screws at each end. They cost nearly a thousand dollars, but Giovanni was worth every penny; besides, she had been saving up for this Christmas season when she learned his family would be visiting. She tucked the precious package into her bag and continued to enjoy wandering past the festive windows.

As she passed the promenade, she noticed Carol ringing her bell in front of the kettle. She had the biggest smile on her face, chatting it up with passersby. Every so often, someone would recognize her as the "lady who got mugged by Santa" and would stop for a chin-wag. She always got a little extra from those folks. Frankie crossed the street and headed in Carol's direction. Carol spotted Frankie walking toward her and proclaimed, "My guardian angel!" The two women hugged and spoke for a few minutes.

"After that day, when you forced me to go to church, well, I have to tell ya, things have been right as rain. My son is back from doing two years overseas and will be in the States again. My sister got a clean bill of health after her chemo, and I sold my house for way over the asking price. I'm planning on moving to a quieter place where I can be near my son and his three children." She stopped for air. "And it's all because of you!"

Frankie blushed. "Hardly. It's all because of the good faith we sent out to the universe. It does come back. Sometimes not as fast as we may like, but with patience, we're rewarded."

"How did you get so smart?" Carol looked up at Frankie's beautiful eyes.

"Smart? More like having faith and hope," Frankie responded. "But being smart can surely help get you out of a jam or two!" she said, chuckling. "I hope you have a wonderful holiday, and I wish you all the best with the next chapter of your life." Frankie gave her a big bear hug and dropped a fifty-dollar bill into the kettle.

By the time she got back to her apartment, it was time to get ready for the Andrea Bocelli concert. This time it was Giovanni's treat for his mother, aunt, and their companions. He was relieved that Frankie would be seated next to him instead of running across the stage.

Rosevita and Lucia were teary-eyed through most of the concert. They were overwhelmed with the magnificent voice of the celebrated tenor, especially when he sang "Time to Say Goodbye (*Con te Partirò*)" in English and Italian, in a duet with his son. By the end of the song, they were bawling. It was glorious.

After the concert, Giovanni sent them back to New Jersey in a town car. He could hear the two women nattering loudly as the car pulled away.

"This may have been the highlight of their trip," Giovanni said, as he put his arm around Frankie.

"Better than my performance?" she said, chuckling.

Pinewood

Charles unloaded his sacks of goods he purchased from Eataly and the farmer's market. Myra looked at the spread of food, from cheeses to vegetables. "We do have brussels sprouts in Virginia, you know."

"I know, love. But it was much more exciting buying them at the farmer's market. And I was able to chat it up with the people who actually grow the food." Charles patted her on the fanny. "Are you going to help me or simply stare at this bounty?"

"Not before I have a piece of that wonderful cheese," Myra said and pointed to the taleggio cow's milk cheese.

"At your service, madame." Charles opened the pungent package. "And it's the perfect temperature." He began to cut a loaf of bread.

"And some of the robiola." Myra nodded at the soft cheese made from mixture of cow and sheep milk.

"Shall I fix us a charcuterie?" Charles offered.

"I thought you would never ask."

"We should probably invite Fergus and Annie. He will be very displeased if I don't."

"I'll phone them now."

"Besides, we have to feed our guests at some point this evening," Charles said, and pulled out a large wooden plank.

Myra opened the variety of olives and unwrapped one of the salamis. Within ten minutes of the invitation, Lady lifted her head, signaling that company was coming. Myra heard gravel being churned up as Annie whooshed the golf cart toward the kitchen door.

"Oh good, you're here," Charles said to Fergus, handing him an apron.

"I think the only reason you invited us was so I could help," Fergus said, and pretended to pout.

"You are too smart for me," Charles said with a twinkle in his eye.

Annie pulled out a chair and sat. "How are our guests doing?"

"They're fine. I believe they will miss the fine cuisine we have been offering."

"No. Really, Charles?" Annie asked.

"We're not barbarians!" Charles chortled. "Leftovers, dear."

"Speaking of guests, how many are we having for Christmas?" Charles asked.

Myra began to count. "Maggie, Kathryn, Yoko, Harry, Nikki, and Jack. Plus us, makes ten."

"Excellent."

"What's on the menu?" Annie asked as she grabbed a piece of cheese.

"We shall begin with a roasted squash soup; then a beet, goat cheese, and arugula salad. The main course will be a pork roast stuffed with spinach, apples, walnuts, garlic, and herbs. There will be extra stuffing as well as Hasselback potatoes, lemon pea salad, and green beans almondine."

"Is that all?" Annie teased.

"No. We shall also have corn bread and biscuits."

"Sounds yummy!" Annie said approvingly.

"Nikki, Maggie, and Kathryn are each bringing a dessert, and Yoko is bringing the centerpiece."

"Splendid," Fergus remarked.

"I spoke to Desie and informed her that she has less than a week to get the street in shape for a New Year's Eve block party," Annie said. "She was a bit dumbfounded, but I explained I contracted a cleanup service to take care of the sidewalks and power-wash the buildings. Once everything is dry, a crew is going to string lights overhead, back and forth from each side of the street. Five-feet stone-looking planters filled with winter foliage will be placed ten feet apart along each side of the street."

"Sounds wonderful!" Myra said. "Your ability to get things done in a flash never ceases to amaze me."

"Thank you. I do my best," she said, and gave a graceful nod, then snatched another piece of cheese from Myra's plate.

"Hold on there, your highness," Charles said, and shook his finger at Annie. "Your gentleman friend Fergus Duffy and

I shall present you with a platter fit for a countess," he said with authority.

"Get busy, you guys," Annie replied.

"Why don't we fix something for our guests while they're working on our snack," Myra suggested.

"There's some roast beef in the fridge, cheddar cheese, lettuce, and tomato. The bread is in the pantry."

Annie and Myra began to assemble the sandwiches for Jimmy and Vinny, who were resigned to their situation. Fergus paused from cutting thin slices of prosciutto. He reached into the fridge and took a jar of gravy from the shelf and spooned some on the meat. "Hot roast beef sandwiches are much more delicious."

"They've been very appreciative of our hospitality," Charles said over his shoulder.

"I think they're appreciative that we haven't maimed or tortured them," Fergus said, and chuckled.

"Have they asked questions? Any conversation?" Myra queried.

"Just 'what day is it?' I think they're too afraid to ask anything else."

"When are you going to deliver their fate?" Myra asked.

"The blitz for the block starts tomorrow. I'll tell them in a few days. We still have to get them back to New York before New Year's Eve," Annie said.

"You're not inviting them to the block party, are you?" Fergus asked with a bit of an edge.

"Absolutely not. I have something else planned for them."

"You're still not going to spill the beans, eh?" Charles replied.

"I suppose I can trust the two of you with it." Annie turned to Myra. "What do you think?"

Myra played at looking the men up and down. "They look alright to me."

Myra and Annie brought the sandwiches and water down

to the basement. She snickered at the small Christmas tree. "Nice touch."

"Gentlemen," Myra announced, "we are serving hot roast beef sandwiches tonight."

"Thank you," Vinny said quietly. "You guys have been really nice to us. I gotta be honest. It's a little scary."

"Scary? Why?" Myra asked, and slid the tray through the small opening.

"We kinda think we know why we're here, but what about Bucky? What has he told you to do to us?" Jimmy was much more talkative. Maybe it was because he was in the presence of women, whom he believed would show more mercy. Good thing he didn't know anything about them; otherwise, he would faint.

"Bucky? Oh, you mean Buchwald Barflow?"

"Buchwald?" Jimmy said with surprise. "Is that his real name?"

"Yes, but he will no longer present himself as a nuisance," Myra put it mildly. "He seems to have left the country."

"No foolin'?" Jimmy asked enthusiastically.

Vinny finally spoke, "You said Bucky left the country?"

"Yes. For good," Annie replied.

"But what does that mean? I mean, for us?" Vinny asked.

"That is up for discussion at another time," Myra responded. "Meanwhile, enjoy your sandwiches." The two women turned and went back upstairs.

Vinny and Jimmy didn't know what to make of it. They had no idea where they were, or who these people were. More importantly, what were these people going to do to them?

Christmas Eve
Marco's House

As predicted, Rosevita and Lucia took over the kitchen, much to Anita's relief. Keeping the kids under control was challenging enough. They were normally well-behaved, but as with any other kid, the days leading up to Christmas were an exception.

A feast of seven fishes was mandatory. Rosevita and Lucia began preparing a few days before. After all these years, they were pros at it. Dinner for ten was a walk in the park.

Frankie helped with the tablescape. She set the table and lit the votive candles. Again, she showed her flare for creating a perfect atmosphere.

Frankie's parents arrived at six-thirty, carrying several wrapped gifts. The children's eyes widened when they saw the glittery packages. Bianca asked Anita if it would be alright for them to open the gifts after dinner so she and William could see the expression on their faces. Sophia was yearning for a ballet outfit, and Lorenzo asked for a Mario Brothers interactive Lego set.

Dinner was served at seven to allow time for everyone to enjoy the meal, have dessert, and then get ready for midnight mass.

With each course, moans of delight and groans of overeating were rampant around the table, which gave Rosevita and Lucia the utmost satisfaction. Classic Christmas music played in the background, and lively conversation filled the room. It was a wonderful gastronomic experience.

By nine-thirty, it was time for dessert, and Lorenzo and Sophia were allowed to open their gifts from Frankie's parents. They squealed with glee and effusively thanked Bianca and William.

With many hands and offers to help, the table was cleared, and the kitchen had no evidence that a feast had been prepared.

Giovanni hired a small van to take everyone to church except for the children, who were going to be supervised by their favorite babysitter. Anita hoped they would be pooped enough to fall asleep and stay asleep so she and Marco could put their presents under the tree when they returned. As the children had gotten older, hiding the gifts became more of a challenge. This year they put everything in the attic, which required access by a disappearing ladder, something the children could not maneuver.

Anita and Marco put the children to bed and wished the sitter good luck.

With some time to spare, the group relaxed in the living room. Frankie was anxious to give Rosevita the memory book, and they decided to exchange gifts before they left for church. Frankie was a little surprised that Giovanni asked if they could exchange their gifts privately, but she preferred that moment of intimacy and was happy for the suggestion.

It didn't take long for the beautifully wrapped gifts to quickly turn into piles of crumbled paper and ribbons and bows strewn about. Giovanni looked around and chuckled. "A paper explosion. I don't know who is worse, you or the children!"

People were gushing over their presents while trying to keep their enthusiasm at a low decibel level. The last thing they wanted was to keep the children from slumberland.

When most of the gifts had been opened, Frankie presented the book to Rosevita. For a moment, Rosevita had a perplexed expression on her face, until she noticed the dried flowers on the front and recalled the bouquet she carried when she got married to Giovanni's father. Frankie hoped it wouldn't make Elio uncomfortable, but everyone has a past. It's the present that counts. As the expression goes: *The gift is in the present.*

Rosevita's eyes welled up. She gingerly untied the cord and opened the book. With each turn of the page, she sniffled a little more. But it was all good. Frankie kept handing her tissues as Rosevita studied the entries, photos, tickets, and memorabilia.

Rosevita looked up at Frankie, who was also wiping away

a few tears. "This is the most beautiful gift you could give me. I cannot explain." The woman was truly overwhelmed, and filled with gratitude, so much so that words escaped her. She put the book aside, stood up, and gave Frankie the biggest hug she could muster. For Frankie, that hug was the best gift Rosevita could have given her in return.

Giovanni, too, was taken by the thoughtfulness of the gift, and his mother's reaction. He pulled out his handkerchief and wiped a tear from his eye, then handed it to Frankie.

Giovanni spotted the headlights of the van he'd hired pull into the driveway.

Hats, coats, new gloves, and scarves were donned, and everyone exited toward the van. As they began to climb into the vehicle, Frankie elbowed Giovanni, noting how Elio and Anthony graciously assisted Rosevita and Lucia. "Kinda sweet, don't ya think?" she whispered.

Midnight mass was a beautiful experience. Frankie began to sing from her pew. All eyes were on her while her melodious voice followed along with the choir, yet she continued as if no one was watching.

By the time they returned home, it was almost two.

Frankie and Giovanni rode back to Frankie's parents' house, where the two of them finally found some private time.

Frankie handed Giovanni the beautifully wrapped box. He caught his breath at the gift box with the iconic logo. Something from Cartier.

He was stunned when he saw the beautiful cuff links, kissed Frankie amorously, and began to chuckle.

"What is so funny?" Frankie had no idea what was going on in his head. Laughing? At a gift?

"No. No. These are beautiful. But please, open your gift." Tears of laughter were forming in the outer corners of his eyes.

Frankie quickly ripped the paper off the box. It, too, had the iconic Cartier panther logo on it.

Inside was a bracelet made with two half-circles; each half held two diamonds. To complete the enclosure, one must join them together with small screws with a tool that was provided. The purpose was for one partner to fasten the bracelet on the other one, declaring "forever love."

It was the style that inspired the design for Giovanni's cuff links. Tears were rolling down Frankie's cheeks. What were the odds? Incredible.

Pinewood

It was only the four of them that evening. The rest of the crew would arrive for a Christmas Day feast. Charles prepared a simple dinner of pasta with a lemon and caper sauce, shrimp scampi, and a crisp salad.

"Charles, you said it was going to be a light meal," Myra said, feigning a protest.

"It *is* light. Except for the garlic." He grinned as he finished combining the ingredients for the scampi sauce.

"Good thing all of us will be eating it!" Myra laughed. "Where's your sous chef?"

"I gave him the night off. It's Christmas Eve, after all."

"And tomorrow?" Myra teased.

"Tomorrow he'll be back in an apron," Charles said, and chuckled. "Speak of the devil, I hear Mario Andretti pulling in," he said, joking about Annie's fierce driving, even if it was only a golf cart.

Fergus made his entrance with his hands in his pockets, waiting for Lady and her pups to greet him.

Once they received their treats, they got out of his way.

"Smells bloody good, mate!" Fergus said, and slapped Charles on the back.

"Yum!" Annie said in agreement.

"Should be ready in short order," Charles announced.

"I'll get the dishes," Annie offered.

"I'll open the wine," Fergus said, holding up a bottle of Sancerre. "White for fish, ay?"

"So, you've learned a few things about pairing food, have you?" Charles said.

"If he wants to take the credit, but I picked the bottle," Annie replied with a grin.

"I am learning," Fergus said, "to keep my bloody mouth shut."

Just before they were about to sit, Myra suggested they fix plates for their basement guests. "I'm sure Vinny will enjoy two fishes for Christmas Eve."

Charles plated the food and placed two dishes on a tray. "I am not certain they deserve such culinary pleasures, but. . . ."

Fergus jumped in with, "We're not barbarians!"

Myra went into the atrium, fetched Vinny's phone that was sitting on her desk, and slipped it into her pocket.

"What are you doing with that?" Annie asked.

"He has to call his mother and wish her a Merry Christmas. I am sure he is in deep trouble, and I don't want her to worry. She wasn't the one who created this situation."

"You are right, my friend."

Myra and Annie returned to the kitchen and brought the food downstairs.

Vinny immediately recognized the aroma. "That smells like home," he said half-heartedly.

"Speaking of home, you are going to call your mother."

"I am?" he said with a sense of fear. *Was this going to be his last meal? His last goodbye?*

"I am going to put you on speaker. One false word, and the call is over. Do I make myself clear?" Myra said in a stern tone.

"Crystal."

"Good. Now dial her number and read what's on this piece of paper." Myra wrote out a little blurb for him to say. This is how the conversation went:

"Hello, Ma. It's me, Vinny."

"Vincent! Where are you? Where have you been? Why aren't you home?"

He read from the script:

"I'm sorry, Ma. I got caught up here in Atlantic City. I was winning really big, and they kept comping me rooms and meals. It was too hard to break away from the craps table."

He looked at Myra, wondering how she knew his weaknesses.

"That's your problem, Vincent! You never know when to stop. I want you to come home right away. And Jimmy's aunt and uncle are worried about him."

Vinny kept reading the note in front of him.

"I'll be back in a few days. Jimmy twisted his ankle, and he's laid up right now. He's okay, but the doctor said he can't travel for a couple of days."

"Good thing your Uncle Richie is here to help, but I'll tell you something, if you plan to keep staying in my house, you are going to have to get on the straight and narrow. *Capisce*?"

"*Capisce*, Ma. I'm sorry. I gotta go. See you soon."

Myra ended the call. "Very nicely done."

Vinny looked at her and asked, "Will I really be going home in a couple of days?"

"There are certain conditions, which we will discuss at another time. Meanwhile, enjoy your dinner," Annie said, and turned and followed Myra up the stairs.

"How come you told your Ma I sprained my ankle?" Jimmy whined.

"Because that's what was written on the page. You gonna argue with someone who has you locked behind bars?" Vinny answered in frustration.

Christmas Day

Giovanni and Frankie drove over to the church to help set up for the dinner. Mateo and his crew were already hustling.

"Thanks so much for pitching in," Frankie said, and gave him a big hug.

"For you? Anything," Mateo said with a warm smile. He shook Giovanni's hand. "Good to see you."

"Likewise," Giovanni answered. When he first heard of this young, charming, handsome chef who was working with Frankie, he couldn't help but be a little jealous. But when Frankie went missing in Lake Tahoe and Mateo offered some of his flight time to hustle Giovanni, Peter, and Richard to the resort, Giovanni's opinion turned to extreme gratitude. He had to admit, it was easy to love Frankie, and it was clear Mateo loved her, too. As a sister and a friend.

Amy and Peter arrived soon after, followed by Nina, Richard, and Robert. Rachael, carrying a big box, was the last one in the door. Robert quickly approached her and relieved her of the package that was almost as big as she was. Frankie and Nina eyed each other. It appeared things were moving nicely for Rachael and Robert.

"What gives?" Frankie whispered.

"Robert seems to like her. He said she's funny and quirky," Nina said in a hushed voice.

"She told me she enjoyed his company, and she's been keeping her cool. She said he makes her feel grounded."

"We should try to bottle that!" Nina said, a little louder than she wanted to.

"Bottle what?" Rachael said as she strutted over.

"This energy. All the congeniality," Frankie said with an excellent save.

The men began to set up the tables and chairs, and the girls followed with tablecloths and small sprigs of fir cuttings with red ribbons to make it festive. Rachael began to unpack her box that was filled with strings of lights and garlands. "I figured the place might need a little *zhuzh*."

"Tell me about the New Year's Eve plans," Amy said as she bounced from table to table.

Frankie gave her the breakdown. "Dinner at Del Frisco's, and then we can walk to Sniffen Court. That's if the weather holds out."

"How did you meet these people?" Amy asked innocently. "A countess and a confectionary mogul?"

Frankie realized that Amy was the only one who had not been informed of the stakeout, which ultimately led to the impromptu parade behind the Rockettes. Frankie was certain Amy had heard about it on one of the newsfeeds, but wasn't aware that it was her pals who were "wanted for police questioning." Although Frankie wasn't sure if they were or not.

"It's a bit of a long story. I'll fill you in during the week. Myra and Annie are lovely people."

By the time they were finished decorating, the once plain and stark community room looked like a winter wonderland—a vast improvement, for sure.

Families began to arrive. Everyone had expressions of amazement when they entered the room. Once they were seated and plates piled with food were set in front of them, ministers from different denominations said their version of grace.

Frankie and her crew were overcome with emotion as they witnessed the joy and gratitude on everyone's faces.

This is what Christmas is really all about.

Pinewood

Charles and Fergus were busy in the kitchen, preparing the Christmas meal for the Sisters and their guests. This year was a smaller group than usual, if you could call ten dinner guests small. It was no challenge for Charles since he'd begun experimenting in the kitchen, watching cooking videos, and reading books. With each holiday or mission, he seemed to outdo himself with new recipes.

Maggie and Kathryn arrived early to help set the table. By now everyone knew what their assignments were. Yoko was in charge of the floral arrangements, Nikki and Jack were in charge of the wine, and Annie was the official champagne lady.

The aromas of the tenderloin filled the entire house, beckoning Maggie into the kitchen. "You should make that into a scented candle," she said as she peered toward the stove.

"Scoot!" Charles scolded, and flagged her away from the oven with a towel. "I know. You're hungry. I'm one step ahead of you." He opened the second oven and slipped out a tray of hors d'oeuvres. "A bit of amuse-bouche," Charles said, using another term for a small item not usually on the menu.

Maggie couldn't wait and tried to pluck one from the tray. She withdrew her hand quickly. "Ouch!"

Charles gave her an incredulous look. "Are you daft? Didn't it occur to you they may be hot?"

"Yes, but I can't help myself," Maggie said, and wrinkled her nose.

"Have at it, but you're not getting any sympathy from me."

Maggie reached for a spatula and added several of the delectable delights to a plate. Charles gave her a disparaging look.

"I'm sharing them! Geez. I'm not a barbarian," she sniveled.

Charles burst out laughing. "Seems that expression is going to be the slogan for the season."

Maggie returned to the dining room that was taking shape and passed the plate around. Half an hour later, Yoko arrived with ten bouquets of amaryllis in short vases, tied with silver ribbons.

"Everyone can take one home with them later," she said as she placed them down the center of the shimmering metallic table runner. It complimented the Noritake Odessa silver-trimmed dinnerware perfectly. White tealight candles in silver holders brought even more sparkle to the table.

Myra looked over at Kathryn, who was busily folding napkins. "What's this?" she asked, noticing the napkins were folded into the shape of a Christmas tree. "I don't remember you having any interest in domestic decorating."

Kathryn raised her eyebrows. "You'd be surprised at what I've learned all those nights spent in my rig. Had to watch something."

"Well, well. Who knew we had our own Martha Stewart among us?" Maggie teased.

"Don't get funny. At least I didn't eat my way across the country," Kathryn jibed back, as she plucked one of Maggie's mini quiches off her plate.

"Ha ha. Very funny." Maggie was used to all the ribbing about her appetite. For someone who ate round the clock, she was petite.

When everyone was satisfied with the illuminated dining room table, Annie popped a bottle of champagne. She poured two glasses for Fergus and Charles and brought them into the kitchen. "Cheers, dear fellows!" she exclaimed.

"Cheers to you!" Charles said as he stirred something aromatic on the stove.

"Here's to all of us!" Fergus responded.

Annie promptly returned to the dining room, where the others waited. "Here's to those who wish us well, and all the rest can go to. . . ." She didn't have to complete the toast. Everyone knew how it ended.

Charles entered the dining room. "Dinner is served. Please take your seats."

The women complied, and Fergus appeared with a large platter of sliced pork tenderloin. Charles returned to the kitchen and gathered the side dishes.

Everyone *ooh*ed and *aah*ed over the presentation and the aromas. Charles and Fergus offered compliments about the table.

"Clever napkin folding," Fergus remarked.

The women began to giggle.

"That's Kathryn's handiwork," Annie announced.

"Blimey!" Fergus howled. "Where did you learn that?"

"YouTube," Kathryn said, smiling. "There isn't a whole lot to watch when I'm on the road."

"Origami," Yoko said, and nodded.

"Exactly!" Kathryn replied.

When everyone was seated, they held hands around the table and said grace.

Myra began, "Thank you for the many blessings in our lives. Our friends, family, good health, and most of all, the love we share."

"Amen!"

Conversations included the New Year's Eve party, then moved on to their houseguests in the basement.

"What's the plan?" Charles asked for the third time.

"We have one more thing to do with them, and then I shall read them the requirements that they must abide by unless they want to spend the rest of their lives in the basement."

"We can't have permanent occupants," Charles said in disagreement.

"Of course not. But they don't have to know that. I think after a week here and our instructions, they will remain on the straight and narrow," Annie replied.

"Here! Here!" Charles raised a glass, and everyone followed with their version of "Cheers!"

New Jersey

Frankie, Giovanni, Anita, and Marco returned to the house, where Rosevita and Lucia were putting the final additions to their dinner of lasagna, stuffed mushrooms, and eggplant rollatini.

Rachael's son was with his father, and Nina announced to Richard and Robert that she'd invited Rachael to join them with her parents. Robert had no objection, and the four of them headed to the Hunter house. Her parents spent most of the year in Florida, and the house was big enough to accommodate a few houseguests, Richard and his brother included. They feasted on the traditional glazed ham, sweet potatoes, macaroni and cheese, and string beans.

Amy and Peter spent the day with Amy's parents, both sets of the divorced pair. Amy was overjoyed when she learned that the once-estranged couple was actually being civil to each other as they enjoyed a traditional turkey dinner.

Nina, Richard, Robert, Rachael, Amy, and Peter joined their friends at Marco's later that day. They wanted to present their gift to Rosevita, Lucia, Anthony, and Elio as a group. The two couples were thrilled. They had discussed going to a casino but didn't think there would be time. Rosevita whispered to Lucia, "I think we're going to need a vacation after this one!"

At the end of the day, everyone felt satisfied, overfed, appreciated, and grateful.

Chapter 20

New Year's Eve—Late Afternoon

Annie and Myra had arrived in New York the night before and were waiting to hear from Charles and Fergus. They had a big day ahead of themselves.

Meanwhile in Pinewood, Charles and Fergus went to the basement and instructed the men to shower. Once they were finished with their morning hygiene, Charles and Fergus handed Vinny his freshly laundered Santa suit. Jimmy was given an elf costume.

"These are kinda tight," Jimmy complained.

Charles stared him down and said nothing.

"Okay. Okay. Okay," Jimmy said, then sniffled and wriggled himself into the snug-fitting clothes.

Charles handed over two plates and waited for them to finish their turkey sandwiches. When they were done eating, Fergus ordered them to stand up and turn around. He zip-tied their hands behind their backs, placed burlap bags over their heads, then gingerly marched them up the stone steps.

Fergus eased them into the rear of the SUV, while Kathryn and Maggie were waiting in another car. When everyone was buckled in, they drove to the airport, where Annie's jet was waiting. They shuffled Jimmy and Vinny up the stairs to the plane and seated them in the back row. No one had said a word until the pilot announced, "Wheels up in ten."

As much as Vinny wanted to know what was going on, he figured it was better if he kept quiet. Besides, what would it matter? He had no control over the situation. Apparently, Jimmy was of the same mindset.

Ninety minutes later, they arrived at Teterboro. Charles and Fergus decided it was better to transport their guests by car rather than the helicopter they originally discussed. There would be too many eyes watching. A stretch limo was waiting inside the hangar as their "cargo" staggered in the direction they were nudged. The Sisters had employed the limo driver many times, so nothing surprised him, not even Santa and an elf wearing burlap bags over their heads.

Charles sent a text to Myra to let her know they were approaching Midtown:

I have a permit, so I can park on a side street for as long as you need me to.

She replied:

I'm thinking a little before ten. Does that work or is that too long?

His response:

Why don't we come up to the townhouse and leave the blokes in the car. This way Kathryn and Maggie can get themselves sorted.

Myra:

Great idea. See you soon.

At the same time, Annie reached out to one of her contacts at the FDNY, Captain Dag Dorph of Engine 54.

"Hello, Captain! Happy holidays! It's Annie De Silva," Annie said with a lilt in her voice.

"Countess! Nice to hear from you. And to what do I owe the pleasure?"

"Please call me Annie," Annie said, and proceeded to explain what she had in mind. "Can you do that for me?"

"For you? Absolutely. And where do you want this equipment delivered to?" he asked.

Annie gave him the address of the townhouse. "Thanks, Captain. I'll give you the usual holiday donation and then some."

Later that Evening

Frankie and her crew met up near the famous tree, just outside of the restaurant. Reservations were for seven-thirty. The mystery of Rachael's plus-one was finally resolved. No one was really surprised that it was Robert, Richard's brother. As different as they were, they seemed suited for each other. At least for the time being.

Everyone was dressed in festive holiday attire. Amy's hair was gleaming with glitter, Rachael had a rosebud tucked next to her ear, Nina wore a white and gold lamé headscarf, and Frankie was in her ponytail with fairy tinsel running through it. They were certainly a dazzling bunch.

They were seated in a quiet corner, quiet for New York City on New Year's Eve. Cheesesteak eggrolls and Thai meatballs started their feast. The choices of pan-roasted branzino, braised short ribs, and fish and chips were debated. Then there were their famous steaks.

"As if Keens wasn't enough," Frankie said as her mouth began to water for another excellent cut of beef. The bone-in prime rib eye was calling her name. "Shut up!" she said to the menu. Frankie often spoke to inanimate objects. She insisted it was a sign of intelligence, which brought howls of laughter to the table. It was a quiet corner no more.

Just as the group was finishing dessert, sirens and flashing lights engulfed the promenade. Almost everyone in the restaurant either had their phone in front of them or were craning their necks to see what the commotion was about. No one seemed terribly unnerved. New Yorkers are accustomed to unruliness and confusion. The expression "a New York minute" was added to the lexicon for good reason: anything can change at any given moment.

Peter logged into a live feed from Times Square. Anderson Cooper's brow furrowed, and he announced into the camera that there was something quite interesting going on at Rockefeller Center. He listened from the earpiece and repeated what they were telling him. Apparently two men, one dressed as Santa and the other an elf, were dangling from the golden statue of Prometheus. The outstretched arms of the eighteen-foot sculpture held the "ornaments" above the ice-skating rink on the lower level of the plaza.

Frankie pulled out her phone and called up the Anderson Cooper feed. "Wait! What?" She recognized the one dressed as the elf. He looked very much like the bad Santa who'd stolen the money from Carol. She grabbed her purse and motioned for everyone to follow her and the several folks heading out the door. There she saw two fire trucks flanking the north and south sides of the plaza. She spotted Captain Dorph and made her way through the crowd. Next to him were her new friends, Annie, Myra, Kathryn, and Maggie. Close by were the Colin Firth and Patrick Stewart look-alikes.

"Annie?" Frankie said in a state of confusion.

"Frankie! So glad you could make it!" Myra said, grinning ear to ear.

Captain Dorph looked at the women in front of him. "You all know each other?"

"We do now!" Annie said, offering a high five to Frankie.

"What is going on here?" Frankie asked with wide eyes.

"Apparently, the reindeer kicked Santa and one of his helpers off the sleigh, and they got caught on big Prometheus." He nodded toward the section where the action was taking place.

Frankie was beside herself. She was doubled over with laughter. Nina moved past her and peeked over the side. She, too, began to howl.

It took four firemen to rescue the "ornaments." Once the crowd realized the two men were okay, they broke out into laughter and cheers.

When Vinny and Jimmy were finally on terra firma, two police officers began to immediately question them.

"What were you two guys trying to pull?"

"How did you get here?"

"I need to see some ID."

Vinny and Jimmy were dumbstruck. They had no answers for either of them, nor did they have any identification.

"You're coming with us." The officers escorted them to a van.

Everyone was speaking at once. Finally, Myra held up her hands. "Let's take this up at the party later, shall we?"

"Absolutely! I have a rib eye calling my name," Frankie said playfully.

"I thought you told it to shut up!" Rachael teased.

"It wasn't listening."

During dessert, Frankie explained the whole story to those who had heard about it but were not aware that two of their pals were part of it.

Frankie thought Robert may have doubts about carrying on with this outlandish bunch. But the big smile on his face erased all of her concerns. This was a good bunch. Make that a great bunch.

Chapter 21

Later that Evening

Santa's crew strolled across town to East 35th Street, where they could hear music coming from a courtyard. A security guard stood in front of the wrought iron gate.

"Good evening," Giovanni said. "We are guests of Annie De Silva."

The man took out his tablet, ticked off their names, and let them pass through.

The courtyard was alive with song and laughter. The atmosphere was as spectacular as any celebration could be. A bar was set in each corner, waitstaff presented bites of mini dessert offerings, and servers glided through the crowd with trays of glasses filled with champagne. It took almost fifteen minutes for everyone to be introduced to one another.

Around eleven-thirty, Annie suggested the couples from Santa's crew join her crew and toast the New Year on her rooftop patio. Frankie hesitated for a moment until she heard a familiar sound began to play. "Doot . . . doot-doot-doot.

Doot-doot-doot." It was "Uptown Funk" by Mark Ronson and Bruno Mars.

Frankie excused herself and joined the line on the dance floor featuring Amy, Rachael, and Nina. After two years, Giovanni, Richard, and Peter had no option but to join in. To be honest, they really enjoyed it. Richard watched the expression on his brother's face. He yelled over to him: "Get used to it!"

Annie, Myra, Kathryn, Maggie, Fergus, and Charles stood with their mouths open. Very little surprised them, but Santa's crew blew them away with their flash mob choreography.

When the dance number was over, Annie asked the band to play a conga song. The two crews joined together and zigzagged their way to the top of Annie's townhouse. They arrived just in time to hear the fireworks and see the glow.

It was truly a very Happy New Year!

Epilogue

Kathryn decided to take a break from the highways and byways of the country. She hung up her keys and renovated her cottage. It was time for her and Murphy to have room to run and play. Kathryn welcomed the change and went to work with Yoko in her new landscaping and nursery business.

Vinny and Jimmy were released from jail, thanks to someone who posted bond for them. Neither had anything to offer the police except that they had been kidnapped, put in a cell, and then found themselves hanging from the sculpture. The story was so bizarre, the judge decided it wasn't worth pursuing, and fined them for disorderly conduct.

As Santa and the elf were leaving the detention facility, a familiar face met them outside. Annie once again went over the rules. Myra reminded them they had an opportunity to lead a decent life.

Vinny's mother forgave him for skipping Christmas, but insisted he begin to pay rent. In addition to rent, he made a deposit each month into an account he believed was repayment of the loan but was actually a savings account Annie set up for his mother. Once the full amount was repaid, Mrs. Massella would receive a "special benefit" check into her retirement.

With the renovation of the pizzeria, and the revitalization of the block, business started to boom. The residents reclaimed their neighborhood, with new shops and cafés opening. Celebrations were now the norm, as residents gathered on the clean and safe street, enjoying fellowship. Bucky Barflow was never heard from again, and the rest of his gang was also "relocated," assuring harmony and peace.

From that point on, Vinny was an upstanding member of the community, in a neighborhood that was revived because of two separate groups of women—who, when they put their minds to it, made something happen. And if it wasn't something good, they would change it, lickety-split.

Official Notice: The participants of the Radio City commotion were never identified by the authorities, and the matter was considered closed.

Look for the new novel in Fern Michaels's #1 bestselling
The Sisterhood series. . . .

CODE BLUE

The Sisterhood: a group of women from all walks of life
bound by friendship and years of adventure. Armed with vast
resources, top-notch expertise, and a loyal network of allies
around the globe, the Sisterhood will not rest until every
wrong is made right.

Theresa Gallagher has never met her Aunt Dottie, though she
remembers her mother's stories about the wild sister who left
home at seventeen and moved out west. When a letter arrives
from one of Dottie's neighbors telling Theresa that her aunt
is now incapacitated and in a nursing home, Theresa decides
to fly out to Arizona to see her. After all, family is family.

The staff at the Sunnydale Care Facility seem pleasant and ef-
ficient, but Theresa finds it strange that she's only permitted
to "observe" her elderly aunt from a viewing room. It's the
first of several red flags that lead Theresa to start asking
questions. Is it just coincidence that as soon as she does, her
car is almost run off the road?

Theresa contacts her attorney friend, Lizzie Fox, who just
happens to be connected to a group of women uniquely
poised to get answers. Soon the Sisterhood is on the case,
uncovering evidence suggesting that behind Sunnydale's com-
passionate image hides a greedy, cruel enterprise. At Sunnydale centers all over the country, seniors are mistreated, duped,
and drained of their savings. And with powerful political figures at the helm, staying one step ahead of legislation and in-
vestigation, it seems like the perfect scam.

But no one is beyond justice—not when the Sisterhood's ex-
traordinary women are involved, making wrongs right as only
they can. . . .